BEFORE SHE SAID I DO

MARTINA MONROE
BOOK 14

H.K. CHRISTIE

This is a work of fiction. Names, characters, businesses, places, events and incidents are either the products of the author's imagination or used in a fictitious manner. Any resemblance to actual persons, living or dead, or actual events is purely coincidental.

Copyright © 2025 by H.K. Christie

Cover design by Odile Stamanne

All rights reserved.

No part of this book may be reproduced in any form or by any electronic or mechanical means, including information storage and retrieval systems, without written permission from the publisher, except for the use of brief quotations in a book review.

If you would like to use material from this book, prior written permission must be obtained by contacting the publisher at:

www.authorhkchristie.com

First edition: September 2025

ISBN: 978-1-953268-35-8

121025

For everyone who has walked through the darkness and found their way to the light braver, stronger, and more unbreakable than before.

1

ZOEY

As I stepped off the plane, a wide grin broke across my face. I was so excited to be home, back in the Bay Area to see my mom, family, friends, and to get *married*. When Henry kissed me goodbye at the airport in Eugene, he'd whispered, "I can't wait to be your husband."

And I'd whispered back, "I can't wait to be your wife."

We'd shared one of those epic airport goodbye kisses. The kind that makes strangers nearby cringe. I didn't care. We were young and in love. The two of us were so blessed. After months and months of planning, the big day was just over a week away. With nearly all the details in place, I was ready to start my life with Henry.

And I couldn't think of a better way to kick off my wedding week than to surprise Mom with one last Friday night movie night. It was something we'd done together since I was a kid. It was one of the few times my mom embraced eating pizza, ice cream, Red Vines, and drinking soda. It was one of my favorite things about growing up with the infamous Martina Monroe. And I wanted one last night, just the two of us, before I became a married woman.

Mom didn't usually like surprises, even the good kind. She liked to be prepared. I didn't blame her. But I did like surprises, and I knew she'd be happy. No one knew I was flying in. The only trace of me was an appointment I'd made with my mom using an alias so she wouldn't know it was me. That way her calendar would be clear so she could take the rest of the day off. I couldn't let anyone know I was flying in early so that no one could spill the beans. I'd been tempted to tell Selena, but I didn't want to put her in a position to lie to Mom. That's a scary place to be, even if you're trained in combat.

I walked through the airport, checked my watch. Right on time. It was just the way I liked it.

At San Jose Mineta Airport, it wasn't too busy. It wasn't one of those crazy hectic airports like you see on TV where people are shoving and screaming at flight attendants. Very civilized. I made my way to baggage claim, and right as I arrived, the blinking light signaled our bags were about to be unloaded. A beep sounded, and colorful suitcases began rolling out onto the carousel.

It was all happening.

I was getting married.

And I'd just finished my second year of veterinary school at Oregon State.

Two years down. It was wild to think about. The next time I walked those campus halls, I'd be someone's wife. Married. I'd been warned the third year was one of the toughest with long clinical days, packed schedules, and real-life cases. But I was ready for it. Nervous? Sure. But I felt like I was on the path I was meant to walk. I'd worked so hard to get there. Life felt full with school, love, and the future. So full, it almost didn't feel real. Not everything was perfect, though. Nothing ever really is.

My thoughts drifted back to the look on Mom's face when I told her I wanted a chair reserved for Dad at the wedding. Her eyes welled up. Even after all these years, losing him still ached. I felt him with me through my entire life. Sometimes I worried I wouldn't remember his face, but Mom always told me I had his eyes. That was all I needed to know. Still, I liked flipping through old photo albums to see his face. He was so handsome with his dark hair, strong jaw, and bright blue eyes just like mine. Strong. Fearless. I tried to be like him. And like Mom, too. But his spirit... I had always felt it in me, even when I was a little girl. He was a fighter. Someone who went after what they wanted. And that's exactly what I had done.

I hadn't had my biological father with me, physically, for so long, but I was gaining a father-in-law. Graham would be a second father figure in my life in addition to Charlie, my stepdad. Charlie was great, but I hadn't lived at home when he and Mom were married. But one thing I loved most about him was how clearly smitten he was with Mom. I couldn't ask for much more than that in a stepdad. Even so, I got a sister in the deal. Selena and I were different in a lot of ways, but we'd gotten close over the years as if we had always been sisters. She was tough and cool but had the biggest heart of anyone I've ever known. Her life had been rough before she came into our lives, but she never let it keep her down for too long. In comparison, losing my dad as a kid felt like a big loss, but hers? Losing her mother and almost her life on *too many occasions* was beyond unfair. Selena without her mother and me without my father had connected us. We understood each other in ways no one else could. There was so much loss, but we had each other and our blended, patched-together, fierce, and loyal family. And I was about to get a whole other one too. Henry's family. The Ashfords.

Could I really ask for anything more? How about my suitcase?

There it was—my suitcase. I grabbed it, hauled it off the

carousel, and wheeled it toward the exit. I was half-tempted to stop at Dunkin' Donuts for a snack but decided against it. I headed outside into the cool September air. The sun was shining, people bustling about.

I pulled out my phone, requested a rideshare, and followed the signs to the pickup zone.

Only a four-minute wait. Score one for Zoey.

The car pulled up with its rideshare logo on the dash and a matching license plate number displayed on my screen. I opened the back door.

"Zoey?" the driver asked.

"Yep, that's me," I said.

He got out, popped the trunk, and offered to lift my very heavy suitcase into the back. I smiled gratefully.

Thankfully, Mom had let me store all our wedding supplies at her house each time we came down to California for planning. Her house was bursting with things for the reception. She'd insisted we hire a coordinator, and we had, but I'd wanted to do most of the planning myself since I had the summer off. I'd enjoyed it. I wanted sparkle everywhere. No way I could hand off something that important to someone else.

With the trunk slammed shut, I climbed into the back seat.

"Ready to go?" the driver asked.

"Ready!"

He drove out of the airport and onto the highway. I admired the familiar Bay Area the hills, the traffic humming, and the stadium off in the distance.

But then something felt off. "Wait," I said. "We're supposed to be going north, not south."

"The map says north. Don't worry, we'll get you to your destination," he said without turning around.

I opened the maps app and typed in the address for Drakos

Monroe Security & Investigations. "This isn't right. I just checked my phone. We should be going north. This direction is completely wrong."

He paused and tapped the map on his smartphone. "Sorry, you're right. This thing's been giving me trouble all day."

I leaned back, relieved. Thank goodness I checked. Where would we have ended up if I hadn't said anything? I needed to surprise Mom while she was still at work.

The driver exited the highway, but to my surprise, he didn't head toward the return on-ramp heading north. Instead, he turned onto a quiet residential street.

"This isn't right," I said again. "You need to get back on 101."

"Hold on, hold on. It's the right way. There's a detour."

I glanced at the map on my phone again. There was no detour listed, and there were no orange signs on the road. "No," I said firmly. "You need to turn around. Right up here at this street. Turn around."

"Hold on, hold on," he repeated. "Don't worry."

Despite the license plates and the official logo, unease started to slither into my chest. Something wasn't right.

We were only thirty minutes from Mom's office. Why couldn't this man just follow the GPS? My frustration twisted into dread as the car suddenly accelerated. "What are you doing? Stop the car! I want out!"

"Oh, really?" he said with a smirk.

My heart pounded as he pulled over sharply and slammed the brakes. My seatbelt caught me just in time. If it hadn't, I'd have slammed my head into the headrest in front of me.

Adrenaline racing, I scrambled to undo the belt and fumbled for the door while I tried to tap out a text. I needed to call Mom or get another ride. And most of all, I needed to get out of the car and away from this man. I hadn't gotten very far when the door flew open and a hand came at me fast, something in it, and he pressed it against my mouth. I fought, twisting, and kicking.

But my limbs slowed and everything blurred. My muscles gave in and then I succumbed to the darkness.

2

MARTINA

GLANCING up at the corner of my monitor, I saw it was 4:05 PM. My four o'clock appointment was late. Tardy clients weren't terribly unusual, but it was Friday, and it was my last appointment before I would be out of the office for a week. I had assumed the appointment was important, given the person who scheduled it had insisted on meeting with me specifically and that they needed to see me before my time off. I'd wondered if that was ominous. Maybe it was a big case. Maybe someone had heard of my reputation. Maybe someone who'd come across Hirsch or me and was part of one of our old cases. But if that were true, wouldn't they at least bother to show up on time?

I shook my head, pushed myself out of my chair, and headed into the office area toward reception. I opened the door to the waiting room and glanced around. It was empty, except for Mrs. Pearson with her magenta lipstick, sitting behind the desk. She looked up at me. "I haven't heard from your four o'clock."

"Did you try calling? Maybe they need to cancel or they're stuck in traffic."

Mrs. Pearson nodded, picked up the phone, and dialed. I

waited, tapping my finger against my thigh. Part of me hoped they'd cancel. I wouldn't mind getting out of the office early. Zoey was flying in early tomorrow in preparation for the wedding. Tomorrow night was her bachelorette party and then a week of finalizing all details for the wedding next Saturday. I still couldn't believe my little girl was getting married. Though she wasn't so little. She was twenty-five years old, starting her third year of veterinary school, and engaged to be married. Sometimes I didn't know where all the years went. It seemed like yesterday she was spilling glitter all over the dining room or begging for a dog. But as I thought about it, Zoey had always acted like she was a grown-up, even when she was seven years old. The way she talked and acted. She had always been fun and loving, yes, but with a seriousness to her too. Like how she insisted on punctuality and hated to be late for anything. Unlike my four o'clock appointment, who, it seemed, had stood me up.

Mrs. Pearson hung up the phone and shook her head.

"No answer?"

With a pinched face, she said, "No. Must be a cell phone. It's out of service."

"That's strange."

"It's only five after. Maybe she'll walk through the door any moment."

"Sure. I'll just finish up some work until she gets here."

"I hear Zoey's coming home tomorrow?"

"She is."

"Everything ready for the wedding?"

With a nod, I said, "Just about."

Mrs. Pearson smiled, her lips curling fondly. "I remember her when she was just a baby. Those big blue eyes, just like Jared." Sadness slid into her voice.

It struck me too. I didn't think there was ever a time I looked at Zoey and didn't think of Jared, but it wasn't always in a sad way. It made me happy to know a part of him lived on. We'd lost him so many years ago, and so much in life had changed.

Sometimes I wondered what it would've been like if he'd still been there for every step of the way, raising Zoey. Life would certainly have been different. I probably wouldn't have become an alcoholic or met Charlie. I wouldn't have gained Selena, a stepdaughter who now felt like my own flesh and blood.

Life rarely turned out the way you thought it would. But I'd been blessed. Somehow, I always ended up with something just as good as I'd expected, maybe even better. There's no way to know for sure what roads untaken lead to.

Mrs. Pearson giggled. "Remember that time Zoey came in here covered in glitter and wanted to show you and Stavros the photo she made with the nanny? I thought Stavros was going to have a heart attack when she got rainbow glitter all over his office."

That memory brought a smile to my face. "Glitter is hard to get rid of."

"So, are *you* all set for the wedding?"

"I am. Zoey helped me pick out a dress, and Charlie has his suit. Selena and the other bridesmaids have their gowns. Wait until you see Audrey in her junior bridesmaid dress! She looks like a mini version of Kim."

"Oh my gosh. Oh, how the years have changed things."

"That they have." And yet, some things never changed, or at least not completely. Maybe they were just a slightly different shade of the same color. Mrs. Pearson had been here as long as I had, since it was just Drakos Security & Investigations before I became a partner.

Stavros had always been like an uncle to me, a godfather to Zoey. People had come and gone from the office. I'd done a long side contract with the Sheriff's Department, working cold cases with Hirsch. He'd since retired, and I was back at the firm full-time. But I still saw him regularly, and he had worked a few cases with us in his retirement. It's funny how we collect people along our lives and then somehow they quietly become family.

"I bet you're anxious to get out of here. It's now fifteen after. If Miss Lemontree shows up, I can tell them to reschedule if you'd like to scoot out early."

"No, that's not necessary. I'm just about wrapped up, but I'll check if there's anything else I can help with before I'm off for the week."

"Whole week off—that oughta be fun."

"Lots of meetings with Zoey's soon-to-be mother-in-law. The bridal shower, rehearsal dinner, rehearsal at the church, and getting to know all the out-of-town family. One big happy gathering."

"Well, I, for one, cannot wait to see Zoey walk down that aisle in a beautiful gown, with sparkles, no doubt."

I nodded. "Oh, there are sparkles. Don't worry. She may almost be a veterinarian, a doctor, but she still loves her sparkles."

"And I love that about her."

"Me too. I'll get out of your hair. Let me know if Miss Lemontree shows up. I'm going back to my office to see if there's anything left to finish."

"You got it, Martina."

I headed down the hallway and spotted Vincent with his messenger bag slung over one shoulder.

"Heading out?"

"I am," he said. "Anything you need from me?"

"Nope, all wrapped up. I just got stood up for my four o'clock, but I'm heading out at five. Next time I see you will be at the wedding."

"I'm looking forward to it. Makes me think about how one day, Caden will be all grown up and getting married. He's only seven now, but it's like you blink and five years have gone by."

Isn't that the truth. "That's how it seems to go."

"I'm assuming Hirsch and Kim will be at the wedding?"

"Of course. Audrey is a junior bridesmaid, after all."

Audrey was Hirsch's thirteen-year-old daughter. Thirteen going on fourteen going on twenty-seven. Hirsch and Kim had their hands full with her. Delightful, but a firecracker. She gave Hirsch a run for his money.

"All right then," Vincent said. "Have a great weekend. I'll see you soon."

I waved and returned to my office.

Seated again, I scanned my inbox. No new messages. No update from my four o'clock. I'd already tidied up, prepped my desk for the week off, cleared my files. I was ready to have a week filled with bouquets and celebrations.

But something wasn't sitting right with me. Something was off. I didn't know what it was. Was it my missing client? Were they in danger?

I peeked at the appointment notes. There wasn't much. Just that I'd been requested to help find a family member. That wasn't a lot to go on. Maybe it was a high-profile case or something sensitive. Maybe Miss Lemontree was trying to find a child she'd given up for adoption, or she herself was looking for her birth parents. There were a hundred reasons why people didn't show up to launch an investigation. They were scared and maybe worried about what we'd find. It was understandable. Reconnecting with long-lost loved ones could be emotional and life changing. Maybe Miss Lemontree simply wasn't ready. I could understand that, but I would've appreciated a phone call.

After forty-five more minutes of checking and rechecking, I shut off the lights and closed my office door. It was time to spend a week celebrating my beautiful girl and her new husband. Tears welled in my eyes. I wiped them away, shaking my head. I was being silly. Sentimental. But how could I not be? My little girl wasn't so little anymore. She was a woman. A professional. Brilliant and dazzling, both inside and out. How had I gotten so lucky to have such a blessing like Zoey in my life?

3

MARTINA

As I walked toward the exit, I noticed a light still glowing in Selena's cubicle. *Of course she's still here.* I swore she worked nonstop. At least I knew she was taking the week off too in order to spend time with Zoey, her new family, and all the friends flying in for the big day.

I walked over to her cubicle. She had her phone pressed to her ear, eyes wide. When she glanced up at me, her jaw dropped.

"Hold on, Henry," she said, her voice tight. "Martina's here. I'm going to put you on speakerphone."

My body went rigid. Why was Henry calling Selena?

"Can you hear me?" Henry's voice came through the phone, anxious and uneven.

"I can hear you, Henry," I said, stepping in closer. "This is Martina. Is something wrong?"

"It's Zoey," he said. "I haven't heard from her."

Heart racing, I said, "What do you mean? Where is she supposed to be?"

"With you."

I frowned. "What do you mean she's supposed to be with

me? Henry, can you start from the beginning? I'm not following."

I waved Selena to follow me as I turned and led us quickly back to my office. There weren't many still in the office, but we needed privacy.

Henry's voice trembled. "So... Zoey wanted to surprise you. She flew into San Jose today. I dropped her off at the airport in Eugene. She was supposed to land at San Jose Mineta at 3:15 PM. She said she made an appointment with you at 4 under a fake name. It was a setup so you'd leave early and she could... I don't want to ruin the surprise if I'm overreacting."

I flicked the light on in my office and shut the door behind us, heart pounding. "Henry," I said calmly, "tell me everything. From the beginning. No skipping anything."

He took a breath. "She wanted one last Friday night movie night with you before we got married. Just the two of you. That's why she set up the fake appointment, so you could leave early and the two of you could spend the evening together. She told me she'd call or text when she got to your office, but she never did. I've been calling her over and over. She's not answering and not replying to texts."

I glanced at Selena. That weight in my chest settled deeper. The missed four o'clock. The no-show client. It had been Zoey all along. She'd set up a fake appointment to surprise me. Tears stung my eyes. *My girl.* Trying to stay focused, I said, "Are you sure her flight wasn't delayed?"

"I checked online. It landed on time."

"How was she planning to get to the office?"

"She said she'd take a rideshare from the airport."

My mind was spinning now. I turned to Selena. "She's still on my cell phone plan."

Selena nodded.

I turned back to the phone. "Henry, I'm going to do a search on her phone line and see if I can track her. Since she's on my plan, I can access her call and text records, even her data usage, and if location services are on, I might be able to see where her phone last pinged a tower. Just hold on, okay?"

"Okay," he said, his voice breaking.

I flipped on my monitor and logged into my mobile account dashboard. Under shared family plans, I selected Zoey's line. Her call and text logs hadn't updated yet. I knew it sometimes took an hour or two. I checked her recent data activity. It showed a burst of use shortly before 3:30 PM, then nothing. No activity since.

I switched tabs and pulled up my iCloud access. "Henry," I said, "do you and Zoey use location sharing? Like through Find My Friends?"

He gasped. "Oh my god. Yes. I forgot. Yes, we do!"

"Okay, good. Open the app and tell me if you see a location for her. You might only see the last ping if her phone's off or out of service, but anything helps."

I bit my lip, thoughts racing. Why didn't she call him? Why didn't she text? I'd disabled location sharing between us when she moved to Oregon. It had felt like giving her space to be her own adult. But she and Henry shared it now, which made me feel a little better.

Henry finally said, "There's a location. From about an hour and a half ago. It's in San Jose. Looks residential. But the dot just stops. There's no movement since then."

I looked at Selena.

"I can drive," she said.

"Give us the address," I told Henry.

He read it aloud. I typed it into my phone. "Thank you for calling us, Henry," I said. "We're going to that location. We'll find her. And we'll call you as soon as we do, okay? I'm sure this is all just a misunderstanding."

"Okay," he said softly. "Thanks, Martina. Thanks, Selena."

Selena ended the call, her face pale. "I don't like this, Martina."

Fear gripped my insides. "I don't either," I said quietly. "Let's go find Zoey."

4

MARTINA

I HAD a bad feeling about this, and I was glad Selena was driving. Normally, I liked to be in control, but my emotions were heightened, and I had to focus on keeping a clear mind. Yes, there was a possibility this was all just a misunderstanding. Maybe Zoey was picking something up for the wedding before she came to see me. But that didn't explain why she wasn't answering her phone. And why had her location stopped on a random street in San Jose? None of it made sense.

Selena said, "Should we call in reinforcements?"

"We don't necessarily know that we need reinforcements yet, right?"

Selena glanced over from the driver's seat quickly, then returned her focus to the road. "True. But you're worried."

"You're right," I said. "Who do I call? My daughter hasn't answered her phone for the last—" I looked at my watch. "Two hours."

Selena's expression tightened. Her gut must've been saying what mine was: something was very, very wrong. It was Friday night. Who could I call? The truth was, there were a lot of people I could call. There were people I'd worked with over the years. Anybody from Drakos Monroe. Hirsch. They'd all drop everything to find Zoey, if needed.

"Maybe you're right," I said. "I'll at least call Hirsch and let him know what's going on. Maybe we'll all laugh about this in a few minutes. Who knows, maybe this is some elaborate game Zoey's playing. Like a scavenger hunt. First item is Zoey."

Selena wrinkled her forehead. "You're her mother and you know her best, but do you really think Zoey would pretend to be missing?"

It would be a terrible game. Maybe she thought it would be fun for me, but... no. She wouldn't do that. That would be absurd. "You're right," I said. "I don't think she would." I grabbed my phone and called her number one more time. Same message —out of service.

Swallowing hard, I scrolled to my contacts and clicked on the one person I knew I could always count on in an investigation. This wasn't an investigation. I was probably just being overprotective, like I'd been accused of being *many* times over the years, pretty much since the day Zoey was born.

"Hey, Martina. How's it going?"

"I'm not sure. Have you heard from Zoey?"

"No. I can check with Kim and Audrey."

"Okay."

As I waited, I prayed they had. His voice came back on the line. "They haven't. Is something wrong?"

I explained quickly that we couldn't get a hold of Zoey, that she was supposed to be in the Bay Area, and we were heading to her last known location.

"What's the address?" he asked.

I glanced down at my phone and read him the address.

"I'll meet you there."

"This could be nothing," I said, trying to talk myself down.

"This could be a misunderstanding. Maybe she lost her phone or left it in a rideshare or taxi—"

"I'll meet you at the address," he said again. Then the line went dead.

I was grateful that Hirsch was dropping everything to help us, but at the same time, I wished he would've told me I was overreacting and that there was a logical explanation for the situation. But everything inside me was screaming that something *was* wrong.

"What did Hirsch say?" Selena asked.

"He's going to meet us there."

"Good. He's got pull with law enforcement."

"True, but let's hope we don't need his law enforcement connections tonight."

Neither of us said anything else as we drove past the San Jose airport, tension thick. I called Charlie to see if he'd heard from her. Maybe she'd gone to the house instead of the office. But disappointment sank in quickly when he said he hadn't. Call ended, I began to process all the things we needed to check out. Like had she actually gotten on the airplane? Was she on the manifest? Did I even have any legal right to ask for that? Maybe that was it—maybe she never got on the flight. But then... how was her phone in San Jose?

She had to have gotten on the airplane. She had to have landed and left the airport. Still, we'd double-check everything, just in case we couldn't find her. At least we were in the tech hub of California, where there were likely security cameras on every block and on people's front doors. Those cameras could help us if Zoey wasn't simply visiting an old friend or picking up something for the wedding. I didn't know what else she could be doing or why she wouldn't tell anyone.

Selena pulled off the highway and turned down a quiet residential street, following her navigation system until it stopped and pointed to the location where Zoey's phone had last pinged.

It was a quiet neighborhood, and I didn't see anyone out. It was a Friday evening in September, and the sun was already dipping low in the sky. It was going to be dark soon.

Selena parked the car and said, "Knock on doors?"

I nodded and climbed out of the car, rushing to the front door of the first house. I whispered a quick prayer that Zoey might be inside. Before I could even knock, the door opened.

A man stood there. He was middle-aged with dark hair, a short beard, and tan skin. He looked at me with confusion. "Can I help you?"

"Yes, my name is Martina Monroe. I'm looking for my daughter, Zoey. I believe she was at this address a few hours ago."

The man stepped back, his brow furrowed. "I'm sorry. I don't know anyone named Zoey. Are you sure she was here?"

"We don't know if she was inside your house," I said quickly. "But her fiancé used the Find My Friends app. This is where her signal stopped."

"I'm really sorry, ma'am. We haven't had any visitors today. Do you have a photo?"

I pulled out my phone and opened the engagement photo of Zoey and Henry. Her smile was so wide and beautiful. I handed it to him. He studied it for a few moments, then handed it back. "I'm sorry. I haven't seen her."

If I had to trust my instincts, I believed him. "Do you have a doorbell camera?"

"Sorry, I don't. But I know my next-door neighbor does and probably several others. I'm sorry I couldn't be of more help. I hope you find your daughter."

"Thank you." I turned back to Selena. "You hear that? Let's go."

Selena marched straight to the house next door, and we knocked. The door opened slowly to reveal a woman of about sixty, wearing glasses, joggers, and a sweatshirt.

"Can I help you?" she asked.

"Yes. I was just at your neighbor's house. I'm looking for my daughter, Zoey. She's twenty-five. Her phone last pinged here, and we haven't been able to reach her." I showed her the photo of Zoey and Henry.

The woman looked at it and nodded sympathetically. "Beautiful girl. No, I haven't seen her."

"Your neighbor mentioned you might have a Ring camera. I was wondering if we could check the footage to see if she was on the street or in a car?"

"Sure. Just wait here."

I nodded, and Selena gently placed her hand on my arm.

"We're going to find her, Martina."

I nodded again, fighting the tightness in my throat.

The woman returned carrying a laptop. "I logged in to my security system. If you want to take a look at the footage... actually do you have any identification?"

"Yes, I'm so sorry." I pulled out my business card. "I'm Martina Monroe. I'm a private investigator. And this is my other daughter, Selena Bailey. She's a PI too."

The woman examined the card and nodded. "Okay, come on in," she said, ushering us inside.

We sat down in the living room while she set the laptop on the coffee table. "Can you bring it back about two hours ago, starting around 3:30?" I asked.

"Of course."

She scrolled back and we watched in fast forward until the time stamp hit 3:40 PM. "Pause it." I pointed at the screen. "There's a car." The dark sedan parked abruptly, tires jerking to a stop.

Selena leaned in. "There's a sticker on the windshield. It's an Uber."

The driver, a large man, maybe six-two, two-fifty rushed around to the passenger side, flung the door open, and shoved his arm inside.

Something was happening. A struggle maybe.

Then the door slammed shut, and he got back in. He remained in the vehicle for a minute before driving off. It was hard to make out the passenger in the back seat, but it was someone with dark hair.

"Can you rewind that again?" I asked.

The footage was decent, but it was difficult to make out the license plate number. Still, I knew someone back at the office might be able to enhance it.

"Would you be able to email me a copy of the footage?"

The woman nodded. "Did you see her?"

"Maybe. I can't see her face clearly, but it looks like a woman with dark hair and that matches her description. I've got people back at my office who might be able to enhance the image. And I have friends in law enforcement who might be able to help too."

My voice wavered, and I realized I was about to cry.

Selena said softly, "Martina... we're going to find her."

I nodded.

The woman took the laptop back and said, "Can I get your email address?"

I gave it to her, and she tapped away on the keyboard. A few minutes later, I verified the footage had landed in my inbox. We exchanged contact information, and I thanked her profusely.

"I hope you find her," she said at the door.

"Me too."

We stepped outside just as Hirsch came striding toward us.

"Did you find her?" he asked.

I shook my head and showed him the video on my phone.

"Are we even sure that's her?"

"The timestamp matches. She would've taken a rideshare from the airport. This is where she was. That has to be her in the car. It looks like her. It's a woman with dark hair."

Selena said, "It could help to get additional footage from other homes. Maybe they captured a better angle and maybe a clearer view."

"You're right. Let's try across the street and see what we can find."

We needed to be sure it was her, and every minute counted.

Hirsch said, "I'll come with you. Once we positively ID it's her in the car, I can get her missing person's case started and we can get *everyone* looking for her."

I wiped tears from the corners of my eyes. *Zoey is missing.*

5

ZOEY

I woke in a dimly lit space. Through a haze, I could see the walls were cement and the floors were concrete. There were no windows. To my surprise, I wasn't tied up. They had placed me on a ratty old couch, covered in yellows and browns that looked straight out of the '70s or '80s. It was hideous. And dirty.

I couldn't hear anything. Where was I? What were they going to do with me? Who were they? All kinds of horrible things rushed through my mind and my pulse raced. Were they human traffickers? Were they going to sell me into slavery? Keep me drugged up? Ship me overseas to the highest bidder?

My family—my mom, Henry, Selena, Charlie—they might never know what happened to me. The irony stung. My mom, the fearless private investigator, the one who solved decades-old cold cases that no one else could crack, and she might never know what happened to her own daughter.

I stood up; rather, I tried to. My legs were wobbly, and my head throbbed. They must have drugged me. Instinctively, I checked for my phone. *Gone.* Of course, they'd taken it.

I sat back down. It was easier than standing, and it wasn't like there were many places to go. The room was mostly empty aside from an old shelf, a metal chair, and a dining table draped with a sheet. I didn't see any food or water.

Were they planning to move me? Take me somewhere else? You're never supposed to let someone take you to a second location. I replayed it back in my mind. The rideshare going south instead of north. Arguing with the driver. The sudden slam of the brakes. That was the last thing I remembered before waking up here.

A doorknob turned.

My eyes flicked to the staircase. The door creaked open, and footsteps pounded down, one pair, and then a second.

There were two of them.

They flicked on a switch, and the basement burst into bright light. I raised my hand to shield my eyes until they adjusted.

"You're awake," one of them said.

"Who are you? Where am I?"

"Don't worry, Miss Zoey Monroe. Everything is being taken care of."

My heart slammed in my chest. "How do you know my name? Who are you?"

I studied their faces. I didn't recognize them. One was heavyset and maybe six-two, with mean eyes. He was the driver. The other was thinner but solid, with blondish hair and sharp features. He looked a bit Nordic.

"We just have a few questions for you, Zoey. Do you think you can answer a few questions?"

"I'll answer yours if you answer mine. How do you know me? Why did you take me? What are you going to do with me?" I tried to stay calm, but how could I? *I've been abducted.*

"That's fair," the blond man said.

"Yeah," the big one added.

"Who are you? Why did you take me?" I asked again.

The blond one said, "I'm Mark and this is Gil."

"And why did you take me?" I asked again.

Gil said, "Truthfully, it's unfortunate you've gotten wrapped up in this. Let's just say we have a message to deliver. And we figured the clearest message would be to take you and keep you with us until it's been received and they have complied."

"So, you're using me? To get to someone else? My mom?" I stared at them. "Do you even know who she is?"

The two exchanged a glance. Mark said, "Yes. We know all about the famous Martina Monroe."

"And you're not scared?"

The larger man, Gil, chuckled. "Scared? Hardly."

"Really? Because it's not just my mom. She works with serious people—ex–Special Forces, military types. Law enforcement. The FBI. They get the job done."

"Pretty bold words for someone who didn't even see it coming," Gil said. "I'd have thought your mother would've taught you better."

A pit opened in my stomach. They knew all about my mom. This was personal. Maybe they were tied to one of her old cases, maybe someone she and Uncle August helped put away. Didn't they realize by taking me, Mom and her team would come after them and wouldn't stop until they found them? Not to mention, if they hurt me, she wouldn't let it go. Nor would Stavros or Uncle August.

So, who were these people? What did they want? And why weren't they more afraid of being caught?

"What message are you trying to send?" I asked.

"That's not for you to worry about," the big man, named Gil, replied. "Now we have a few questions for you."

I swallowed. "Okay."

"Who knows you're in the Bay Area other than Henry?"

How did they know about Henry? "No one." In hindsight,

that was stupid. Maybe they wouldn't even know I was missing until it was too late.

"Good."

Why was that good? *Because it means Mom isn't looking for me.*

"Why not?" Mark asked.

"I flew in a day early to surprise my mom. She's expecting me tomorrow."

"Good. Now, we don't plan on hurting you, as long as you cooperate."

"What do I have to do to cooperate?"

"Great question. Well, as you can see, you're being treated very well. You're not tied up. You're free to roam—at least here, in the basement. We'll bring you water. Some food. All we need is for you to sit tight. But if you get funny ideas like trying to escape or fight us, then all bets are off. And you may not come out of this alive. No white wedding for Zoey Monroe."

They knew I was getting married.

"So, what you're saying is all I have to do is sit here and cooperate, and you won't hurt me?"

"Exactly," Mark said.

"How long am I going to be here?"

"Don't worry. If everything goes according to plan, you'll get to the church in time to marry your fiancé."

Part of me believed them. Part of me didn't. You couldn't trust criminals. But either way, I couldn't risk it. Not yet.

One of them had a weapon under his jacket. I could see the bulge. Even without that, they were twice my size. There was no fighting my way out unless I caught them off guard or could snatch the weapon away from him.

I let my shoulders slump. "I won't fight."

Not yet. Not until I came up with a better plan. I'd been taking self-defense since high school. Kicking myself, I wondered why I didn't just have Selena pick me up. But I couldn't always be worried of the monsters hiding in the shadows, right?

"That's good to hear," Gil said. "Now, we'll get you something to eat, some bottled water. We'll be back. We'll also need a few photos, so get yourself together."

I nodded. "I'll do whatever you want. I'll take the photos. I'll sit here."

"Awfully calm, considering your circumstances," Mark, the blond man, said.

"What else am I going to do? You're obviously bigger than I am. I don't have a chance at fighting you off. Your weapon looks pretty secure. It would be hard for me to grab it and use on the two of you. I've assessed the situation." I said it with far more bravery than I felt.

The truth was, I was terrified and too scared to fight, too scared to test their limits. Maybe I was just hoping I'd make it out alive. Or that this was all a bad dream. But I knew it wasn't. I would comply because I would do anything to see my mom, my family, my friends, and Henry again.

6

HIRSCH

IT WAS no small feat to convince Martina that we needed to go to the local police station to report Zoey missing. There were things the police could do that we couldn't, at least not legally. I knew she didn't care about legal boundaries in that moment. Honestly, I wouldn't either if I were in her shoes. But notifying the San Jose Police Department meant more eyes looking for Zoey. More people was always better than fewer.

It was just Martina and me at the police station since Selena had already gone back to the office to meet Vincent. They were going to review the footage we'd gathered from the neighbors' security cameras, hoping to track down the license plate of the vehicle Zoey had been seen in.

Martina was holding up, but I could tell she wasn't her usual calm and collected self. Truth be told, if it had been Audrey who was taken, I don't think I'd be calm either. All I'd want to do was find her.

And that's exactly what Martina wanted. Still, I truly believed that getting the police involved was necessary. Stranger abductions were notoriously difficult to solve. Assuming it was a stranger who had taken her. At this point, we couldn't assume anything, and we could use all the help we could get.

Martina walked back over to the counter and placed her phone down, her fingers trembling slightly.

"I just got off the phone with Charlie," she said. "He's going to stay by the phone in case Zoey calls."

"That's good. And how about Vincent? Is he already back at the firm?"

"He's on his way."

"I know this is hard, Martina, but there's only so much we can do. And we've got a lot of people helping. We're going to cover every angle. We're going to get Zoey back."

She nodded but didn't look convinced. "I know. I just... I also know how these things can go wrong. I can't help but think through all the worst possibilities."

"Have you told Henry we can't find her?"

She shook her head, eyes wet. "I'm not quite sure what to say. Your fiancée is missing—all because she wanted to surprise me. Hirsch, this is my fault."

"No, it's not. You and I both know who's to blame: the criminals who took her. It's not Zoey's fault she wanted to spend a little special time with her mom before she got married." My voice cracked, and I had to stop. The truth was, Zoey was like family to me too. I wouldn't stop at anything until we found her.

"You're right."

"We're here, Vincent and Selena are at the office. As soon as we're done, we'll go back to the office and help find her. Have you requested cell records?"

"She's on my plan," Martina said. "I already submitted the request to the provider. They're compiling everything—call logs, text data, GPS, and internet usage. But it could take some time."

"All right, we'll follow up on that right after we're done here."

Just then, a man in uniform walked through the lobby toward us.

"Here he is now," I said.

"Hey, Hirsch. Martina. Good to see you both, though I hear you've got a problem. Come on back to my office."

We followed Lieutenant Blackwell down the corridor. We'd worked with San Jose PD before, on a few different cases. One of them had been high profile. Martina was shot during that one. No one forgot it, and we'd kept in touch from time to time.

We sat across from him, behind his oversized desk, stacks of folders and files surrounding him.

"So," he said, lacing his fingers. "What can I help you two with?"

Martina took a breath. "My daughter is missing. We have reason to believe she was abducted at approximately 3:40 PM today."

Blackwell's expression darkened. "Why do you think she was abducted?"

Martina explained the situation clearly and efficiently. We showed him the timeline and the location we believed Zoey was taken from.

"We also have security footage from the street. We think it captured the abduction," she said.

"All right," he said, raising a finger as he picked up the phone. "Hold on." He barked into the receiver, telling someone to come down immediately.

A few moments later, a guy in khakis and a faded Nirvana T-shirt walked in, holding a laptop.

"What can I help you with, Lieutenant?" the man asked.

"We've got security footage we need reviewed ASAP. Then we'll need to pull traffic cam data and figure out where a vehicle went."

"Sure thing. Where's the footage?"

Martina pulled out her phone. "I have it. I can email it to you."

"Great," the tech said, rattling off his email address. Martina forwarded it on the spot.

"I'll get working on it right away," the tech said.

"Walker," Blackwell said, "this is our top priority. Above all else. This is Martina Monroe and retired Detective August Hirsch from CoCo County. They're one of us, and Martina's daughter is missing. We believe she was taken roughly three hours ago."

"Nice to meet you both," Walker said, eyes serious. "Your reputation precedes you. I won't let you down."

"Thanks, Walker," Martina said softly.

He ran out of the room.

"Walker's good," Blackwell said. "He'll figure out exactly where that car went. You have my word."

Relief flickered across Martina's face. This was why I wanted her there. Filing a missing persons report, having the footage logged officially—it allowed us to escalate everything, legally and quickly. Having plainclothes PIs roaming neighborhoods was one thing. But having that same neighborhood surrounded by cops? That could save Zoey's life.

"We'll get some additional details and keep following the trail," Blackwell said. "We're going to find Zoey."

"Thank you, Lieutenant," Martina said.

"Not a problem. I'm so sorry this is happening."

"Me too."

"Once we get that traffic camera data and security footage processed, we'll keep in touch. Are you sticking around?"

"I was hoping to get back to my firm," Martina said. "We've got some other angles we're pursuing."

"Cell phone records?"

"She's on my plan. I've already requested them. They should

be arriving soon, hopefully by secure download. We'll get pings, GPS history, tower logs—anything we can work from."

"Mind if we make the request too, as part of our investigation?"

"Go ahead," she said.

Martina was cooperating, and I was sure this was the right move. Especially if this wasn't random. If it tied to one of our old cases, then we were dealing with something much worse than a stranger abduction. We both knew the risks our work brought. We'd been lucky that no one close to us had been hurt. Until now.

After wrapping up the report, we shook hands with Blackwell.

Martina turned to me. "Now let's get back to the firm."

"Yes, ma'am. Why don't you call Henry on the drive back?" I asked gently.

She hung her head. "I will. Thanks, Hirsch."

"I'd do anything for you and Zoey. You know that."

"I do."

And I meant it. I wouldn't stop until we'd found Zoey.

7

MARTINA

My hope was slowly being restored, knowing that the San Jose Police Department had their top guy checking traffic cams. It made me feel a little better, like maybe we could track where the car had taken Zoey. But I couldn't believe it was all happening, and it wasn't a nightmare that I'd wake from in a minute. After all the missing person cases we'd worked, other people's tragedies, I never imagined Zoey would be one of them.

Now, I had to do something terrible. Something I didn't want to do. I had to call Henry. I had to tell him that Zoey was missing. That I didn't know where she was. That she was probably in danger. That we might... I couldn't think like that. I forced the swirling thoughts to stop and shut my eyes. Instead, I prayed. *Lord, please let her come home safe.*

I opened my eyes, picked up my phone, and dialed Henry.

He answered quickly. "Hi, Martina. Did you hear from Zoey?"

I swallowed the lump in my throat. "Hi, Henry. No, we were just at the San Jose Police Department. We reported her missing. We have reason to believe she's been abducted."

There was a sharp gasp on the other end. "I'll get on a plane right now," he said, voice cracking. "I'll be there on the first flight."

"We'll find her," I said, trying to steady him and myself.

"I want to be there. I want to help. Oh my God... if—if I never see her again—" He broke off, overcome with emotion.

For a moment, I had no words. I couldn't promise him he'd see her again. But I also couldn't let myself go to that dark place. *We will see Zoey again. She will be married on Saturday.* That was the only way we could think.

"Henry, listen to me. Positivity and hope is important. We will find Zoey. You will see her again. But we need to stay focused."

"Okay. I'm booking a flight. I'll call my parents too and let them know what's going on."

"Great."

"They'll probably want to come down too. After we book our flights, I'll let you know what time we'll be in the Bay Area."

"Okay."

It would be useful to have Henry here. He may have insight into anything unusual that may have happened before she left Oregon.

"Thank you, Martina."

"We're going to see her again," I said firmly.

"Yes, we are."

I ended the call and glanced over at Hirsch, who had been quietly giving me space.

"How'd he take it?" he asked gently.

"As expected," I said. "He's getting on the first flight. He wants to be here to help."

Hirsch nodded. "It'll be good for him to be here when we find her. She'll want to see Henry."

"You're right. She will."

My phone buzzed with a new email notification. I opened it

and scanned the screen. "I got an email. The phone records are in. It shows all her internet usage."

"Perfect. I'll pull over so we can take a look," Hirsch said, before taking the next exit and pulling the car over. He turned to me and said, "Let's see what she was doing before she disappeared. It might give us a lead."

We both leaned over the screen, hearts racing, ready to follow the digital trail to bring Zoey home. I opened the email and clicked the secure download link. The report populated a spreadsheet with columns of timestamps, IP addresses, domains, and data usage logs.

Hirsch leaned over my shoulder as I scrolled to the timeframe we cared about just after 3:15 PM, when Zoey's flight had landed.

"Here," I said, pointing. "Looks like her phone came back online at 3:20 PM."

A flurry of activity followed. It was mostly standard postflight syncing: apple.com, icloud.com, imap.gmail.com.

"Here's something," Hirsch said, tapping the screen. "3:21PM. Connection to api.uber.com. She likely ordered a ride."

I nodded. "Then maps.apple.com at 3:35 PM, and then 3:37 PM and again at 3:39PM, with increasing data usage each time. She kept checking the route."

"She was suspicious," Hirsch said. "Probably realized they weren't heading where they were supposed to."

"Exactly," I said, my stomach tightening. "Then at 3:40 PM she hits messages.apple.com—maybe trying to send a text. Then one more maps.apple.com ping at 3:41PM... and then—nothing."

The logs went dead after that. No more syncing. No background apps. No idle connections. Not even push notifications. "The phone went dark," I said. "Either it was shut off, put in airplane mode, or destroyed."

Hirsch's jaw clenched. "That's the exact time the car pulled away in the neighbor's security footage, 3:41 PM."

"She knew something was wrong," I whispered. "She was watching the map. Maybe trying to figure out where they were taking her."

"Maybe she was trying to text someone before they stopped her," Hirsch said. "That messages.apple.com ping. We should have SJPD request metadata from Apple, see if she sent anything out before the signal cut. If she got even one message off—one clue—we'll find it. I'll call Blackwell."

I stared at the screen, picturing her in that car. Holding her phone. Watching the route twist away from what she expected. Feeling the dread set in. Wondering if she should jump out or stay calm.

"She tried," I said quietly. "She tried to tell us."

"I'll call Blackwell and give him this new information. You call Selena and Vincent and tell them the latest."

With a nod, I thought, *We'll find you Zoey. Just hang on a little longer.*

8

MARTINA

Hirsch and I charged through the doors of Drakos Monroe Security & Investigations. We'd been in constant contact with Vincent and Selena on the drive back, and Hirsch had already spoken with Lieutenant Blackwell from the San Jose Police Department. Everyone was looking for Zoey, but it was going to take time. And on a good day, I wasn't the most patient person. With my daughter missing, that patience had dwindled to a solid zero out of one hundred.

As we entered the cubicle area, I noticed the overhead lights were blazing, and the space buzzed with energy, fingers tapping on keyboards, voices echoing over phone calls, and the occasional ping of incoming messages. Soon, Selena and Vincent spotted us and hurried over.

"What's the latest?" Selena asked.

"Like Martina told you," Hirsch said, "there was activity on Zoey's phone. It shows she accessed a rideshare app, Uber, around the time she landed. San Jose PD is submitting an emergency subpoena to Uber. If it goes through quickly, it should give us a full trip report. That includes Zoey's account name, pickup and drop-off coordinates, driver identity, vehicle info, time and route of the ride, and payment details. Sometimes, even the driver rating and comments."

"If it's all legit," Selena added, "we'll know who picked her up. And hopefully, why. Maybe that will lead us to where she is."

"Are they also checking traffic cams?" Vincent asked.

"They are," Hirsch said. "Still parsing through the footage. It might take a while."

"Sure, sure."

I turned to Vincent. "Is the team making progress?"

"We are," he said, throwing a glance at Hirsch, who, no longer officially law enforcement, was now skating the line of legal risk. "We're pulling out all the stops. But it looks like San Jose PD is, too. From what we've gathered, we've got Zoey's location on camera for about five minutes before she vanished. Not a lot, but enough to confirm the timeframe of the abduction. Everyone's working it, Martina."

"Who's here?" I asked.

"Everyone," Selena said with no hesitation.

"How did they know?"

"I called Stavros. He sent the word out to the whole team asking if anyone was available to come in. And just like that, they showed up."

At the mention of him, Stavros appeared from a nearby hallway. Semi-retired but still an imposing figure, his silver hair and deeply tanned skin stood out beneath the harsh fluorescents. His wide brown eyes were intense and focused. Built like a tank, he came straight for me.

"Martina. Anything new?"

"Just the subpoena San Jose PD is putting in for the rideshare data."

"Good. I don't know if Selena and Vincent told you, but we've got everybody here. We're not stopping until we find Zoey, and we're going to find her tonight."

My body tensed with emotion partly from terror about what my daughter might be enduring, partly from the overwhelming gratitude that so many had dropped what they were doing on a Friday night to help.

"Thank you, Stavros."

"Of course. We're family."

"What can we do?" Selena asked.

"She accessed the rideshare app," I said, "and we think she was trying to send a text before her phone went dark. If we could—"

I glanced up at Hirsch, silently asking the question.

He didn't flinch. "I didn't hear a thing," he said flatly. "And I'm not law enforcement anymore."

Even without the badge, Hirsch was a Boy Scout through and through. He didn't like breaking rules, even now. I didn't blame him. But I also knew that if it were his daughter in danger, he wouldn't hesitate to cross a few lines.

"If we could get into her iCloud or Apple account, maybe we could see what she was trying to send. Anything could help."

"We've set up a situation room," Selena said. "And there's food coming in. Gotta keep everyone fueled."

I nodded, emotion lodging in my throat again. If Zoey had her way, we'd be curled up on the couch right now, watching a movie, eating pizza, Red Vines, ice cream, and soda—just like old times. It had been so long since those nights. It felt like another lifetime. I cleared my throat.

Stavros gestured toward the glassed-in conference room. "While the tech teams track traffic cams, Apple data, and the rideshare info, let's start putting together a full picture. Everyone Zoey spoke to. Everywhere she went. Everyone she might've trusted—or avoided. We work this like any other case."

"But... nobody would want to hurt Zoey," I whispered.

"Of course not," Stavros said gently. "But someone might

want to hurt someone close to her, and they could use her to do it."

My stomach turned. Someone like me. "Okay," I said. "Let's do it."

Inside the conference room, Vincent had already set up the whiteboard. I still couldn't believe this was happening, a full-blown investigation into my daughter's disappearance, just one week before her wedding.

"Okay, so who knew about the trip?" Vincent asked.

Selena spoke first. "Henry knew. She was supposed to call him as soon as she got to the office to surprise you. But she didn't call, and she didn't respond to any of his texts. By five o'clock, he was worried and called me to see if I'd heard from her. That's when you found out, Martina. We used the Find Your Friends app from Henry to find her last known location."

"I think we should talk to Henry," I said. "See if Zoey mentioned her trip to anyone else. She may have told someone in passing, or maybe we can get access to airport security footage."

Vincent looked over at Hirsch. "That's going to have to come from SJPD. They're the only ones who can request access to airport surveillance systems. It's too risky to try backchannels. Nobody here is interested in a stay at a federal prison."

Hirsch grimaced, grinding his teeth. "That's fair," he said, pulling out his phone. "I'll call Lieutenant Blackwell."

We continued outlining strategy. We needed to know every step Zoey took from the moment she stepped off that plane until she accessed the rideshare app and got in the car. Sometime after that, she was abducted. She tried to send a text—and then her phone went dark.

The clock was ticking.

She'd been missing for approximately four hours. By now, she could be anywhere. If this was a stranger abduction, we would hope the abductor wasn't particularly smart or careful. It would make it easier for us to find her.

After reviewing logistics like the surveillance footage, people to interview, and subpoena timelines, Stavros leaned back and rubbed his jaw.

"Now for something more sensitive," he said. "Assuming this isn't a stranger abduction... who would want to hurt Zoey? Anyone come to mind, Martina? Any threats against you? Or her?"

I exhaled. "Sure, I've been threatened plenty of times over the years. We've had surveillance at the house, and security protocols in place. People have tried to get to me before through Zoey, even. But that was years ago."

"Nothing recent?" Stavros asked.

"Not that I know of. But we could pull up case files and maybe look at all the high-profile convictions. People I helped put away."

"You've locked up quite a few," Stavros reminded me. "Some real monsters like human traffickers, organized crime, serial killers, dirty cops. It's not impossible someone's been waiting for the right moment."

Hirsch returned. "Blackwell says no one's going home until we get everything we can on Zoey. They're putting in all the emergency subpoenas now."

"That's good," I said quietly. "Really good."

Hirsch nodded. "So, what's next?"

"We need a list," I said. "Anyone who might have a reason to go after me—by taking Zoey."

Hirsch crossed his arms. "That's a long list, Martina."

"We have to start somewhere."

Selena stepped up. "I can pull files."

Vincent added, "I'll reach out to CoCo County. They can

Before She Said I Do

send over the old cold case files you worked. We'll compile a list and start sifting through it."

"I'd appreciate that," I said.

Stavros stood and paced to the front of the room. "One more thing. If we're considering this might be someone trying to get to you, Martina, they may try to get to Hirsch too. Are your wife and daughter secure?"

Hirsch froze, stricken. The realization hit me at the same time. If someone was targeting me through Zoey, then Audrey could be in danger too.

"I'll call the house," he said quickly, stepping into the hallway. I prayed that Kim and Audrey were okay and that Hirsch had enough time to arrange protection.

Back in the room, Stavros glanced at the group. "There's still one part of Zoey's life we haven't talked about."

"Henry," I said.

He nodded. "Yes. What do we know about him? What does his family do? Could there be someone from vet school, or someone close to him, with a motive? A stalker? An ex? Anyone who might want to harm Zoey for reasons unrelated to you?"

He was thinking rationally, and I needed to as well. "You're right. We always have to look at those closest to the... victim."

Stavros winced as he caught the word. *Victim.* None of us wanted to think of Zoey that way, not yet.

"He's coming in on the next flight," I said. "We can talk to him in person."

As I picked up my phone to call Henry, my future son-in-law, I considered whether this could be connected to him or his family. They'd always seemed friendly, polite, and supportive, but I didn't know them well. I'd done a background check on Henry when they first got serious. He was clean. But I hadn't looked deeper. I hadn't checked out the rest of the family. Was it possible they had secrets—secrets that could hurt my daughter?

9

HIRSCH

After one last "I love you" to Kim, I hung up the phone. Until Stavros had said it, it hadn't even crossed my mind Audrey could be in danger. But he was right. Martina and I had worked a lot of cases together and put away a lot of criminals. If one of them wanted revenge, they wouldn't just go after Martina's loved ones. They'd go after what mattered most to me, too. Kim and Audrey.

Audrey was thirteen, energetic, bubbly, and loving. But she was also a teenager, which meant she didn't always like to follow the rules. I wasn't sure how Kim and I ended up with a daughter like that. Both of us were rule-followers from birth. Of course, we got the rebel.

At least for the moment, Kim and Audrey were safe at home. We had a solid surveillance system in place, cameras that would catch anyone trying to hurt them. Still, I'd feel a lot better if someone were outside watching the house 24/7. Someone who could follow Audrey if she had to leave for school. Thankfully, it was Friday night. The weekend was here. She could stay home. She'd be safer there.

I couldn't believe this was happening. Back when I was in law enforcement, I'd always known there was a risk that someone might retaliate. But I'd been lucky. That threat had never materialized. Until now. The sick feeling in my stomach wouldn't go away. The idea that someone would hurt Zoey or Audrey or Kim was unbearable. I was heading back to the conference room when my phone buzzed. I glanced down and saw the name: Lieutenant Blackwell.

"Blackwell," I answered. "What's going on?"

"Our tech team is done with the traffic cam footage. We were able to get the license plate number, and we have a team headed to the registered owner's home now. Not sure if he'll be there."

"Sounds like progress. Do you have the vehicle's current location?"

"Unclear at this point. The team tracked the sedan into an underground parking garage at a shopping mall in San Jose. The sedan entered at approximately 3:57 PM. They've been watching the footage for the last twenty minutes, and nobody's come out. We still have several hours to get us caught up to real time."

"Do you think she could still be inside?" *Or long gone.*

"We don't know. It's nine PM now. I've dispatched units to the garage to check it out. They should arrive in about five minutes."

What were the odds she was still there? "What's your take?"

"If these are experienced kidnappers, they might've switched vehicles or taken her out through another exit. It's underground. She could've been moved into the trunk of a different car, or she could still be in the original vehicle. I'll let you know what the team finds."

"Thanks. Any news from the rideshare company or Apple?"

"Not yet, we're still waiting, but it shouldn't be too much longer. What else is happening over there?"

"We're pulling together a list of known threats."

"If you've got intel, I'd appreciate a copy."

"Absolutely. I'll get it to you."

"I'm extending you professional courtesy here, Hirsch, keeping you in the loop. I'd appreciate the same."

"Of course," I said. "We all want the same thing: to bring Zoey home safe."

"Talk soon," he said, and the line went dead.

Fueled by adrenaline, I rushed back into the conference room. "I just got a call from Blackwell," I said, catching Martina and Stavros's attention.

"What'd they find?" Martina asked, stepping toward me.

"They followed the sedan into an underground parking garage. They've been watching the video feed for twenty minutes. Nobody's come out yet. They sent a team."

"I'm going," Martina said, already reaching for her bag.

"I don't think that's such a good idea."

"Really?" she snapped. "If Audrey was in there, would you go?"

I nodded. "Yeah. But I still think we should wait here and let Blackwell's team do their job. They're five minutes out, but it would take us at least thirty. They'll keep us updated," I added. "Blackwell's sharing info as a professional courtesy. We're in this together. What have you all been working on?" I asked, trying to refocus Martina away from running to a scene.

"We've been digging into Henry," Martina said. "His family, vet school contacts, different angles, not just the cases we worked."

"That's smart. When's Henry supposed to arrive?"

"He should land within the hour."

"Have you spoken to his parents?"

"They're on a flight too. They're coming in from Washington state."

"So, they're out of communication for now."

Stavros looked at Martina. "I'm assuming you know his parents' names."

She nodded. "Yes, actually, I have a list of all their family and friends from the wedding invitations."

Just then, Vincent hurried into the room. "What's up?" he asked.

"We need to go through the wedding guest list from Henry's side," I said. "Start doing background checks. See if there's anyone who might pose a threat. Anyone with a criminal history or ties to something shady."

"But would they even know about Zoey?" Vincent asked.

"Well, his family's pretty wealthy," Martina said. "They're part of the country club scene. The engagement was announced in the local paper. It's not exactly a secret that my daughter is marrying their son."

"Country club circles," Stavros muttered, exchanging a look with the rest of us.

"I'll get on it," Vincent said, turning to Selena, who'd just walked in. "I'll fill you in." He ushered her away to explain the task.

Martina looked at us, her eyes burning. "There's nothing more we can do here. I'm going to the parking garage. If you're not coming with me, I'll go alone."

Stavros gave me a look, and I said, "I'll go with you."

"Okay," she said, then paused. "What about Audrey and Kim? Did you talk to them?"

"They're still at the house. Safe."

"We'll put a security detail on the property," Stavros said. "We've got the address."

"I appreciate it."

"Of course." He nodded. "Now go find Zoey."

Martina and I didn't need another word. We jogged out of the building and into the night, hearts pounding, hoping and praying we'd find Zoey and that we weren't too late.

10

ZOEY

WITH MY ARMS wrapped tightly around myself, I couldn't help but wonder how long I'd be here. Mark and Gil, my two *charming* captors, had given me a sandwich, chips, and a bottle of water. They hadn't hurt me. Not yet, anyway. But I didn't know how long that would last if they didn't get what they wanted.

Problem was, I had no idea what they wanted.

But they knew who I was. They knew my mother and Henry. That meant they hadn't picked me at random. I'd been targeted.

I wasn't an investigator like Mom. I didn't have her instincts or training, but even I could tell these guys weren't your run-of-the-mill low-level crooks. They were too careful, too organized. Nobody had found me yet, and that alone told me they were good at what they did. Still, I had to believe Mom would find me. She and everyone back at the firm. They'd be tearing the Bay Area apart by now, right?

I tried to stay positive, but my mind started spiraling. I thought about the past. The future. The mistakes I might've made. Was I making the right decisions in my life? Was Henry really the one for me? Was I too young to get married? Should I just wait until we we're done with school first? Why hadn't I thought of this before? I was only twenty-five, and it wasn't like we were going to start having children right away. We had a plan. We'd finish school and establish ourselves in our careers and then at thirty we would try to start a family. I shook my head. In my heart I knew it didn't matter if I waited another year or two to marry Henry. He was it for me. He was loving. Smart. Supportive. His family had welcomed me with open arms. Mom had welcomed Henry, too, though not without a thorough background check, of course.

I missed them. All of them. If I didn't get out of here—

No. I couldn't think like that.

I would get out of this.

I still had one thing they didn't expect, the element of surprise.

They hadn't locked the door every time they left. I'd seen that. Maybe if I could get to the top of the stairs fast enough, I could... the sound of the twist of the door handle broke my thoughts.

The creak of the door was followed by heavy footsteps descending the stairs. Not two sets this time. There were three. The man who followed Mark and Gil was different. He had dark hair, darker eyes, and wore an expensive suit. Shiny shoes. He was confident and controlled. The boss?

He smiled when he saw me and something in my gut twisted. Was I wrong? Was this not about my mom and a past case? Had they simply taken me, then discovered who I was? Maybe they ran a quick background check or saw that I was headed to Drakos Monroe Security & Investigations. Maybe this man... was here to buy me.

He sat in the cold metal chair across from me. "Zoey Monroe," he said calmly.

I stiffened. "Do I know you?"

"No, I don't believe we've met," he said, raising a brow, amused. "But I know about you. And your family."

My breath caught. "Oh? How do you know them?"

He chuckled. "In due time. I just came down to see how you're doing and if there's anything I can get to make you more comfortable."

I blinked. "Well... I guess a blanket? Something to read? Or, I don't know, you could let me go."

He grinned. "Very clever. I'd expect nothing less. I hear you're in veterinary school. Going to be a doctor?"

"Yes." I tried to keep my voice neutral.

"You're very intelligent. I can see that about you. I can sense it."

"Thanks," I said, unsure how to respond.

"So," he continued, folding his hands in his lap, "I think you can use that intelligence to help us out and keep yourself safe."

I nodded slowly. "Okay..."

"I have something I need you to read. We're going to film you as you read it. Now, I know you're smart, so I need you to listen carefully to the rules. There will be no hidden messages or secret hand gestures or signals. Just read what's on the paper. Not more. Not less. I think you can do that, Zoey. Don't you?"

"I can do that." That was a good sign. If they were filming a message, they were likely planning to send a demand. A demand in exchange for my freedom. *This could all be over soon.*

"As long as we're clear," he said, reaching into his suit jacket and pulling out a folded white piece of paper, "I think we can get this done quickly."

"Okay."

"Excellent," he said. "Now, my associates will set up. Mark will hold the camera. Gil will assist. All you have to do is read."

He reached into a sleek leather folder and pulled out a

printed newspaper. "One more thing," he said. "Proof of life." He held it up. "Got it right here. You know what that means?"

I nodded. "I've watched movies."

"No investigations of your own?"

"Not really my thing."

"All right, then." He handed me the newspaper and then stood. "It was very nice meeting you, Zoey. You take care."

Without another word, he turned and walked up the stairs, disappearing behind the door with a quiet click.

I didn't know his name. I didn't know who he was or what he wanted besides the video. Maybe it was about money. But my mom wasn't rolling in it. She had to pay for vet school, for my rent, her house, her retirement... I just couldn't imagine what they thought she could give them.

Gil said, "Lift the newspaper below your chin."

I did as I was told.

"Perfect," he said. "Now I'll hold the script. Mark will run the camera. Are you ready, Zoey?"

I swallowed. "I'm ready."

"All right. Smile and say it like you mean it."

The red light blinked on. I forced a smile and began to read.

11

MARTINA

Staring out at the traffic on the highway, I locked my mind on one thing and one thing only: bringing Zoey home. Despite Hirsch's reservations, I drove while he was in the passenger seat feeding me directions as I needed them. My adrenaline had kicked in, pushing aside the sadness and fear. I was in full investigation mode and ready for anything. I glanced quickly at Hirsch. He was on the phone with Lieutenant Blackwell. They exchanged a few words I didn't quite make out. I hoped it was good news and that they'd found something, anything, that would help us find Zoey.

"All right, we'll see you at the parking garage," Hirsch said, ending the call.

"What was that about?"

"The team went to the home of the registered owner of the sedan we saw Zoey in. He was home, swears he doesn't know anything about her, and he's not an Uber driver. He walked the officer out to the driveway to prove his car was parked in the driveway, but to his surprise, the vehicle wasn't there. He appeared shocked and then proceeded to file a stolen vehicle report."

"So, the car was stolen?"

"Most likely. They're running a background check on the car's owner now. He has dark hair, but he doesn't match the description of the driver caught on video. The guy is only five feet five inches tall."

"So, what do we think? They stole a car and put up a fake profile on Uber? Can someone do that?"

He shook his head. "No, they think that the kidnapper might have used an existing driver account and simply added the vehicle to the driver's profile. In most cases, it can be updated and approved in less than 24 hours."

The information sank in. "This was a planned attack on her."

"I'd say my gut is leaning that way too."

"I wish we had that rideshare profile and the driver's identity."

"SJPD is working on it."

I shook my head, frustration burning in my chest. Nothing was happening fast enough. Stavros and I had already authorized Vincent and the entire team to do *whatever* it took to find her. They had strict instructions to pull out all the stops. Hack into whatever system they needed, other than anything federal. Everything else was fair game, as far as I was concerned.

I spotted the exit ahead and veered off the highway. The city buzzed with traffic, lights stacking red up the line. A shopping mall in the distance. I swerved into the right lane, fingers tapping anxiously on the steering wheel as I waited for an opening. As soon as I could, I turned and sped through the parking lot, pulling up at the entrance of the underground garage.

Five black-and-white patrol cars barricaded the way. In the distance, I could see at least a dozen officers spread throughout the garage. Some were directing traffic and others were checking undercarriages with flashlights and shining lights into backseats. Two officers held clipboards. They hadn't spared any resources, and I appreciated that. Hirsch going to the police had been the right move. I just hoped they found something. Something that would bring my daughter home.

I threw the car into park and jumped out, heading straight for the first officer I could find near the entrance.

"Hi, I'm Martina Monroe, and this is August Hirsch. We're here to see Lieutenant Blackwell."

"Yes, of course. He's right down at the entrance. Go ahead."

"Thank you," I said, not even catching the officer's name. I was already jogging forward.

The garage was about ten percent full, and the lower levels echoed with the low hum of voices, footsteps, and two-way radios. It shouldn't take too long to complete the search. I spotted Lieutenant Blackwell and waved.

"Hey," I called out. "Have they found anything yet?"

"We've been going car to car," he said. "There are only three levels. They're almost finished. They haven't found anything yet."

"What about the car?" Hirsch asked.

"Haven't found that either."

"So, they had to have left," I said. "Is there an APB out on the license plate and the car?"

"Not yet. As soon as the search is done. If we don't find it—"

He was cut off by static on his radio. He barked a code, then said through the speaker, "We found the vehicle. It's on the bottom level."

My pulse jumped. I glanced at Hirsch, then Blackwell. "I'm going down there."

Lieutenant Blackwell hesitated, starting to protest, but I was already sprinting toward the stairwell. My thoughts swirled as I ran, feet pounding the concrete. If she was here, I wanted to be the first to reach her. I needed to wrap my arms around her and tell her I loved her.

Sweat trickled down my back as I hit the bottom level. It wasn't hard to spot the car since they had it surrounded. Several officers, maybe five or six, stood in a semicircle with weapons drawn and flashlights pointed at the dark windows. The tension was thick, every movement calculated, every breath shallow.

Someone touched my arm and I jumped. It was Lieutenant Blackwell.

"Hold on. We don't want anybody getting trigger-happy."

I nodded, barely restraining myself. My chest was tight with hope and dread. I slowed my pace but still walked as fast as humanly possible. As we approached, one of the officers who had been peering into the vehicle stood up.

"Empty inside."

"Open the trunk," Blackwell ordered.

They nodded. One officer stepped forward with a crowbar, wedged it into the seam, and cracked it open.

I held my breath. Everyone did. The trunk creaked open. Relief and disappointment hit me like a blow to the chest. It was empty. She wasn't there.

They had gotten her out. They must have switched vehicles and slipped out of the garage. They could be anywhere.

I turned to Hirsch. "They need to check the security footage. Every single car that's exited this garage since the sedan first entered. And if there are cameras outside, leading to the mall, they need to check those too. There must be cameras just about everywhere, right?"

"It's likely," he said.

I shook my head, scanning the dimly lit parking garage. "Are you sure she's not hidden in another car?"

Blackwell looked at me, his voice steady. "They've done a visual check of all interiors. We haven't gone through the vehicles, but the officers were instructed to listen for any sounds or visual indications someone may be concealed inside."

"What about K-9's? I could give you something of Zoey's, and the dogs could track her scent and determine if she's inside one of the other vehicles."

"It's a good idea. We could make arrangements. We'd need that scent."

It would take at least forty minutes to get home and pick up something of Zoey's and then another forty minutes to bring it back. "I'll call Selena and have her pick up some of Zoey's clothing or a coat she has at the house. She'll bring it here."

"Okay. In the meantime, we'll continue viewing the security footage for any vehicles that exited with the driver and Zoey inside. We won't go anywhere until we're sure she's not here."

I nodded, but inside, I knew the truth. She wasn't in this garage, not anymore. She was gone, and we had no idea where she was.

12

MARTINA

It was nearly 1 o'clock in the morning when I stepped back into the office of Drakos Monroe Security & Investigations. Both Hirsch and Selena were quiet as we entered the space, which was still humming with activity despite the late hour.

The dogs hadn't picked up on Zoey's scent. My gut had told me she wasn't in that parking garage anymore. They hadn't seen the driver emerge in a different vehicle, which meant there was more than one person involved in the abduction or they'd waited a long time to leave the garage in a second vehicle. Somehow, they'd left without a trace.

The most frightening thing was that if my suspicions were correct, this was a relatively sophisticated operation. They had stolen a vehicle, intercepted a rideshare app, abducted Zoey, brought her into what was essentially a dead zone, an underground garage, then transferred her into another vehicle possibly with a different driver, and vanished into the night.

She had been taken nine hours ago. My sweet, sweet Zoey had been held in captivity for nine hours. I shuddered at the thought of what could be happening to her.

If whoever took her wanted revenge, I couldn't imagine

they'd keep her safe. If they wanted to hurt me, they would hurt her. Because there's nothing worse they could do to me. Zoey was my heart. If something happened to her...

"Martina?"

I glanced up and saw my mother. She ran over and squeezed me harder than I thought she ever had.

In my ear, she said, "We're going to find her. We will." She stepped back, her eyes searching mine. "I'm guessing no news?"

"She's not in the garage," I said quietly. "We don't know where she is."

My mother nodded solemnly. "I brought more food. I baked some cupcakes—chocolate peanut butter. One of your favorites."

"Thanks, Mom."

"I also brought good coffee. From home. Ted offered his assistance, and he's helping the team in the conference room. Vincent has him helping sift through old case files, flagging any names that could be a threat. They've been working on it for hours. I've been helping too."

"Thank you, Mom."

"We'll do anything we can to help."

"Let's go see if they've found anything." I headed toward the situation room. Mom followed, and inside, I was grateful to see eight people, heads down, scanning case files, calling out names to Vincent, who was recording everything into a spreadsheet that was projected on the wall.

Vincent glanced over and said, "Hey," before he stepped away from his computer and walked over. "We're pretty close to getting into the rideshare data."

"Good. The police haven't received the records yet. Let me know as soon as you get anything."

He nodded just as my phone buzzed.

"Hi, Henry," I answered.

"I'm downstairs, Martina. And my parents are here too."

"Great. Come on up. I'll let you in."

"Thanks."

I turned to Selena and Hirsch. "Henry and his parents are here."

Just then, Stavros walked in, his face serious. It was a look I remembered from our years working together. He'd found something. He strode up to me. "Martina, we might've found something."

I moved in closer. "What is it?"

"We've been doing a background check on Henry and his family. There are some darker elements they may have once been associated with. We're still compiling data, but Zoey's abduction may be linked to the Ashfords."

"Do you have names?"

"We do. We're still running checks. But I don't think everything in their past is squeaky clean."

"Well, they're downstairs," I said. "We can ask them anything we want."

"All right. Let's do it."

"Let's go easy on Henry, though, Stavros."

"I can be cordial," he said.

I smiled and patted him on the arm. He was physically intimidating, and when he spoke, he had a way of commanding attention. He wasn't someone you wanted to mess with. And Henry and his parents? They weren't exactly the tough-guy types. They were more... well, the country club set. Wealthy blue bloods who played tennis as opposed to pumping iron and participating in cage matches.

We headed toward the lobby, and I could see them through the glass just outside the door. I unlocked it and let them in. "Hello, Henry, Margot, Graham," I said. "This is Stavros Drakos. He's my business partner. We're going to bring you into a conference room. We have a few questions, but before we go, do you need a restroom, something to drink, anything?"

"I'll have some water," Margot said. She looked nearly picture perfect in her navy suit and full make-up, despite traveling for hours.

"Yeah, that would be good. Maybe coffee," Graham added. Henry's father was tall and lanky, a bit like Henry, and was also wearing a suit. It wasn't wrinkled, which made me think they'd flown in first class.

"Of course. We have food, we have coffee, and my mother baked cupcakes," I said, offering a small smile.

They nodded and followed Stavros and me through the hallway into the back office area.

"So many people here," Margot said, glancing around.

"Nearly everyone at the firm is looking for Zoey, and so is the San Jose Police Department," I explained. "There are dozens of people tracking her down right now, trying to find out what happened."

Margot looked stricken. This wasn't normal for her. It wasn't normal for any of us, but for some of us, it was familiar. But not when it hit this close to home.

Inside the small conference room, I brought in coffee, snacks, and water. I also brought in Selena and Hirsch, familiar faces I hoped would put them at ease while Stavros stepped in with a list of questions.

Seated around the table, I said, "So, usually with a missing persons investigation, we interview those closest to the missing person." I couldn't bear to say the word victim again. "And as you know, Hirsch and I have worked a lot of cases. We've put away some very bad people, people who might be looking for revenge. We have to consider the possibility that this could be tied to one of those cases. But we also have to consider that it might not have anything to do with me. It could be related to someone Zoey met in Oregon or someone connected to your family or Henry."

Margot's voice trembled. "It's so terrifying. I can't believe this is happening."

Henry shook his head. "Why would somebody do this? Are there really people out there who would take Zoey just to get back at you?"

Graham spoke up, his voice low and steady. "I've thought a lot about this since we got the call. I think it's good that you're looking into our background as well. We have considerable means. Someone could have easily seen that Zoey was engaged to Henry and took her for ransom."

"That is a possibility," I said, thankful that they were open to all angles, not just focused on my past.

Hirsch said, "Right now, we don't know who's taken Zoey. We don't know the motive yet. It's still possible that this was a stranger abduction and not connected to anyone in her life. It could've been a crime of opportunity. Although... usually, crimes like that aren't as sophisticated as this one appears. Which makes us think it was planned. Can you think of anyone who may have reason to take Zoey?"

Henry shook his head. "Everyone at school loves her."

"Anyone love her too much? Maybe someone who gave her the creeps? Maybe she received strange phone calls or messages?" I asked.

"Not that she ever said. I can't think of anyone who would do this."

I said, "Was Zoey acting normal? Was she more nervous than usual or did she make any new friends recently?"

"No, she's been pretty normal. She's been really excited about the wedding and visiting home. She hasn't made any new friends that I know of."

"When you dropped her off at the airport did you notice

anything suspicious or odd? Maybe someone paying too much attention to Zoey or you?"

Henry shook his head.

"Was there anything, no matter how small, that seemed out of the ordinary over the past few weeks?"

With sad eyes, he said, "Nothing."

A reel of silence fell over the room.

Then Stavros said, "How about the two of you?"

Graham said, "There isn't anyone who comes to mind."

Margot remained silent.

Stavros continued, "We've been looking into your background, and we have a few questions about associates you've done business with in the past."

Graham crossed his arms over his chest and nodded. "We're an open book. Ask us anything."

I was relieved to hear that. At least they were willing to do anything that might help bring Zoey home.

Stavros glanced down at his notes. "Okay. We have one associate here. It looks like you were business partners some years back. A guy named Daniel Caburn."

Graham shut his eyes like the name triggered something deeply unpleasant. "We had brief business dealings," he said. "We haven't spoken in years, at least fifteen. We don't run in the same circles anymore. Let's just say Daniel didn't always like to follow the rules."

"Yeah," Stavros confirmed. "He has a record for money laundering and embezzlement. The charges came about a year after your business was dissolved."

"I got wind of the charges and pulled out of the deal," Graham said flatly.

Stavros nodded. "All right. I have a few more names to ask you about."

As he flipped the page, I watched the Ashfords carefully.

They remained composed, but their nerves were showing. Were they afraid we'd uncover some deep secrets? Or simply upset because Zoey was missing?

Margot pulled out her phone, swiped the screen, and then she gasped.

"What is it?" I asked quickly.

Her face went pale. "I just got a message. It's a video."

13

MARTINA

With zero hesitation, I leapt out of my seat and hurried over to Margot. "Press play," I said. She did as I asked, and my heart nearly stopped.

It was Zoey.

She didn't appear to be hurt or restrained, but her face was pale and her expression tight. Then she spoke. "Hi. It's me, Zoey. I'm okay. I haven't been hurt. They've been treating me well. I've had dinner. I hope all of you are doing okay and aren't worrying too much. There's no need to worry yet." She paused, and then continued. "You'll be getting another message with demands. Do not involve the police. Please comply." She shivered visibly and then said quietly, "Or they will kill me."

I paused the video and studied the background. Zoey sat on what looked like a basic couch. The wall behind her was cement or concrete, cold, gray, industrial. There was nothing else distinguishing about the space.

"We have to run this number immediately," I said. "Find out who the sender is. Do you recognize the number, Margot?"

Margot looked stunned, frozen.

Hirsch gently asked, "Margot?"

She remained silent, and Hirsch said, "I'll get Vincent in here to take a look."

I nodded. To Margot, I said, "Do you recognize the number?"

It came out harsher than I intended, but my daughter had just told us they would kill her if we didn't comply.

"I don't know the number. I don't recognize it."

I turned to Graham. "How about you? Do you recognize it?"

Despite his earlier calm, he now looked rattled. "I don't recognize it either."

Stavros stepped forward, his voice even. "Can you think of anyone who would do this? A ransom scheme? Anybody at all? Here's my list." He handed over a folder, thick with names.

Graham immediately started flipping through the pages, eyes scanning each line.

"Honestly, I guess any of them could be capable," he admitted. "I mean, I've never known any of them to commit a violent crime, but I don't know them that well. Our associations were limited, like I mentioned with Daniel. As soon as I found out he was shady, I cut all business ties. Your guess is as good as mine. We've never gotten threats before."

"No one's ever threatened Henry?" I asked.

Henry looked at his parents, mouth agape. "It's because of me. They took her because of you, because you're my parents. They took her for money. This is my fault."

"Henry, this is not your fault," I said, my voice rising. "It is nobody's fault sitting in this room right now. It's the criminals' who took her. They're at fault. Not you. Not your parents. Okay?"

I realized I was shouting again. I placed a hand on my chest and took a breath before saying, "She's okay. This is good news. Wanting money is better than revenge. Because if this was someone trying to get revenge for one of my cases, then they would want to hurt her, to hurt us. But if this is just money..." I looked at Stavros. "We can work with this. Right?"

"We don't know it's money they want, Martina," Stavros said. "They said there would be demands but didn't specify what. It could be money, but we just don't know yet."

"You're right. We don't know. We have to wait," I agreed. "We have to assume the next message will go to you, Margot." I turned to her. "There's no one in your past that could do something like this?"

Margot shook her head slowly. "I don't know. I don't think so."

"It is possible," Graham said. "In our family, we've always had concerns. We keep a relatively low profile, but we do participate in a number of public charities. We know the risks. But this has never happened before. Not to anyone in our circle. It's frankly shocking they took Zoey." He hesitated. "This may sound cold, but I would've thought if they wanted ransom from us, they'd have taken Henry. Not Zoey. Please don't take that the wrong way. We love Zoey."

I raised a hand. "No explanation needed. I understand what you're saying. And yes—it is a little strange that they took Zoey as opposed to Henry, but maybe they saw her as an easier target. We just don't know."

He nodded, and silence fell again until Hirsch and Vincent entered the room. Vincent said, "Hirsch filled me in. Can I see the video?"

I handed it to him. When he pressed play, I squeezed my eyes shut as I heard Zoey's voice. When it was over, Vincent said, "I'll download it to analyze the shadows, the lighting and see if we can figure out where it was filmed or trace the phone it came from, as well as figure out who the number belongs to." He glanced at me. "No law enforcement, no problem, right, Martina?"

There was a flicker of his usual flair, and I appreciated it. "That's right, Vincent."

"So... we're not even going to tell the police about this?" Henry asked.

Stavros took a moment, looked to Hirsch, then back at us. "Let's let Vincent and the tech team handle it. Trace the call. It's likely a burner phone. If these people are as organized as we think they are, they won't be using anything traceable." He looked over at Margot. "Which means you need to be in the presence of one of us at all times for when the demands come in. If they've done their homework, they know Martina is part-owner of this firm. They'll know we have resources."

"So, we just wait for the demands and then give them whatever they want?" Margot asked, wide-eyed.

"Let's take it one step at a time," Stavros said. "First, we wait for the demands. Once we know what they want, we come up with a plan."

It had been a long time since I'd worked with Stavros on an active case, but he still commanded a room better than anyone I knew. In that moment, I was so glad he was here and so glad to have someone strong, experienced, willing to pull out every stop to get Zoey back. Not that Hirsch wouldn't do the same. But Hirsch had Audrey and Kim to think about. Stavros had loved ones, too, of course, but they weren't directly in the line of fire. Although, if Zoey's kidnapping was related to the Ashfords' wealth, then Audrey was safe.

I turned to Margot. "We can set you up at our house."

"We rented a home for the entire week for the family coming in from out of town for the wedding."

"When do the first guests arrive?" I asked.

"Monday. My sister and her husband. They're staying with us all week. We were supposed to check in tomorrow."

"Well, until they arrive," I said, "you can stay with us. At least until we hear what the demands are. It may only be five minutes or it could be two hours or it could be eight."

Graham nodded. "We'll do whatever you need us to do, Martina. Anything to get Zoey back."

Now, we wait.

14

HIRSCH

THE TEAM HAD BEEN DIGGING into the Ashfords' background, trying to uncover anything that might explain why someone had taken Zoey. It was surprising how little we knew about them, how little *I* knew about them. It made me wonder if we'd only scratched the surface of Graham Ashford and his vast web of business associates.

No one in his circle, or his family, for that matter, had ever been kidnapped for ransom before. So, why now? Why Zoey? Why *not* Henry? The way Zoey was taken had been elaborate, carefully planned. It seemed like it would've been easier to grab Henry. He was back in Oregon, not at an airport, not getting into a rideshare. They could've snatched him off the street.

Was it possible the Ashfords weren't telling us something? Or maybe they didn't even realize what they weren't telling us. Maybe there was something buried deep, something forgotten. Whatever it was, the feeling gnawed at me. We were missing something.

Martina looked physically shaken, understandably so. Given the circumstances, anyone would be. But I still questioned whether having the Ashfords go back to her house was the best idea. Maybe they should stay here at the office. If the kidnappers made contact again, we needed every resource at our fingertips. I said, "Martina."

She turned quickly. "What is it?"

I waved her over and stepped out the door with her, lowering my voice. "Are you sure it's a good idea to bring the Ashfords back to your house? How much do we really know about them, anyway? What if they're in on it?"

She gave me a curious look. "Are you getting a vibe off of them?"

I hesitated. "Graham and Margot both seem awfully nervous. Concerned, too. A little too nervous for people who are supposed to be innocent."

"I've met them several times. They're very reserved. Maybe they're worried about something else, something unrelated," Martina said. "We've seen it time and again. People act cagey during investigations, not because they're guilty of the crime at hand, but because they're hiding something. Infidelity, taxes, or business secrets. An investigation threatens to expose everything."

"Maybe," I said, unconvinced. "But we don't know. And the kidnappers could make contact anytime. I think the Ashfords should stay in the office. There must be a place they can rest if they need a nap. It's not like any of us are getting sleep tonight anyway."

Martina agreed. "One of the lounges has a pullout couch, and a few offices have sofas too. If they need a nap, they can sleep there."

"Good. I think we stay put. As soon as we get any information, we act. Getting them settled into your house will just waste time. You said yourself, it could be as short as five minutes or as long as eight hours."

Martina nodded. "You're right. The demand could come in asking for one of the Ashfords to drop off the money. If that's what the kidnappers ask for, we'll need to be able to act in real time. I'll let them know. What about you? Do you need to get home?"

"No. I'm here until Zoey's back safe and sound."

"I appreciate it."

Martina gazed into my eyes, and in them, I saw a blend of fear and hope. It wasn't the first time Zoey had been threatened, but it was the first time someone had actually gotten to her. The last time we thought there had been a kidnapping attempt, it had turned out to be a scare tactic by the people Martina had been investigating in relation to the death of my brother.

The criminals responsible didn't want the truth coming out. People had tried to intimidate her, to force her to walk away from the case. They didn't know Martina very well. She never backed down from a challenge or from seeking justice. "Let's let them know the new plan. And why don't you take Henry and Margot out for a break. Get some tea or a snack so we can question Graham alone."

Reluctantly, she agreed. Knowing Martina, she'd want to question him herself, but it wasn't a good idea for several reasons.

We stepped back into the situation room and explained the revised plan: everyone was to stay put within the walls of Drakos Monroe Security & Investigations. Food had already been brought in, and support staff filled the space, ready to assist.

Stavros nodded in agreement. "I think that's a good idea."

I continued, "Maybe we can set up a rotation schedule for anyone who needs to go home to refresh and get some rest. Just make sure we have backup coverage. I'm assuming we've got enough people for that?"

"We do," Stavros confirmed.

Graham chimed in. "Sure, anything you need."

Henry looked stricken, barely processing the conversation.

"Has everyone gotten something to eat?"

"I don't think I can eat," Henry said softly.

Similar sentiments rippled around the room. The faces in the room were pale, movements sluggish, and eyes heavy with worry. "We need to keep our strength up," I said, gently but firmly. "If we need something like food, water, rest, we stop and take care of it. My former sergeant back in CoCo County used to drill that into us." With that said, I eyed Ted across the table.

He returned a nod.

Ted, my former sergeant, was now married to Martina's mother and was helping search through old files. With that, my thoughts drifted for a moment. It felt like decades ago, because it had been, since Martina and Zoey entered my world. Life had changed so much since we'd met. Martina always had Zoey to protect. I used to only have myself. Now we all had a lot to lose.

"Well, how about caffeine?" I offered, trying to inject a sliver of normalcy. I glanced at Martina and tilted my head toward Margot. She remained composed, but the adrenaline and worry were etched into every line of her face.

Martina picked up on the cue because she turned to Margot and said, "Why don't you come with me? We'll get some air. Maybe some tea?"

Margot nodded without a word, too drained to speak.

Just before leaving, Martina glanced back and added, "Henry, why don't you come too?"

Henry stood wordlessly and followed them out.

I took a seat next to Graham, across from Ted and Stavros. Vincent had already slipped away, off to trace the phone and dig into the video's metadata hoping to find any distinguishing characteristics that could help us.

"So, Stavros," I said, turning to him. "What more do you have on Daniel Caburn—the man currently in prison?"

He leaned forward. "Just that he's serving time. But as you and I both know, most criminals don't work alone."

I nodded, then turned my attention to Graham.

"Any of Daniel's associates come to mind? Anyone who might target you, maybe out of revenge? Payback for pulling out of a deal? A partner of his, perhaps?"

Graham rubbed the back of his neck and let out a breath. "No, it was just Daniel. He and I started the company. It was a securities exchange. Small brokerage-type setup. We had big dreams. We wanted it to be the next Bear Stearns." He paused, then winced. "Bad example, I know, considering how that ended. But back then, it all seemed above board. Then came the whispers."

"Whispers?" I asked, narrowing my eyes. "I thought you said it was just the two of you."

He nodded. "It was. But friends, people who used to work with Caburn at Morgan Stanley, they warned me. Said there were questions. Apparently, there were inconsistencies in his client accounts. Nothing proven, but enough to raise red flags. They told me to watch out."

"So, you did some digging?"

"Yeah. And that's when I pulled out."

"And that was how long ago?" I asked.

"Fifteen years ago."

I glanced over at Ted, who was flipping through a file, half-listening. I gave him a subtle nod. He had decades of law enforcement experience and could read people like a book. Right now, that skill might be exactly what we needed.

"Who else do you know," I asked, "who maybe hasn't done anything criminal in the past but maybe has fallen on hard times? An old business partner who lost everything? Bad bet on a bad stock? Anything like that?" Desperate people did desperate and sometimes horrifying things.

Graham shook his head. "The people I associate with are doing very well."

Stavros crossed his arms, skeptical. "Sometimes people look like they're doing just fine. They've got the shiny cars and the house on the hill, but it's really a crumbling mountain of debt that is close to collapse. I'm sure there's at least one or two in your circle. Maybe you don't even know about it."

"It's possible," Graham said after a pause. "If that's true, I can give you names and numbers of everybody I associate with. Friends at the club, business contacts. Maybe you're right. Maybe there is someone I know who is moments away from bankruptcy and I don't know about it. It happens."

"What about your associates' families?" I asked. "Children? Black sheep who got cut off financially? Someone who saw Zoey as a quick payday?"

He frowned and shook his head. "All of our friends' children are very successful. We've been fortunate."

I exchanged a look with Stavros.

"How did you get into the business?" Stavros asked.

Graham cleared his throat. "After my undergraduate degree, I worked in the field and then later went back for my MBA. After that I started a few businesses. I always wanted to be in finance. It was a pretty standard path."

Before I could press further, Vincent rushed into the room.

"What's up?" I asked.

"Just traced the call," he said, breathless. "Burner phone, as we suspected."

"Any location data?" I asked, cutting him off.

He frowned. "It was turned on in San Jose and was active for approximately two minutes. The current location is at the bottom of Almaden Lake."

I finished the thought aloud. "So, the phone they used to call is a dead end."

"Exactly."

It wasn't good news, but it was expected. "Thanks, Vincent."

Stavros leaned back in his chair, arms crossed again, watching Mr. Ashford closely. After a beat, he glanced at me, then at Vincent. Stavros was likely thinking what I was. This wasn't an act of desperation. This was sophisticated, and perhaps Graham's pals at the club weren't as clean as he thought.

Turning back to Graham, he said, "Mr. Ashford, why don't you start a list. Your current associates. List anyone who didn't come up in the background checks we ran. Friends, clients, and business associates. Then I'd like your earliest contacts too. Starting with your college days."

Graham looked incredulous. "You really think that's necessary? I mean, my gosh, I'm in my fifties. I can hardly remember people from thirty-five years ago. There were a lot of parties, a lot of faces. I can list the people I'm still in contact with, of course."

Graham's reluctance surprised me. On second thought, was he reluctant or was he simply shaken by the entire ordeal?

Stavros gave him a knowing look. "Okay. Let's start with that," and he pushed a pad of paper across the table and placed a pen on top of it. "Why don't you get going on that, Mr. Ashford. I'm going to grab a coffee. Mr. Ashford? Hirsch? Vincent? Can I get you anything?"

Graham said, "No, I'm fine thank you," and picked up the pen and began writing.

Vincent stood up and said, "I could use a coffee. I'll come with you."

"I'll join you as well."

We had surrounded the coffee machine when Stavros lowered his voice and said, "What's your take?"

"I don't know," I said, glancing back at the war room. "But I think there's something in his past he doesn't want us to know about."

Stavros nodded. "My thoughts exactly."

Vincent eyed us. "Whatever it is, we'll find it."

15

ZOEY

THE TURN of the doorknob jolted me awake. My heart pounded so loud I could hear the thud in my ears. Cold sweat clung to the back of my neck, soaking into my already-damp collar. The harsh fluorescent light cut through the darkness, searing into my eyes. I winced and lifted a shaky hand to shield my face.

It took me a moment to remember where I was. The cement walls and the grimy couch beneath me. The sharp, metallic tang of rust lingered in the air, mixed with the faint sour scent of mold and stale breath. Last night had been a living nightmare. Part of me couldn't believe I'd actually fallen asleep. I'd been so sure I wouldn't. Not here. Not with the fear squeezing my lungs. Had they drugged me?

I blinked away the bleariness and looked up.

It was the blond-haired man, Mark, followed by the man in the suit again. Different suit this time: dark blue, crisply pressed, but the same icy presence radiated from him. Had he gone home and gotten ready for the day as if he hadn't been part of a kidnapping?

What time was it? What day was it? I couldn't tell. The room had no windows, no sun, and no way to track time.

I sat up straight, my spine rigid against the couch back, every muscle taut. I was ready for whatever came next. The man in the suit walked with slow, deliberate steps and lowered himself into the chair still stationed in front of the sofa. "Good morning, Zoey. How are you feeling?"

His voice was calm, too calm, like a doctor speaking to a patient about to undergo surgery.

"I'm feeling okay, I guess. Is it morning already?"

He nodded and gave a small smile. "Bright and early. Six AM. It's always good to get an early start. Don't you think?"

"Yeah. I'm usually up pretty early, actually," I said, my voice steadier than I felt. There was something about him that made my skin crawl. He was too composed, too calculating. "This isn't my usual setting, though."

He adjusted his cufflinks, gold and gleaming under the dim light. "I just wanted to give you an update on where we're at and what we plan to do. We need your help once again."

"Help? With what?"

"Well, first we're going to feed you. Get you some breakfast. Breakfast is the most important meal of the day." His lips curled into something like amusement. "Then we'll get you cleaned up. And then we're going to create another message."

The word "message" hung heavy in the air. He meant another video. The demands, whatever they were, had been kept from me so far.

"Okay." My mouth was dry.

"Excellent. Any requests for breakfast?"

They were taking my order? Seriously? "Anything is fine, I guess."

"Perfect. How does a breakfast burrito sound? My friend Mark here makes a great one. Coffee too?"

I hesitated. "Okay," I said, reluctantly. The kindness in his tone was unnerving. Was it real? Was it part of a game? A setup?

I couldn't tell. I just wanted it to end. I wanted to go home and scrub the memory of this place off my skin.

The man in the suit glanced at Mark. "Go ahead and get a burrito and some coffee for Zoey."

"Yes, sir," Mark said, already heading up the stairs. The door clanged shut behind him with a final-sounding thud.

So, he *was* the boss. That much was clear. Mark had called him sir, and the way he moved, confident, unhurried—it wasn't just authority. It was control.

He turned back to me. "So, Zoey, since I'm here, I'd love to hear all about your life. Who is Zoey Monroe?"

"Well... honestly, I thought you knew," I said cautiously. "I mean, you seem to know my name. My mom. Henry. His family..."

"True. Those are just facts about Zoey. I mean, what is it you really want from this life, Zoey?"

He leaned forward slightly, hands clasped loosely between his knees.

"I know you're studying to be a veterinarian, and I know your mom is someone who likes to solve cases and seek justice, or what she perceives as justice, anyhow. But what about you, Zoey? What do you *really* want?"

I stared at him, surprised by the question. Did he really want to know? Or was it part of the weird game he was playing? But to be honest, I wasn't sure anyone had ever asked me that before. Not like this. People asked what I wanted to do for a living. If I wanted to get married and have kids. But what I wanted from life? That was different. "I love animals," I said quietly, the words dry in my throat. "So, I'm becoming a veterinarian. I want to try to make the world a better place, even if in just some small way."

He gave me a sidelong glance, like I'd just told him I believed in fairies.

"And you believe you can make the world a better place by becoming a veterinarian and marrying Henry Ashford?"

I opened my mouth to respond, trying to piece together my thoughts. Would being a veterinarian really help make the world a better place? Better, at least, for animals. But then again, animals were such a big part of people's lives too. They brought comfort, joy, emotional support. They helped children with disabilities, veterans with trauma, and elderly people facing loneliness. Animals healed in ways most people never truly appreciated. And not just pets, livestock too. They fed families, powered farms, and sustained entire communities.

"I think so," I said slowly. "I mean... animals can bring so much joy. Not to mention food. And help on farms. Transportation. They matter."

The man nodded, tapping one finger thoughtfully against his knee. "Interesting. So, no bigger scheme? No running for president one day? Or becoming an advocate for animal rights?"

There was something cold in the way he said it. Like he was amused. No one had ever minimized my dreams before. It stung more than I expected. There was a cruelness in this man, coiled beneath his calm exterior. I lifted my chin. "I'm not sure yet. Maybe. Why?" I met his eyes. "What do you do to make the world a better place?"

He shrugged, slow and deliberate. "It's not my ambition to make the world a better place."

No kidding. "Then what is it?" I asked, my voice rising. "Why did you take me? Are you so hard up for money? Is that what you want? You're going to ask for money?"

That earned a wide, almost predatory grin. Like a Cheshire cat. "My motivations are not solely about money," he said smoothly. "It's more of a message, Zoey. I have plenty of money."

The hairs on my arms rose. The room felt colder suddenly, though nothing had changed. The way he said it, with that eerie calmness, didn't sound like a boast. It sounded like a warning.

"Then what is it that you want?" I asked again. "Why did you take me?"

He tilted his head slightly, studying me. "That's an excellent question. And one that I will answer for you because I think it's important. From what I understand, you're a bright, caring young woman. And I *know* the family you're marrying into. Do you?"

My stomach clenched. "Of course I do," I said. "I've been with Henry for over a year. I've gotten to know his parents, his siblings. They're great. They're generous, caring, thoughtful—"

The man chuckled. Not kindly. "Is that right?"

"Yes," I said firmly. "They've never been anything but kind to me."

"Maybe that's how they present themselves," he said, his tone sharp, almost condescending. "But maybe... there are a few things you should know about the Ashfords before you marry into their family."

My breath caught. "Like what?"

"Well," he said, leaning back slightly, "for starters... you should understand a little more about your future father-in-law, Graham Ashford."

And then he told me everything he knew about Graham. About their family. Things that unraveled the neat, warm picture I thought I knew. With every word, I felt the color drain from my face. My hands grew cold. My lips parted, but no sound came out.

I barely noticed when Mark returned with my breakfast. The scent of eggs, tortilla, and coffee wafted into the room, but it barely registered. The food sat in my lap, untouched, forgotten. Because what the man was saying, what he was claiming, couldn't be true. It just couldn't be.

16

HIRSCH

WE'D BEEN QUESTIONING Graham Ashford for hours. The research team had worked through the night, digging into every name on the list he gave us. So far, not a single promising lead. It could easily be that the connection wasn't obvious. Or maybe, just maybe, Graham wasn't telling us everything.

He seemed open, even overly helpful, rattling off names with ease. But had he left anyone out? Or were we all just too tired to see the truth? With our first break in hours, Ashford went into the office lounge to try to get some rest. I stayed behind, sitting at the table with Martina as we picked at breakfast.

Her mother had graciously gone home and cooked: scrambled eggs, toast, bacon, and a batch of warm muffins. The scent of butter and bacon hung in the air. Betty had so much energy, especially for her age. I didn't know how she managed it.

Martina set down her fork with a quiet clink. "This is taking too long."

"It'll take as long as it takes," I said, trying to keep my tone upbeat. "Let's take it as a good sign. Maybe they wanted Zoey to get some rest. She looked okay in the video. We don't want them to do anything hasty." I said it calmly, trying to be a cheerleader for Martina. But deep down, I was just as terrified. What was happening to Zoey? Why hadn't they sent any demands yet? It didn't add up. A part of me agreed with Martina that it was taking too long. "I'm sure we'll hear soon," I added, trying to reason it through. "Maybe they're moving her to a new location, one that doesn't point back to whoever's behind this."

I leaned back in the chair, forcing logic through the growing unease in my chest. As a detective, I'd worked cold cases, missing persons, and homicides, but active ransom kidnappings? Not many. They were very rare. And this one wasn't following any pattern I knew.

"That's true." Martina sighed. "I just want this to be over, Hirsch. It's just..."

The door swung open.

Charlie stepped into the room.

Martina sprang up from her chair like she'd been lit from within and threw her arms around him. Right behind him was Selena and bounding at her side on a leash was Barney.

The moment Barney saw Martina, he whined, tail wagging furiously. Martina melted to her knees and wrapped her arms around the dog, running her fingers through his thick fur. A smile crept across her face, the first one I'd seen since Zoey had been taken.

Maybe it was time we got a dog. Audrey had been asking for one since she could talk, but it had always felt like too much responsibility. Yet watching how Barney lit up the room and how he seemed to heal something in Martina just by being there... maybe it was worth reconsidering.

I walked over and extended my hand. "Good to see you, Charlie."

"You too, Hirsch. Any new leads?"

I shook my head. "No. But I think I'm going to call Audrey and Kim. See how they're holding up."

"All right," he said with a nod.

I stepped out of the room and pulled my phone from my pocket, just about to dial Kim's number when it buzzed in my hand.

The screen lit up. It was Lieutenant Blackwell. My heartbeat kicked up a notch. "Hirsch here."

"Hey, Hirsch, we got some news."

"What did you find?"

"We got the rideshare data for Zoey's trip. We've got the name of the driver and his address. We're heading over there now."

"Where is he?"

"Lives in San Jose. We're bringing full tactical."

I stood straighter, pulse ticking up. "Do you really think it's the guy? Does he match the driver in the video?"

"It's close. Hard to tell because the video's grainy. I don't think we could make a positive ID off that alone. But either way, Hirsch, he could have information. If it's not him, maybe someone stole his phone, used his account. Or he lent it to someone. Wouldn't be the first time someone gave login info to a buddy so they could pick up a few extra bucks delivering food or running rides. Maybe he knows the guy who took Zoey. That's what we're hoping. Any lead we can get, we'll take it. Anything new on your side?"

I hated lying to a fellow detective, especially Blackwell, but we couldn't jeopardize the ransom situation. If the police found them on their own, technically, we wouldn't be violating the demands.

"Nothing yet," I said. "We've been questioning the father-in-law, seeing if there's anyone in his past who might've wanted revenge. They've got considerable means, so it could still be a ransom play. Don't know. We haven't received any demands yet."

It wasn't a total lie. We hadn't received the demands, we'd just been told they were coming.

"It's possible," Blackwell said. "These people could be sophisticated. Might be part of a larger organization, we can't rule that out. But nothing in the Ashfords' past?"

"Not yet. He gave us a full list of known associates going all the way back to college. We're running backgrounds, checking for anything that smells off. So far, just a few shady characters, but no one who stands out. We're still digging."

"What about Martina's cases? Could it be connected to something old? I thought you were checking that angle?"

"We've got people combing through files from both CoCo County and Drakos Monroe. We're looking for anyone who might want to take Zoey and is capable of doing so." There was a pause, then I added, "Why don't you send me the address? I'd like to meet you there and question the guy if that's okay."

"You're not law enforcement anymore, Hirsch," Blackwell said carefully. "It's probably best you stay back."

"But it might help if we have Martina there. Maybe this guy won't talk to cops, but he might open up to the girl's mother. Play the sympathy card."

There was a brief silence, then a sigh. "All right, I'll approve it, but you can't go in with the team. You wait outside until we've apprehended him and cleared the scene. Then you can come in and question him."

"Agreed," I said quickly. "Thanks, Blackwell."

"I'll text you the address. See you soon."

The line disconnected. I exhaled slowly, adrenaline humming through my veins, and turned back toward the room.

Martina sat beside Charlie and Selena, her hand absently resting on the dog's back. The moment her eyes met mine, she shot to her feet.

"What did you find out?"

"They got details from the rideshare company," I said. "They have the name and address of the driver who picked Zoey up, at least according to the profile. They're heading there now with full tactical."

"They shouldn't do that, Hirsch," she said, alarm rising in her voice.

"Why?"

"If he's with the kidnappers, they could see it as not complying with their no police demands. They might hurt Zoey. You have to call it off."

"And what am I supposed to tell Blackwell? That I didn't tell him about the kidnappers? That I withheld information in an active kidnapping?"

Martina groaned and began pacing the room. "I don't know," she mumbled. "I don't know."

"It's not us going in. It's the police," I reminded her. "And technically, they said we could be there to question the guy after. We haven't said anything about the ransom."

She stopped pacing and looked at me, uncertainty etched all over her face.

"This is just rideshare data," I added. "If these people are as sophisticated as we think they are, they already assumed the cops would be checking Zoey's internet history and know she took a rideshare. This isn't tipping our hand."

Her jaw tightened, and she gave a small, reluctant nod. "Do you have the address?"

"Yes."

"Let's go."

I muttered, "Yes, ma'am," and headed out the door.

17

MARTINA

Despite my protests, Hirsch drove us to the rideshare driver's house. It was fine, I supposed. I needed to be laser focused on how we were going to get Zoey back. It was eating me up that we hadn't heard back from the kidnappers in more than six hours. Six hours of pacing, of wondering if we'd be able to meet the demands and have Zoey back home.

I knew, and Hirsch knew, that the person who took Zoey wasn't likely to be the person described in the driver's profile. We assumed they were sophisticated, but there was always the chance that they overestimated how long it would take to get the data from Uber or they'd gotten sloppy. Fingers crossed.

Hirsch slowed the vehicle, taking a right turn, and said, "We're almost there. Remember, Blackwell told us we couldn't go inside. We have to wait until they've apprehended him and secured the scene before we question him."

Like I had forgotten. I hadn't. "What if she's inside?" I asked, stomach twisting. I couldn't help it. The image of Zoey trapped in some room, just a few yards away from me, wouldn't leave my head. There was no way I could stand back and not run to her.

"It's not likely," Hirsch said. "They wouldn't go to this level of sophistication and then link her location to a public account on a rideshare app. That'd be too reckless."

"Maybe. But criminals always make mistakes. You know that."

"I do. Let's at least hope the driver has some useful information, something that leads us to Zoey."

"The driver could also have the demands from the kidnappers. He could be in contact with whoever's orchestrating this."

"That's true. If he's in on it, he could be a valuable lead."

"Or we could be walking into a trap. Or... I don't know, Hirsch." My fingers curled into my lap. My heart hadn't stopped pounding since the call from Blackwell.

"We'll find out when we arrive," he said. "We're only a minute out."

I stared out the window at the passing streets. "Still nothing from Graham?"

"No. Maybe we should question Margot. Maybe she knows more than he does."

"But Margot doesn't even work."

"No, but she's involved with a ton of charities and knows a lot of people. Probably more than Graham does. We should have her put together a list once she wakes up."

"That's a good idea." I reached for my phone. "I'll text Vincent and have him get it started."

"Good. The sooner the better. Would be nice to know who we're dealing with."

"Agreed." I started typing out a message to Vincent, asking him to speak with Margot the moment she was up. She needed to give us a list of everyone she knew. Friends, acquaintances, associates. Anyone with access to the Ashfords or their world.

After all, they'd sent the video to Margot, not Graham. Maybe the kidnappers had a closer connection to Margot. It could've been someone she'd encountered but didn't have a close relationship with. A tennis coach. A staff member. A bartender at the country club. Someone who knew her and how wealthy the Ashfords were.

I kept texting Vincent, listing the types of people we needed names for. Gardeners. Housekeepers. Drivers. Anyone employed by the Ashfords at any point in the past ten years. It didn't have to be a criminal mastermind, just someone with inside knowledge who passed it along to someone else with deeper and darker connections. Someone who knew the value of their daughter-in-law to be.

It could be anyone.

Hirsch slowed the car, and we pulled up to a modest home already swarming with law enforcement. Tactical vehicles and black-and-white San Jose PD cruisers lined the curb. Officers stood guard at the perimeter, their bulletproof vests tight against their chests, radios crackling with background noise. The front door was open. That meant they were inside and possibly already questioning the suspect.

My stomach dropped.

I didn't want to be on the sidelines. I didn't want to sit in the car like some helpless parent. This person needed to know exactly what they had done. That Zoey wasn't just a payday, she was my daughter. She was someone's fiancée. Someone's best friend. Someone deeply loved by people who would do anything to get her back. And make whoever did this pay for their crimes by spending the next few decades behind bars or worse, if they chose to put up a fight.

I was never a big proponent of revenge. I believed in justice. In letting the system work. But this was different. Whoever did this to my daughter would pay dearly. If that meant I spent every day hunting them down and ensuring their capture by law enforcement, so be it.

With the car stopped, I climbed out of the passenger seat

and walked with Hirsch toward the front of the house. The sun was going down, casting shadows over the quiet, well-kept street. A uniformed officer stepped in front of us, hand resting on his holster.

"We're here with Lieutenant Blackwell," Hirsch said. "I'm August Hirsch, and this is Martina Monroe."

"He's inside, but I'll need to radio it in. Please wait," the young officer replied.

As he stepped aside to speak into his radio, I listened, straining for any sound. A struggle. Raised voices. A barking dog. A slamming door. Anything. But all I heard were footsteps shuffling inside. They were slow, deliberate. No one was speaking. That was strange.

The officer turned back to us. "He'll be out in a minute."

Not even sixty seconds passed before we saw Lieutenant Blackwell emerge from the open front door. He stepped onto the stoop and gave a short wave.

One look at his face, and I knew it wasn't good.

He shook his head.

"What is it?" I asked, my chest tightening.

Blackwell's expression was grim. "We found the driver. But he's deceased and my guess is that he has been for a few days."

The words hit me like a punch to the ribs.

"What do you know about the driver?" Hirsch asked, stepping forward.

Blackwell rubbed the back of his neck and said, "Jose Juarez. Thirty-seven years old. No criminal record. Lived alone. Uber was his only job as far as we could tell."

I glanced past him to the small house. "How does an Uber driver afford a place like this?" It wasn't a mansion, but a detached home in San Jose wasn't cheap.

"We wondered the same," Blackwell said. "We got here about twenty minutes ago and started questioning neighbors. Apparently, he inherited the house from his parents when they passed. He lived here his whole life."

I let out a breath and stepped away, my shoes crunching on the gravel edge of the driveway. I stared out at the pristine lawns and identical mailboxes. This quiet neighborhood held a dead man and maybe a vital clue to my daughter's fate. I turned back. "Any sign of forced entry?"

"No," Blackwell said. "The door was locked. No broken windows."

"How was he killed?"

"Not totally clear yet, but we're guessing strangulation. There are marks on his neck, ligature bruising."

"He knew who did this to him," I said, the words sharp with certainty. "We need to find everyone who knew him and question them." I heard the edge in my own voice, like I was running point. I wasn't. But I couldn't stop myself.

"My team's on it," Blackwell said. "We suspect he knew his killer too. Could be someone close to him or someone who knew about his job and his schedule." He paused, then added, "It's possible they even looked like him. Jose was about six-two, dark hair, heavy set. The guy in the footage could've been his brother. My guess is our suspect killed him just to use his profile and get to Zoey."

That thought struck like ice. "The kidnappers were willing to kill an innocent man just to take Zoey?"

"Looks like it."

I stared at him, trying to absorb that reality.

If they were willing to kill for money, then there were no guarantees that Zoey would be kept alive, even if they got what they wanted. These weren't people operating out of desperation. They were cold, calculated, and dangerous.

My head spun as the worst thought imaginable popped into my mind. *I may never see my daughter again.*

18

HIRSCH

THE REALIZATION that we were dealing with cold-blooded killers hit hard. I turned to look at Martina's expression. She had gone pale, so pale that, before I knew it, I was reaching out to catch her. She collapsed, fainting right there on the doorstep of a murder scene. She came to a moment later, her eyes fluttering open, dazed but focused on mine.

"We have to get her back, Hirsch," she whispered hoarsely.

"We're gonna get her back, Martina. First, let's get you into the car. What did you eat for breakfast?"

As I lifted her to her feet, she swayed slightly but managed to stand. "Had coffee. Lots of coffee," she muttered, rubbing her temple. "And some eggs my mom made."

"Okay, well, there's not much more we can do here anyway. Let's get back to the office, all right?"

She steadied herself and let go of me, her gaze drifting around the crime scene. I had never seen Martina faint before. Then again, she had never been in this situation before either. Her daughter was in the hands of killers. The situation had just gone from bad to very, very bad.

I looked to Blackwell. "We're going to head back to the office.

I'm assuming you've got everything covered here. Call me if there's anything I can do or if there are any new developments."

He gave a tight nod. "I'll call you as soon as I hear anything."

We both glanced at Martina before I turned back to him. "Thanks, Blackwell."

Neither of us wanted to embarrass her by drawing attention to the fact that she'd fainted. Not that she had anything to be ashamed of, but I knew Martina. She didn't like to seem vulnerable or weak in any capacity. "Let's go, Martina."

She nodded silently, and I kept an eye on her in case she swayed again. I walked her over to the passenger side, made sure she got in okay, then circled around to the driver's seat.

Inside the car, I asked, "Are you okay?"

"I don't know what happened, Hirsch. Maybe I just... I need some more calories. I'll eat something back at the office. Hopefully by the time we get back, Margot will have come up with a new list."

"Maybe it's time for a break. Maybe lay down on one of the sofas in your office?"

"I don't know if I can sleep. Sitting down is good for now. I haven't drunk much water either. I might be dehydrated."

Neither of us wanted to say out loud what we were really afraid of.

But we both knew the truth. The best place for us was back at Drakos Monroe. We needed to figure out who had taken Zoey. It may be our only chance at getting her back alive. We needed to get ahead of whoever was behind this.

The drive back was silent. My mind raced the entire way, calculating our next steps about what we needed to do, who we needed to pressure, and what angle we hadn't thought of yet. Zoey's life depended on it.

Right now, the Ashfords were our closest link to the kidnappers. And I still couldn't shake the feeling gnawing at my gut that Graham wasn't telling us everything. He swore he was. But everything inside me told me otherwise.

Maybe he didn't think what he knew was important. Maybe he didn't think it could lead to Zoey. But at this point, we couldn't afford to be polite anymore. We had to get serious. Stavros was good at digging deep, pressing people hard without sugarcoating it.

Parked in the office parking garage, I glanced over at Martina. "Do you need help walking?" I asked gently.

She shot me a look that needed no words. It was a sharp, definitive no.

In all the years I'd known her, she'd been shot twice and even then, she hadn't passed out. But she was older now. Her body reacted differently to stress. I just hoped she was okay and wasn't pushing herself past the breaking point. Then again, I couldn't say I'd do anything differently if it were Audrey.

Truthfully, there wasn't much I wouldn't do to get Zoey back, except something that would jeopardize Kim and Audrey's safety. They were my whole world. As much as I loved Martina and Zoey, Martina understood my priorities.

Inside the office, I waved at Mrs. Pearson as we walked into the building. She immediately rushed over, arms open, and embraced Martina tightly.

"Anything new?" she asked, her voice filled with hope.

Martina shook her head weakly. "Not really. I need to sit down and get some water."

"Oh, I can help you," Mrs. Pearson offered quickly, already reaching out again.

I gave her a look. "I'll help Martina. It's been a long night. We just need to get her some water and food."

Mrs. Pearson hesitated, then nodded, clearly catching the look I was giving her. Martina wasn't in good shape right now, and the last thing she needed was to be fussed over by multiple people. She barely tolerated me helping her, and I wasn't asking anymore. I was just going to do what needed to be done.

Mrs. Pearson said, "I'm praying for you both."

Martina gave a faint, grateful smile. "Thank you."

She didn't say more before heading back toward the office area.

"Why don't you go into your office?" I said gently. "I'll bring you something to drink and something to eat, okay? Maybe some quiet will do you some good. It'll help you collect your thoughts."

She nodded, her eyes glassy, and walked slowly toward her office. I watched until she disappeared through the door, then turned and rushed to the conference room, where I knew there was still plenty of food and bottled water left from earlier.

Margot and Vincent looked up as I entered. "How'd it go?" Vincent asked.

I exhaled sharply and explained what we'd found at the house and the fate of the Uber driver and how his account had been used to pick up Zoey. Vincent didn't nod or give his usual animated reaction. He simply absorbed the information, the weight of it evident in his silence.

"I need to get some food to Martina," I added.

"How's she holding up?" Margot asked, her brow furrowed. "I'd be a wreck."

"She just needs a minute to take care of herself. She'll be fine."

Vincent gave me a quiet look. He, like me, had rarely seen Martina rely on anyone for care, unless she was laid up in a hospital bed. The stillness in the room mirrored the unease we all felt.

As I grabbed a breakfast sandwich and a cold bottle of water, I asked, "How's the list coming?"

"Just about done," Margot said.

"Good. We need to know who took her. It's our only real shot at getting her back alive."

Margot looked stricken, as she should. Hopefully, she'd be more forthcoming than her husband. Or maybe, just maybe, Graham really was telling us everything. I had no proof either way. Maybe I was just grasping at straws and desperate for a loose thread, a hidden detail, something he hadn't said yet that could unlock the case.

With food and water in hand, I headed back to Martina's office.

She was sitting on the sofa, hunched forward, just staring straight ahead.

"I brought you sustenance," I said softly.

She glanced over, her voice hoarse. "Thanks. Anything new going on?"

"Margot's just about finished her list."

"Good," she said, reaching for the sandwich. She unwrapped it, took a bite, and stopped. Tears welled in her eyes.

"Hirsch," she said, her voice breaking, "I'm really scared. Really, really scared."

I sat down beside her and gently placed my hand on her shoulder. "I know."

"What if I never see her again?" Her voice cracked. "I don't know if I could cope."

"We're not going to think like that. We're going to stay positive. We will stop at nothing to find out who took her and get her back. No one's resting until we do."

"But what if it's not enough?" she whispered. "You and I both know this could go badly."

She sniffed, wiping the tears that had escaped.

"Do you want me to get Charlie in here?"

She shook her head. "He went home. I told him to get some

rest. Plus… if, for some reason, she comes home, I want someone there. I'll call him."

"Anything else I can get for you?"

She took a breath, shook her head slightly. "I think I just need a few minutes."

"All right. I'll be in the conference room if you need me."

She nodded.

I didn't like leaving her alone, but maybe she was right. She needed time to breathe, to think, and to feel whatever she needed to feel. I didn't know what I would do in her position. I only knew that I wouldn't want an audience. I exited her office and gently closed the door behind me.

After grabbing a coffee for myself, I headed toward the conference room. From the corner of my eye, I saw Vincent jogging toward me, his expression urgent.

I rushed to meet him. "What is it?"

"We got another message."

19

MARTINA

SHAKING MY HEAD, I wiped the tears from my eyes and told myself I had to be strong. I had to be tough and focused for Zoey. And to be strong, I needed to eat and hydrate. I needed to take the same advice I would give to anyone else in my position. I had to be alert, clear-headed, and functioning. But most of all, I had to find her.

I finished the sandwich, and reached for my bottle of water. I had just unscrewed the cap when my office door flung open, the sound sharp and jarring.

I jumped. "What is it?"

Vincent stood in the doorway, breathless. "We got another message from Zoey."

My heart slammed in my chest. I grabbed the bottle of water and pushed myself to my feet.

"Where's the phone?"

Vincent crossed the room quickly and handed it to me. My fingers trembled as I pressed play. And then, there she was. My beautiful girl.

Her face filled the screen, and I could hardly breathe. Her eyes looked tired, but she was trying to be brave. Zoey spoke.

"Hello. I'm doing okay still, so don't worry about me. I'm doing fine. The people who have taken me have demands, and I'm about to explain them to you. The same rules apply. Law enforcement cannot be involved in any way. It's the only way that I will be safe. The instructions are this: Deliver five million dollars in cash inside a black backpack to the women's restroom at Almaden Valley Park at 10 AM Sunday. Once the drop-off has been made, you'll receive another message telling you how to get me back safe. I love you, and I miss you all."

The screen went black.

I stood frozen, the phone still in my hand, all eyes on me. The air in the room felt tight, heavy, charged with urgency. I looked up at Hirsch and Vincent. "I don't like this one bit."

Hirsch shook his head. "It's not unusual to ask for the money and then say there will be more instructions."

"Maybe. But something's off about this," I said. "I don't know what, but it's off."

Vincent frowned. "It's pretty standard kidnapping demands. I mean, yeah, it's vague—but maybe they'll be watching the drop. Maybe they're being cautious to ensure the police aren't going to swoop in. She's going to be okay."

"Maybe you're right," Hirsch said.

But my thoughts were already spiraling. Ten AM Sunday. That was tomorrow morning. They were going to keep my daughter for another twenty-four hours.

Which meant we had twenty-four hours to figure out who took her.

"Let's tell Stavros," I said. "We'll get a team in place and figure out how we're going to get five million dollars for the drop."

"You're really going to give them the money?" Vincent asked,

"We need that as a backup," I said firmly, and with a renewed clarity, I added, "I won't call this good news, but they're giving us time. Twenty-four hours. That's our window to figure out who took her, bring her back safe, and make darn sure they never do this to anyone else ever again."

Hirsch sipped his coffee. "I agree. It's buying us some time. They won't do anything to her until they get the money."

"My thoughts exactly." I turned to Vincent. "Is Margot's list done?"

"Just about," he said. "We'll start running backgrounds, compare it to her husband's list, search the criminal databases. Everyone will take a slice. We'll be fast but thorough. No one stops until we've got a trail to follow."

"Good," I said, standing straighter. The fear was still there, but purpose was pushing through it now. "Let's go talk to Stavros."

20

MARTINA

WITH A SOLID PLAN IN PLACE, which was basically to look under every rock and stone to find out who took Zoey, we were ready. If worse came to worst, we were prepared to hand over the five million dollars in a black backpack inside a women's restroom in a public park. That was, of course, the worst-case scenario. Even then, there was no guarantee we'd get Zoey back. That was the part none of us said aloud. All it meant was that we needed to be one step ahead of these people.

As I headed back toward the conference room, I spotted Mom walking through the hallway, her arms carrying large bags, likely more food. I waved to her and saw Charlie come in through the lobby a moment later.

I hurried over, pulling each of them into a warm hug. Charlie took the bags from Mom's hands.

"I've got it," he said gently. "I'll take care of this." He headed toward the conference room.

Mom turned to me, scanning my face. "How are you holding up, honey?"

"I'm hanging in there. We have a plan. We're going to get her back."

"You look pale," she added. "Let's get some food into you. Maybe some more coffee. Or maybe less."

I gave a half-smile. "I can't have too much coffee, Mom."

"Okay, well there's sugar too. More cupcakes."

She nudged my arm and smiled gently.

As we stepped into the conference room, I saw Selena sitting beside Vincent. They were talking animatedly, papers and open laptops spread across the table between them.

"Hey, what's up?" I asked.

Selena glanced up. "Vincent and I have been going over the two lists, one from Margot and one from Graham. So far, there are a few names that weren't on Graham's list."

"Do you think that's significant?"

Selena nodded, already tapping on her tablet. "Look here. Margot's actually really thorough with her notes. She even wrote how she knew each person and where they met. And we found something interesting."

"Oh?" I leaned in.

"Check out this name here: Judy Litman," she said, pointing to the screen. "I looked her up and started researching the names that don't appear on Graham's list. Turns out Judy Litman was someone Margot and Graham went to college with at San Jose State University."

I straightened up. "They're from the Bay Area?"

"Not originally," Vincent said. "But they went to school here."

"Okay," I said, perplexed. "That's news to me. You'd think something like that would've come up at some point in our conversations."

Selena nodded. "Exactly. So, they went to school here, and Judy Litman was the girlfriend of one of Graham's college friends. According to Margot, the four of them used to hang out. They'd go to parties and dinners, that sort of thing. Young couple stuff. But apparently, they had a falling out. Graham had worked with Judy's boyfriend, Jeremy. Graham and Jeremy went into business together, and when the business fell apart a few years later, Graham suddenly stopped talking to him. After that, they never spoke to or saw Judy or Jeremy again."

"And this guy, Jeremy, wasn't on the list Graham gave you?" I asked.

Selena shook her head. "Nope. Not a trace of him. So, obviously, we thought it was weird, and we dug deeper. And guess who Judy Litman had been married to?"

I paused, but they didn't leave me hanging for long. "Jeremy Santo."

I shook my head slowly. The name didn't register. "Okay... and?"

Selena leaned forward, eyes sharp. "Well, Jeremy Santo did ten years at San Quentin for attempted murder."

That got my attention. "Where is Mr. Santo now?"

Vincent jumped in. "He hasn't shown up on any police radars lately, but from what we found, he's still in the Bay Area."

I frowned. "What's he doing here? What does he do for work? I mean, he's got a felony on his record. That's gotta make it tough to land a decent job."

"It does," Selena said, drawing the words out. I could tell something big was coming. Vincent had that tight-lipped smile he always got when he was sitting on something juicy.

"Okay," I said, bracing myself. "What's the punchline?"

"Jeremy Santo is now working as a plumber," Selena replied.

"A plumber. Okay. So...?"

Vincent grinned. "Not only is he a plumber, but he owns a two-million-dollar house in San Jose and drives a Mercedes."

My eyes narrowed. I looked at both of them, Selena's face glowing with discovery, Vincent practically vibrating with excitement.

"He's still crooked," I said. "He's into something illegal."

"That's what we thought," Selena said. "So, we're tracking down everything we can—every known associate of Santo, trying to find some connection to who he's working with. You don't make that kind of dough just from plumbing gigs."

"No, you don't," I agreed. "Do we know who he was working with back when he did time? Or who he tried to kill?"

"We're looking into all of it," Vincent said.

"Have we questioned Graham about this?" I asked.

"Not yet. We only asked Margot," Selena said. "We wanted to come to you first to let you know we found something worth chasing."

"This is good. Have you told Stavros?"

Just then, the door swung open and in walked Stavros, his usual scowl replaced by something close to cheerful.

"Well, this smells awesome," he said, glancing at the food on the table. That tone, light, was rare from him.

My mom smiled from the other end of the room. "Yep, I've got lasagna, some sandwiches, cupcakes, and some bananas. I figured I'd throw in something healthy. But I can get cookies too if you need them."

"This looks amazing, Betty. Thanks." He gave her a warm smile, then looked back at us. "What's going on?"

Vincent stepped forward and filled him in. When he got to the part about Graham leaving Jeremy Santo off the list, Stavros's expression darkened immediately.

"Let's get Graham in here," he said, the cheer in his voice gone. "Let's question both of them. I think it's highly suspicious he left out this little detail, that he had a friend from college, someone he used to work with, who did ten years for attempted murder. And that it didn't occur to him to put the name on the list?" He shook his head, his jaw tight. "Oh, heck no. Let's get him in here *now*."

I looked over at Stavros, and he met my gaze. I gave him a nod, more than just approval. I was grateful.

I needed someone to be the bad guy because I couldn't, not with my daughter's future in-laws. And the rage bubbling in me mirrored Stavros's, and I wasn't sure I could hold back from saying something that could follow us for years to come. But God help Graham if he had been holding back information that could save my daughter.

21

MARTINA

INSIDE THE CONFERENCE ROOM, we had all three Ashfords—Margot, Graham, and Henry—as well as my mom, Ted, and Charlie, along with Vincent, Stavros, Hirsch, and me, all enjoying a much-needed meal. The food was delicious, and the warmth of it settled in our stomachs like comfort against the storm we were fighting. We needed our strength for what was about to happen. It was time to get real with the Ashfords.

Once we'd finished, Stavros pushed back from the table and stood, "Well, that was a great meal. Thanks, Betty. You're incredible."

"Oh, Stavros," my mom said, blushing lightly.

"But now," he continued, shifting tone, "we need to speak with Margot and Graham alone. So Betty, Charlie, and Henry, you guys can go while we work on some official business here."

Henry furrowed his brow. "I don't understand. What kind of official business?"

"Not to worry, Henry. It's okay," I said, gently. "Just go ahead with Charlie and Betty. We'll let you know when you can come back."

Henry glanced around, clearly not thrilled but smart enough

not to challenge Stavros. Most people wouldn't. He gave a short nod and left the room with my mom and Charlie.

Once they were gone, the air shifted. The room felt heavier. Tighter.

Selena, Vincent, and Ted took seats in the corner, watching quietly. Stavros leaned against the wall, with his focus on Graham and Margot. I sat beside Margot, while Hirsch settled in across from the Ashfords.

Stavros leaned forward. "So, we've reviewed the lists you gave us. The names of friends, associates, anyone you've known since college who's been more than just a casual acquaintance."

He glanced at the files on the table.

"Thankfully, we've had Vincent, Selena, Ted, and a few others working diligently on this, so we can resolve things quickly. And they found a few names that gave us... concern."

"Oh?" Graham said.

I studied him closely as I leaned back in my chair. His fingers fidgeted in his lap, a nervous twitch that didn't escape me. He was sweating just slightly along his hairline. He was nervous.

"Yes," Stavros said. "Margot listed a name on her sheet that was not on yours, Graham. That, actually, was our biggest tip-off. It gave us reason to dig a little deeper." Stavros paused, letting the silence do some of the work. "Any idea what name she might've written down that you didn't?"

Graham blinked. "I... I don't know," he stammered. "I can't think of—"

"Okay," Stavros interrupted and stepped toward the table. "I'll just go ahead and say it." He picked up the file and tapped it once against the table. "They found the name Judy Litman. She was dating a man named Jeremy Santo, eventually married him. And, according to your wife Margot, you had business dealings with Jeremy for a few years. But then, one day, you suddenly stopped working with him. And you didn't see either one of them again."

Margot glanced at Graham, lips pressed together.

"She said she thought it was a little strange," Stavros continued, "but you told her you just went in different directions. You wanted to go into finance while Jeremy had other pursuits."

I kept my eyes on Graham. His pupils were dilated now. His jaw clenched.

Trying to remain neutral, I said, "Anything you want to add to that, Graham?"

He blinked again and looked down at the table.

And just for a moment, his entire body seemed to freeze.

"Do you want to explain why a man who did ten years for attempted murder and who was a close friend and associate wasn't included on the list of people we should be looking into?" Stavros's voice was rising now, sharp and accusatory.

The room fell completely silent.

Graham stammered, "It's been so long... I just—I doubt he even remembers me anymore."

Stavros folded his arms tightly across his chest, eyes locked on Graham. "First of all," he said, voice low but fierce, "I don't believe you."

Graham flushed red in the face, visibly rattled.

I stepped in. "Stavros—"

He lifted his hands in a quick, apologetic gesture. "Look, I know this is sensitive. Martina and Zoey are family to me. And I don't really know you two," he said, glancing at the Ashfords, "but I know you're family to them. So, this is a little uncomfortable. But I only know how to work in one mode—and that's this." He looked back at Graham. "We all have the same objective, to find Zoey. Now, I may come off as abrasive, and I apologize. It's just how I operate. Please don't take offense."

I lowered my hands and gave a small nod and let him finish.

To be honest, I was fine if he wanted to go full steam ahead, but I had to at least appear to be on their side. I glanced over at Graham. He was shaking his head, eyes wide, guilt creeping in behind the panic.

"You're right," he said.

I stood up and pushed my chair back. I needed a full view of him now. Rising to my feet, I crossed the room and stood near Stavros. Despite trying my darndest to keep quiet and let Stavros work his magic, I couldn't. I said, "You didn't put him on the list because...?"

Margot turned toward him, her voice rising. "I'd like to know too! They could've taken Zoey!"

"I... I had no idea he'd gone to jail," Graham said weakly. "But I did know he was dangerous and had hurt people before."

Margot's face paled. "You knew he was dangerous?" Her voice cracked. Her composure was unraveling fast.

"I'm sorry, Margot," Graham said, finally meeting her eyes. "It's why I stopped doing business with him. I found out how dangerous he really was and knew we had to get away from him."

"And you didn't think to say anything?" she snapped. "Someone has taken Zoey! They've threatened her life! They're demanding five million dollars to get her back, and even then, there's no guarantee!" Margot was furious but soon she broke down into tears, dabbing at her eyes with a tissue as Graham looked on helplessly.

"I'm sorry," he said again, quieter this time. "The truth is..." He looked at his wife, guilt written across every line of his face. "Margot didn't know about any of this. I tried to shield her from it."

"She should know," I said firmly.

Margot wiped her face and fixed him with a cold stare.

"What exactly were you shielding me from, Graham?" Her tone had changed. She wanted answers, and I loved her for it.

"When I was working with Jeremy," Graham began, "I knew he liked to bend the rules. But I didn't realize how bad it was. Before I started my firm, my first business venture, I was making money on the side."

He hesitated, glancing at us and then at the floor.

"It wasn't legal. Not all of it. Jeremy never did things the legal way. Stolen goods, that kind of thing."

Margot gasped, her hand flying to her mouth.

"I know, I know," Graham said, voice shaking. "I didn't have a lot of options back then. I didn't grow up with money. I didn't like doing it, but it was easy money. And I knew it wouldn't be forever." He rubbed his hands together, nervous energy radiating off him. "Then Jeremy introduced me to some of his associates. Honestly, I don't even know their real names, I swear. They all had nicknames. It was one of those situations where nobody was Jim Jones or Tyler Parker. It was like, 'This is Ratty,' and 'This is Big Carl.' That kind of thing."

He paused.

Organized crime. He was talking about an organized crime ring, one he used to be associated with through Jeremy Santo. This was un-freaking-believable. Fury rose inside me like a tidal wave. He had kept this information from us. He could've gotten Zoey killed.

"Go on," Stavros said, tone clipped.

"Anyway," Graham continued, his eyes flicking to the floor, "Jeremy told me there was a way to make really big money. So, I met with these guys. Only once. When they showed me their product... that's when I was out."

"What was their product?" I asked, even though a knot had already formed in my stomach.

He looked up, his voice barely audible. "Humans. They were trafficking humans."

A silence so thick it was almost physical settled over the room.

"I told Jeremy I couldn't do it," he went on quickly. "That's when we stopped talking. Margot and I moved up to Washington. And honestly, I swear, I've never broken the law since."

Stavros's jaw was tight. "So, what you're telling me is you had associations with organized crime in the Bay Area through Jeremy Santo, your college friend and business partner. You were involved in criminal activity. And you *didn't* think to tell us?"

Graham's hand flew to his chest. "I love Zoey, like a daughter. I wouldn't ever do anything to hurt her..."

Part of me believed him, but another part, maybe the part hardened by years of seeing what people were really capable of, knew he didn't love her the way I did. Or the way anyone else in this room did.

"I was scared," Graham said. "They're dangerous. Really dangerous people."

"And they have my daughter!" I shouted, the fury boiling to the surface.

"I'm sorry," he said, eyes pleading. "I'll tell you everything I know. I hope it's not them who took her. That's the truth."

22

ZOEY

PACING THE BASEMENT, I tried to make sense of what I had just learned about Henry's father. It was difficult to process because I didn't know what to make of it. Did Henry know that his dad had been a criminal?

The man in the suit, still refusing to give me a name, had said something cryptic, something about trying to go clean but never being able to turn your back on your past. That once you were in, you were never really out. Did that mean my soon-to-be father-in-law was dangerous?

One thing the man hadn't explained was why he was trying to get money from the Ashfords. He claimed he had plenty of it. So, what was the point? I had asked him why he'd taken me if he didn't need the money, and he just smirked and walked out after I finished filming.

It didn't make sense. None of it did.

I heard the door creak open and tensed. Footsteps. My heart sped up.

Who would it be this time? Mark? Gil? Or the boss?

The boss gave me the creeps. He had a quiet, composed menace about him. The others were more obvious in their danger, less polished. But the man in the suit? He was cold and always in control. That scared me more.

I glanced up. It was just Mark, the blond one. He had a paper bag in his hand. The smell hit me immediately, fast food. I guessed it was lunchtime. "Hey," he said casually as he stepped inside. He nodded toward the couch.

I moved quickly to sit down. I was supposed to be seated when they came in. That rule had been made clear. He handed me the bag.

Cheeseburger, fries, and judging by the scent, apple pie.

"Thanks."

"So... you're getting out soon," he said, almost playfully.

"Why? What time is it now?"

"Just about one o'clock. Saturday."

I let that sink in. I'd been here almost twenty-four hours. In a strange basement with strange and dangerous people. People who, oddly, were being nice. Too nice. Maybe that would change if I tried to fight back.

Could I take Mark?

He was taller, by a lot, but maybe if I had the element of surprise? He didn't seem to be carrying a weapon. At least, not at the moment. I pulled out a fry and took a bite. It was salty and hot, way tastier than it had any right to be. "So, Mark," I said, keeping my tone even. "What's your role in all this? You just kidnap people and then get paid? Is this your job?"

He smirked, amused. "It's one of my jobs. I don't usually take the person. But I help."

"You meet a lot of people that way?"

He chuckled. "I've met a few. Though you're definitely the most interesting. You've been the most calm."

I shrugged and popped another fry into my mouth. The food was surprisingly good. I'd been on a strict diet lately to fit into my wedding dress, to look perfect on my big day. Now I didn't care. Not even a little. How much weight could I really gain in a week, anyway?

I was supposed to be getting married one week from today. I was supposed to have my bachelorette party tonight. Kaylie had flown in. She was my maid of honor and childhood friend. She and Selena had planned everything. Instead of a fun night with the women closest to me, I was being held in a basement.

"Yeah, well, my mom's pretty tough," I said finally, wiping my hands on the napkin. "And I understand basic self-defense. I also know that you're, well... a lot bigger than me." I looked him in the eye. "I guess I'm hoping that when they pay you the money, you'll let me go."

He said nothing.

"I try to look at the positive side of people," I added, quietly. "Everybody has a good side. Even if it's small compared to the rest."

He smiled faintly, almost like he didn't hate hearing that. But I couldn't tell if he believed it. Or if I still did. "That's interesting, Zoey."

Mark leaned back in the chair, his posture casual, like this was just a normal conversation over lunch and not a discussion between a kidnapper and his hostage.

"Tell me about Henry," he said. "Getting married so young... I mean, I looked him up. Seems all right and everything, but you seem tough. He seems like a wimpy rich kid. A frat-boy."

"He's not," I said quickly. "He's really caring and kind. He's going to be a veterinarian, too. And... he has a good family." I stopped myself. Did he?

After what I'd learned, I wasn't sure anymore. Could people change? Just because Graham had been involved in shady stuff before didn't mean he still was. My mom used to tell me that all the time, after years of dealing with criminals in her work. "Not everybody is all bad," she'd say. "Most of us have some good in us. Some just have more than others, and some have serious deficits."

Mark tilted his head. "So, how are you feeling about him now, after learning about his family's past?"

"It doesn't change my feelings for Henry at all. And I guess I'm trying to look at the glass as half full." I shrugged. "You have to believe people can change. That just because you make bad choices doesn't mean you're a bad person."

He laughed again. "Maybe that's true, Zoey Monroe. But I gotta tell you, in my experience, that's not usually true."

"Am I marrying into a crime family?"

"Maybe." He gave a lopsided smile. "I mean, with his dad's past? You gotta hope he pays the ransom."

The words hit like a slap. It hadn't occurred to me, not really, that they might *not* pay. It was a lot of money, but they had a lot. Did they not think I was worth it? "You really think he wouldn't pay?" I asked, voice smaller than I wanted it to be.

"In my experience, people love one thing above all else. Money. Five million dollars is a lot of money. You gotta ask: does he love his son enough?" He looked right at me. "I mean, if you weren't marrying his son, if you were just some girl? I think he'd ignore the demands and let you die."

I shook my head, not wanting to believe Graham could be so cold. "I get the feeling he'd do anything for Henry."

"I hope that's true, Zoey. I really do."

There was a softness in his voice that unsettled me more than anger would have. Then he added, "Go ahead and eat up. I'll get you more water if you need it, but looks like you've got a couple bottles left."

I looked down at the bag in my lap, then back up at him. "Are you always this nice to people?"

He blinked, caught off guard.

"I mean..." I continued, "you kidnapped me. I'm a victim

right now. And you're nice. Gil's been nice too. And the man in the suit. He seems... cordial." I hesitated, then added, "Is that how it always goes? Not that I want you to rough me up or anything, but... I don't know. I guess I thought kidnapping would be more brutal."

Why was I even saying this out loud? Maybe I was losing my mind. I'd been locked in this basement for nearly twenty-four hours. These people were criminals. And I was... making small talk and asking about their criminal enterprise.

He gave a dry laugh. "No reason not to be nice, don't you think? You haven't done anything to provoke me." He leaned slightly forward. "But let's be clear. If you tried to fight me, I'd fight you back."

The way he said it, I believed him. Every word. No, I couldn't win physically. But could I outsmart them?

I took another bite of the cheeseburger. It was deliciously gooey, salty, and greasy in the best way. I was definitely going to need more water. I finished my last fry and stared at the empty wrapper, my thoughts swirling.

It was funny, in a sick way, how surreal it all was. I was having a weird, almost civil conversation with the guy who helped abduct me. There was something too normal about it. Not that being locked in a basement was normal, but it wasn't like in the movies where scary men in masks threatened with hunting knives for their captives to comply. Come to think of it...

They hadn't worn masks. They hadn't threatened me with a weapon. And then the thought hit me like a punch to the chest.

They hadn't worn masks.

I had seen their faces.

Mark. Gil. The man in the suit.

I could identify them.

And it didn't matter to them that I could identify them to the police... because they had planned to kill me all along. As soon as they got the money, they were going to *kill* me. My heart began to pound. I could feel it in my throat, hear it in my ears. I glanced around the basement, eyes darting for exits that didn't exist. My skin prickled. My breath caught. I had to find a way to escape.

23

MARTINA

Hirsch placed his hand on my shoulder, obviously trying to calm me down.

My daughter's future father-in-law had withheld pertinent information, information that could actually save her life. And I wanted to strangle him more than I'd ever wanted to strangle anyone in my life.

Stavros eyed me, his gaze sharp and knowing. "Okay, now we're getting somewhere. Do you recall if Jeremy Santo or his associates ever kidnapped anybody like this before? Or committed similar crimes? How did they obtain the people they were trafficking?"

"I have no idea how they got those women," Graham said, rubbing a hand down his face. "From what I can remember, and you have to realize, this was thirty years ago, I don't think the victims spoke English. I'm not sure if it was Spanish or another language. I just remember I didn't understand them. Although when they did speak, they were silenced quickly." He hesitated, his voice tightening. "I could just tell they were rough people. But organized, too. And from what I'd heard from Jeremy, ruthless."

I turned to Vincent and Selena. My heart was pounding, but I spoke with purpose. "Let's find out everything we can about Jeremy and his dealings from thirty years ago. Learn who he associated with in prison and who he lived with when he was out. I want to know every single detail of Jeremy Santo's life." I looked between them. "And let's get in touch with his ex-wife. She may have a tale or two."

Selena nodded. "I'll take the Judy Litman angle. I'll try to reach out to her. Let her know we need her help."

Vincent added, "Okay, I'll take Jeremy Santo. I'll check all records, known associates. See if there's anybody who may have been put away for similar crimes, like kidnapping. I may have to make a few calls. The initial background search didn't pull up anything particularly useful. We brought you this news as soon as we got it. But I'll dig deeper. I'll get the rest of the team involved, too. We'll get the information as fast as we can."

"Good," I said, my voice hard. "We have zero time left to waste." I glared at Graham Ashford, letting him feel every ounce of my fury.

Selena said, "I'll step out so I can start making calls."

"Thank you, Selena," I said. She nodded quietly and left the room.

"Vincent," I continued, "let's also get the research team looking into any similar crimes in the Bay Area, kidnapping for ransom or anything that has the same flavor. We've already seen how sophisticated this organization is. Based on how they took Zoey, this can't be their first time."

"Got it," Vincent said. He flipped his laptop shut with a snap and stood. "I'm gonna head to the research room and dole out the work. We're gonna dig hard and look for anything and everything that could lead us to who Jeremy Santo might be in business with. It's likely a large organization."

"That's what I suspect as well," Stavros said grimly. "And this would've been useful information *eight hours ago*."

"My thoughts exactly," I said, shooting another glare at Graham.

Then I turned to the room. "Okay, you've got your orders. Graham, Margot—if you can think of anything else, and I mean *anything*, please don't hesitate." I let out a long breath. "Maybe now, we can give Henry an update."

Graham said, "I don't want Henry to know about this."

"Which part?" I asked coldly. "That you withheld information that could help us find Zoey? Or that you used to be associated with criminals and were one yourself?"

Graham bowed his head, shame washing over his features. Maybe I was being harsher than I should've been. But this was a life-or-death situation. My daughter, his son's fiancée, was out there somewhere, and every second mattered.

"I'm sorry," he said quietly. "Five million's a lot. If... if it comes to that, I can liquidate some accounts. We'll give the money."

Stavros looked over at me, and I glanced back at him. There was tension in the silence, but I gave a slow nod. "I appreciate that," I said. "Let's just hope it doesn't come to that and we can find them before the deadline."

Hirsch stepped closer, his voice gentler now. "Do you wanna get some air, Martina?"

I nodded.

Together, Hirsch and I exited the conference room, stepping through the lobby and out into the cool air. We started walking around the block, and my mind raced with everything we'd just learned, and yet the silence between us felt strangely grounding.

"Can you believe that?"

Hirsch exhaled, shoving his hands into his jacket pockets.

"Some people are ashamed of their past, Martina. But you've got a whole team of people working to find Zoey. This information—sure, it would've been useful earlier—but we have it now. And we've still got a little time. Very little. But still... it's something."

"I suppose you're right," I said, trying to breathe through the storm inside me. "How are Audrey and Kim doing?"

"They're good. Safe and sound."

I shook my head. "Tonight was supposed to be Zoey's bachelorette extravaganza."

He nodded solemnly. "Audrey was really looking forward to it. She was so excited to be invited."

Zoey had requested a rather tame event. She said she wanted something low-key, a PG sleepover at Kaylie's parents' house so that all her girls could be together. And now she was somewhere all alone in a basement. On a filthy couch. And I didn't know if I was ever going to see her again.

My phone buzzed in my hand. It was Vincent. I answered. "What's up?"

"Where are you guys?"

"Just taking a walk around the block."

"We just got the cell phone data back on the ransom demand call."

I stopped walking. "Did you get something?"

"We got a location."

My heart dropped. "Where is it?"

"It's in Mountain View. And the phone is currently on. *Right now.*"

I turned to Hirsch, urgency spiking in my voice. "Hirsch, we gotta go. There's a location. It's live. We have to move."

Vincent's voice sharpened. "Do you want a backup team?"

"Yeah. You and Selena. That should be enough."

"You got it. Meet you in the garage?"

"Meet you in the garage."

We hung up. Finally, a lead. Hope, fierce and fragile, flared in my chest. *Please*, I thought, *let whatever we find lead us to Zoey.*

24

HIRSCH

Martina and I hurried back toward the office building, moving fast but trying not to look like we were sprinting through a crime scene. The cold air bit at our faces as we pushed through the lobby and rushed to the stairwell, skipping the elevator to shave precious seconds.

We burst into the parking garage, the fluorescent lights overhead buzzing faintly. The scent of oil and concrete clung to the air. Just as we rounded the corner toward the row where the agency vehicles were parked, my phone buzzed in my hand.

Blackwell. I answered immediately. "Blackwell, what's up?"

"I think we've got something."

"What is it?"

"Our team finally went through all the security footage from the night Zoey was taken from the parking garage. We're not 100% sure we saw the driver leaving, but we ran every single license plate that exited after we know Zoey had entered, and we found one that had been reported stolen."

I stopped in my tracks, heart thudding in my chest. "Stolen vehicle. That's our best lead."

"Exactly. We put out an APB on the car. And we just got a sighting."

"Where?"

"Mountain View."

I felt a chill run down my spine. "Can you text me the address?"

"Sure. I've already got a team en route. I'll let you know what we find."

"I appreciate it," I said, then ended the call.

My mind raced. The stolen vehicle and the phone that sent the ransom message—both were in Mountain View. Could they be in the same exact location? It was too close to be a coincidence. Unless it was a trap. A diversion. Something meant to see if we were working with law enforcement.

I clenched my jaw, wishing I had more time to talk this out with Blackwell. Compare notes. Form a plan. But we were already moving.

Martina glanced at me. "What was that about?"

I quickly filled her in.

"Well, I'll be darned," she said. "Why don't you call Vincent and let him know. Oh, there he is."

Vincent and Selena jogged up from the far side of the garage, their footsteps echoing against the concrete walls. I waved them down. As they approached, I relayed everything Blackwell had told me. Their eyes widened in sync.

Selena frowned. "Is it possible they messed up? Isn't that kind of strange, like, too convenient?"

"Yeah," I said, "it may mean it's not them. But it might be a clue, something left behind. Something that could lead us to them."

Martina's expression shifted, her eyes lighting with something I hadn't seen in hours—hope.

"All right," she said, squaring her shoulders. "Let's go find that car and that phone."

We all moved in unison, doors opening, engines starting, our convoy ready to chase down the most promising lead we'd had since this nightmare began.

25

MARTINA

As I drove, I could hear Hirsch in the passenger seat, making a series of calls with brief, direct updates about where we were headed and who we might be dealing with. I kept my eyes on the road, barely registering the blur of passing headlights. My only thought: Please let this lead us to Zoey. Anything. Her abductor. Her location. Some clue. Just... something. We were running out of time.

"It's right up there," Hirsch said, pointing ahead.

Not that I needed the help. It was obvious. Up ahead, nestled inside a small strip mall in Mountain View, were half a dozen San Jose Police Department cruisers clustered around a single vehicle. The flashing lights painted the storefronts in red and blue.

I parked along the curb, heart pounding, and spotted Vincent and Selena pulling up right behind us. I gave them a quick wave, and the four of us headed toward the police presence.

I lifted a hand in greeting as Lieutenant Blackwell broke away from a group of officers and hurried toward us.

"What did you find?" I asked.

"It's empty."

"But it's the car?"

He nodded. "It is. We're running it now. The owner reported it stolen a few days ago, but we've also got forensics en route. We'll sweep it for fingerprints, hair, fibers. Anything that could connect back to Zoey."

"Thank you. I appreciate it. Can I take a look?"

"Of course."

"Oh, and Lieutenant Blackwell, this is Vincent." I gestured toward him. "He's on our research team. And this is Selena Bailey, my other daughter, and a private investigator with my firm."

"Nice to meet you both," Blackwell said, offering a quick shake of the hand. "If you're here, I'm guessing you're the best."

They both gave modest shrugs, and I smiled faintly. "They are."

"Okay," Blackwell said, motioning for us to follow. "Let me show you the vehicle." As we walked toward the surrounded car, he added, "Oh, and we also just got the data back from Apple. That message we suspected Zoey was trying to send before we think she was drugged?"

My breath caught. "Yes?"

"Nothing useful. One keystroke. That's it."

"Who was it to?" I asked, already fearing the answer.

"Your phone number."

I let out a long breath, shoulders sagging. She'd tried. Under duress, Zoey had tried to reach out to me.

"Okay," Blackwell said, pausing a few feet from the vehicle. "There it is. No one's touched it. The crime scene investigation van is pulling in now. They'll do the full workup."

In the distance, I could already see the headlights of the CSI van approaching.

If they'd been careless, if they hadn't worn gloves, this car might finally give us something tangible. I'd want to see the garage footage myself later. But something told me whoever drove this car knew what they were doing.

"Excellent," Hirsch said beside me, nodding as the van rolled closer.

Blackwell said, "If they left any clean fingerprints, we'll get a match within the hour."

I glanced around the strip mall, noting the dozens of security cameras mounted along the rooftops and storefronts. Selena stepped beside me, her eyes scanning just as quickly.

"There are cameras everywhere," she said, pointing across the lot.

"Yep," I said, following her gaze. "Let's start talking to the businesses. They've all got security systems, and if we're lucky, one of them caught who got in and out of that vehicle."

Lieutenant Blackwell overheard and stepped toward us. "With all due respect, Martina," he said, "it's probably best if law enforcement makes the requests. We'll have a better shot at getting the footage turned over and it keeps the chain of custody clean."

"Can one of your officers come with us?" I asked. "We know what we're looking for."

"Of course," he said. "I need to stay here at the scene. Hold on." He turned and raised his voice. "Spangler!"

A female officer with her dark hair pulled back in a low bun jogged over.

Blackwell nodded toward us. "Officer Spangler, this is Hirsch, Martina, Selena, and Vincent. They're part of the private investigation team working this case. Martina is also the mother of the kidnapping victim. They'd like to canvass the local businesses for security footage. I want you to accompany them and obtain any relevant evidence legally in case it becomes admissible."

"Absolutely, sir," Spangler said crisply.

"It would help if we could split up," Selena suggested. "Two teams. One go to the left, the other to the right. We'd cover more ground, faster."

Blackwell nodded and turned his head again. "Blaine!"

A young officer with tan skin and a friendly smile jogged over to join us. Blackwell quickly filled him in. "You good with going with Hirsch and Martina?"

"Sure thing," Blaine said.

"I appreciate it, Lieutenant," I said.

"Anytime," he replied. "Now go get that footage."

Selena turned to me. "Want Vincent and me to go together, and you and Hirsch take the other side?"

"Sounds good. Thanks, Selena. Thanks, Vincent."

"Of course," Vincent said. "Spangler, let's head this way."

Though Spangler technically outranked them in jurisdiction, she seemed fine following their lead under the circumstances. Blaine turned to Hirsch and me with an easy grin.

"I guess that means I'm with you two."

With a nod, I said, "Let's move."

We crossed the lot toward the first shop, a sandwich place just in front of the vehicle. The manager was quick to cooperate, letting us behind the counter to view the surveillance monitor. Blaine stood beside him, notebook in hand, while Hirsch and I leaned close to the screen.

We started from the current time and slowly rewound.

Minutes passed.

Nothing.

Then—

"There," I said, pointing while my heart pounded. A man stepped out of the stolen vehicle and casually walked away. "Pause it," I told the clerk.

The footage froze. I leaned in. The man looked to be in his

late twenties or early thirties. Dark hair. Medium build. I took out my phone and snapped a photo. We'd lucked out. Let's hope the streak continued. "He could still be in the shopping center."

"We should search the area," Hirsch said.

"You're right," Officer Blaine agreed. "I'll stay and secure the footage. You two go."

"Thanks," I said, already moving toward the door.

Hirsch and I hurried out of the shop, hearts racing, eyes scanning. We had a face, putting us one step closer to finding Zoey.

26

MARTINA

WE CROSSED THE LOT QUICKLY, heading back toward the stolen vehicle. Lieutenant Blackwell was standing near the hood, talking with one of the crime scene techs. When he spotted us approaching, he stepped away to meet us.

"Lieutenant," I called out.

"You find something?" he asked.

"We did," I said. "A business directly in front of the vehicle had a surveillance camera facing the lot. We caught someone getting out of the stolen car and walking away."

"Male," Hirsch added. "Late twenties to early thirties. Medium build, dark hair. We've got a freeze-frame."

I pulled out my phone and held it out to Blackwell. "Here."

He studied the image, his brow furrowed. "Timestamp?"

"About fifteen minutes ago," I said. "It's possible he's still in the area."

"We're going to do a sweep of the plaza. Fast and quiet," Hirsch said.

Blackwell nodded. "Do it. I'll keep the team focused here and let the other officers know to keep their eyes open. If you see him, don't engage alone. Call me immediately."

"Understood," I said.

We turned and took off across the strip mall again, cutting back to the far end. The shops were scattered with patrons, too few to feel hopeful, but just enough to keep us alert.

We started down the line. First, a dry cleaner with lights still on but no one inside. Next, a nail salon with two technicians cleaning up and a wireless store with a clerk chatting on a headset. I scanned every face we passed, every figure that might match the man in the still.

Nothing.

We ducked into a convenience store with a few shelves half-stocked. A man stood by the back refrigerators, grabbing a soda. I held my breath. It wasn't him. Back outside, we hurried past a taqueria, the smell of sizzling carne asada in the air. A couple sat by the window, laughing. No sign of the suspect.

From the corner of my eye, I spotted movement. At the far end of the strip mall, a figure slipped into the narrow alley behind the last unit. Quick. Quiet.

"There," I said, grabbing Hirsch's arm and pointing.

Without hesitation, we ran down the ally. It was dimly lit, shadowed by dumpsters and the glow of a security light. Hirsch and I turned the corner fast, our footsteps echoing sharply off the concrete. My pulse thundered in my ears as I scanned ahead.

There, just up ahead, a figure moved, cutting between two large trash bins and glancing over his shoulder. Our eyes locked.

"Stop!" Hirsch shouted, but the man bolted.

We sprinted after him. He was fast, faster than I expected, but we weren't far behind. My legs burned as we pushed through the passageway.

He reached the end of the alley, darting around the back of the strip mall toward a small, nearly empty lot. That's when I saw it, a car idling at the curb. The passenger door flew open.

"Stop!" I yelled.

The man dove in, and before we could close the distance, the car peeled away. Tires squealed as the vehicle sped off down the back street. Hirsch pulled up beside me, breathing hard. I reached for my phone, snapping a picture of the back of the car, but it was too far away, and I couldn't make out the plate.

"Dang it. He must have seen the police activity and knew he had to bolt."

I exhaled hard, trying to calm my racing heart. I raised my phone again and opened the still image of the man from the sandwich shop footage. I studied his face one more time. We didn't have his name, but now we had his face and the knowledge that someone else was helping him.

I looked at Hirsch. "Let's go back to Blackwell and see if anyone on the street saw the suspect or car he was in." It was a long shot.

He gave a grim nod.

We doubled back toward the main lot, frustration settling in my chest. We'd been so close. Close enough to see the fear, or maybe the calculation, in that man's eyes before he ran. Close enough to feel like maybe, just maybe, we could bring Zoey home. But close wasn't good enough.

As we approached the scene, I spotted Blackwell where we'd left him, talking with one of the crime scene investigators near the stolen vehicle. He looked up the second he saw us and stepped away to meet us halfway.

"He got away," I said before he could ask. "Took off through the alley. A car was already waiting for him. The driver ready, and the engine running. They were gone before we could get a plate. He probably saw the police activity and called for a ride."

Blackwell gave a small nod, then glanced back at the forensics team. "You might get your ID sooner than you think. My crime scene guys got lucky, and there were clear fingerprints on the interior door handle of the car. And another partial on the rearview mirror. They've already been scanned and uploaded. AFIS is processing now."

My breath caught. "How long?"

"Less than an hour, if the system gets a hit," he said. "If this guy's ever been printed, we'll know who he is before your coffee would've had time to get cold."

I looked at Hirsch. "That's something."

"That's not all we got," he replied. "Techs found long dark hairs in the trunk. They'll run it for DNA to see if it's a match for Zoey to confirm it was the vehicle she was transported in."

The thought of Zoey in the trunk made me physically ill, but at least it was a clue that could help us bring her home.

27

MARTINA

BACK AT THE OFFICE, Vincent, Selena, Hirsch, and I gathered around the conference table, reviewing everything that had just happened. The chase. The alley. The escape. And most importantly, the fingerprint.

We'd been so close. And in my gut, I knew we were still close. But we needed that one final piece to fall into place. We were waiting on AFIS. If the fingerprint got a hit, we'd have a name and hopefully, a direct line to whoever had taken Zoey. If it didn't? All we had was a grainy image from the sandwich shop's camera. And that wasn't going to be enough. Not to find her before the drop at 10 AM the next morning.

"I'll check in with the research team," Vincent said, pushing back from the table. "See if they've uncovered anything like other crimes in the area or more links to Jeremy Santo."

"Thanks, Vincent," Selena said. She turned to me. "Anything else you need from me before I try reaching out to Jeremy Santo's ex-wife? I found what looks like a current address and landline. I'm going to try for an in-person interview."

"That's perfect, Selena. Thank you."

She nodded. "We have to bring her home."

"I know." I stepped forward and gave her a hug. "Thank you. I don't know what I'd do without you."

She smiled softly. "Likewise."

I watched her walk down the hallway, already dialing. Then I turned to Hirsch, who had been uncharacteristically quiet. "How are you feeling?"

He gave a small smile. "Hopeful. You?"

"I feel like we're right on the edge of something. If that fingerprint hits, it could be the break we need to get her back."

Just then, Hirsch's phone buzzed in his pocket. He pulled it out, glanced at the screen, and answered immediately.

"Blackwell," he said, his tone shifting into focus.

I watched his face closely as he listened. First came the nod. Then another. And finally his expression changed. Something passed through his eyes. Relief. Purpose. Satisfaction. He ended the call and looked at me.

"Well?"

"That was Blackwell," he said. "They got a hit on the fingerprint. San Jose PD picked up the suspect a few blocks from where the car was dumped in Mountain View."

My heart leapt. "So, they got him?"

"Yep. He's in custody. They're bringing him in now."

I was already grabbing my coat. "Let's go talk to him."

Hirsch didn't hesitate. He opened the office door for me, his voice steady.

"After you."

28

MARTINA

Hirsch and I busted through the doors of the San Jose police station, the air-conditioned lobby slapping against my face like a cold front. My heart pounded in my chest. I *needed* to see this man, this person connected to my daughter's kidnapping. I needed to look him in the eye and make him tell me where Zoey was.

I could only hope Lieutenant Blackwell would agree to let me question him. Maybe even without the cameras on in the interview room. Near the front desk stood Blackwell, likely anticipating our arrival. Not waiting for Hirsch, I surged ahead, barely able to keep the desperation from spilling out of me.

"Who is he? What has he told you? Where is Zoey?"

"The suspect's name is Diego Gentry," Blackwell said. "So far, he hasn't said a word except when he asked for a lawyer."

"Well, it's a good thing I'm not in law enforcement. I can question him all I want. He can sit there and stay quiet, or he can talk to me. You will let me talk to him, right?"

Blackwell seemed caught off guard by my request. I wasn't sure why. Hirsch stepped in. "When Martina wasn't with the CoCo County Sheriff's Department, we let her question suspects associated with her investigations. It's completely legal," he explained. "He doesn't have to talk, like she said, but she can ask what she wants."

Blackwell nodded slowly, clearly still weighing the risk. "Hirsch, you'll be in the room with her?"

"Of course."

Did Blackwell not trust me? Or did he think my judgment was clouded because my daughter had been taken? Either way, I didn't care. I just wanted to talk to this Diego Gentry, and I wanted to do it now. "Well then, let's go. Where is he?"

Blackwell hesitated slightly, then said, "This way."

He led us down a narrow hallway into a secure room. Inside stood a uniformed officer. I gave the guard a nod, then turned toward the thick glass.

Through the window sat a young man, maybe late twenties. Dark hair. Tan skin. Thin build. Hard to say exactly how tall, but maybe six feet if he stood. He didn't look dangerous. He looked tired. Like he'd been through the wringer. "What do you know about him?" I asked.

"He's twenty-eight. From San Jose, born and raised. He's got a record: petty theft, receiving stolen goods, and a few drug charges."

"Any connection to organized crime?"

"Not that we can tell, but you never know. Organized crime's more rampant here in San Jose than we like to admit. They've got tentacles everywhere. He could be connected, but he's not a big enough fish to be on anyone's radar."

I nodded, understanding. "And he hasn't said anything useful?"

"Nope. Asked for a lawyer almost immediately."

Hirsch said, "So, he's not a complete idiot."

"He's been taught not to talk to cops."

I pulled out my phone and opened the grainy video clip of

the man who took Zoey, that we'd reviewed again and again. "I'm assuming you've reviewed the security footage again?"

Blackwell glanced at the screen. "We don't think it's him. The man who took Zoey was taller. Bigger build. Maybe older. The footage isn't clear enough for a definitive ID. We ran facial recognition, no hits. Too blurry."

"That's what I suspected. Did you find anything on him? A cell phone or any weapons?"

Blackwell cocked his head. "No weapons. But we did find a burner phone on him. We haven't been able to unlock it yet."

Could it be the phone that the ransom was sent from? We couldn't exactly ask Blackwell, or he'd know we'd been withholding information. "But you think you can?"

"Sure, shouldn't be too long."

"Good."

"We're doing everything we can to bring Zoey home safe."

"Thank you."

"I'll let you inside to talk to him, but I don't think I have to tell you to keep your hands to yourself. He can't come to any harm while he's in our custody. You understand, right?"

"Of course."

"All right. We'll be watching."

I nodded, jaw clenched. Of course I wouldn't touch him. I just wanted to talk to him and ask a few questions, like, "Where *is* my daughter?"

Blackwell gave me one last look before stepping aside.

We reached a heavy door at the end of the hall. The metal plate on the outside read INTERVIEW 1. Lieutenant Blackwell slid his keycard through the lock. The door clicked open.

"Mr. Gentry," he said, stepping inside, "we have a couple visitors for you."

"Is it my lawyer?"

"No. Just concerned citizens."

Blackwell pushed the door open wider and gestured for Hirsch and me to enter. I stepped inside and studied the man seated at the table.

Seeing him up close, I thought he was likely the young man we'd chased at the shopping center.

"Who are you?" he asked.

"I'll leave you to it," Lieutenant Blackwell said behind us. "Just holler if you need me."

He pulled the door shut behind him with a soft click.

I moved to the chair across from Diego Gentry and sat down, locking eyes with him. Hirsch stood in the corner, arms crossed, looming quietly like a warning.

"My name is Martina Monroe," I said. "And this is my colleague, Hirsch. I have a few questions for you."

"I asked for a lawyer. I don't gotta tell you nothin'. You can't question me."

"I think you misunderstand," I said calmly. "I'm not law enforcement. Neither is Hirsch. Like Lieutenant Blackwell told you, we're concerned citizens. And I need you to answer a few questions that are related to a kidnapping that took place last night."

A smirk curled across his face, but I saw the flicker in his eyes, the hesitation. He was scared. "I already told the cops," he said. "I don't know anything about a kidnapping."

It was possible he didn't, but I'd bet he knew the person or persons who did. "Where'd you get the car?"

"What car?"

"The black Camry that they found your fingerprints all over. The one parked on El Camino Real in Mountain View. Where did you get it?"

He looked from Hirsch to me, his gaze darting. "I don't know what you're talking about. You got the wrong guy."

I took a slow breath, rolling my neck to relieve the tension mounting at the base of my skull. "Listen carefully, Diego. You may not know who I am, so let me spell it out for you. I'm Martina Monroe of Drakos Monroe Security and Investigations. One of the top private investigation and security firms in California. Maybe the country. I work with ex-Navy SEALs, ex-Rangers, former law enforcement, and the best computer experts in the world. We find things, and we find people. And if I wanted to, I could find out everything about you before the hour's up."

He blinked, trying to stay stone-faced.

"So, it's in your best interest to answer my questions."

"Lady, you got the wrong guy," he said, shifting uncomfortably. "I don't know nothin' about no car or whatever."

I leaned forward. "Listen to me very carefully. Zoey Monroe is my daughter. Someone took her and put her in a car that has your fingerprints on it."

His chair creaked as he leaned back, his face paling just slightly.

"And if I find out you're withholding information that could save my daughter's life," I said, every syllable sharpened with fury, "then I, and all of my resources, will hunt you down and make sure you pay for your role in her abduction."

"You can't threaten me like this," he said, his voice rising, his bravado thinning.

Rage burned in my chest. I stood, leaning over the table, eyes locked on his. "Oh, I can do whatever I want," I said. "Because you're the one backed into a corner. And it would behoove you to tell me where you got that car."

"Sorry, lady. I don't know nothing."

I slammed my hand on the table, the sound sharp and echoing. "We know you're involved. Now I know your face, and I know your name. I will not forget them. Tell me where you got the Camry!"

A sharp knock cut through the air.

I stepped back quickly, straightened my jacket. Hirsch opened the door.

Lieutenant Blackwell poked his head in. "Everything okay in here?"

"This lady is crazy!" Diego snapped, pointing. "I'm gonna file a complaint. She's threatening me! She can't do that!"

I turned to face Diego, eyes hard. "This isn't over."

Brushing past Blackwell, I stormed out of the room into the open space of the conference area. Hirsch caught up to me seconds later. "Are you okay?"

"He's lying, Hirsch."

"I know. But getting arrested for threatening a suspect in custody won't help Zoey."

"I didn't lay a finger on him."

"Look, he's obviously not going to talk to us, not right now. We need to find something to make him talk, without threatening him."

I clenched my fists and nodded once. "Fine. You're right. Let's call Vincent and find out everything we can about Diego."

The clock was ticking, and I was afraid we were running out of time.

29

SELENA

SHAKING MY HEAD, I stared at Vincent. "I don't like what I'm seeing."

"There's a pattern," he said quietly, tapping his screen. "Six kidnappings over the past decade. Wealthy targets. Similar M.O. —taken quickly, ransom demanded, no police involvement."

"And all of them..." I trailed off, unable to say it aloud.

Vincent nodded. "The bodies were found days later. All of them were killed after the ransom was paid."

A cold wave moved through me. I glanced at the clock. 5:57 PM. We had just over sixteen hours until the deadline. That was all the time Zoey had left if this played out the same way as the others. I wrapped my arms around myself, trying to steady my breathing. Zoey wasn't just my stepsister, she was the sister I never knew I needed. My closest friend. And if we didn't stop this...

"What do we tell Martina?" Vincent asked gently.

"We don't. Not yet," I said. "She's already barely hanging on. If we tell her about the other six... it'll destroy her. And she needs to stay sharp."

He gave a slow nod. "All right. But if we find a solid lead, something that changes the picture, we loop her in immediately."

"Of course. And I'm not keeping it from her forever. I just... I don't want her to lose hope."

Before Vincent could respond, his phone vibrated on the table. He answered it after one buzz. "Yeah?" followed by, "Uh-huh... okay." Pause. "Got it. Thanks."

He hung up and turned to me. "That was Martina. The suspect's name is Diego Gentry. She wants us to dig into everything. Background, contacts, and anything he's ever touched. He's stonewalling."

It was like we were constantly changing directions. Find everything on Judy Litman and on Jeremy Santo. Find any similar crimes in the area. Now, learn everything we can on Diego Gentry. Thankfully, we had a full support team to pick up where we left off, so we could handle each new urgent request ourselves. With a nod, I said, "No surprise there. Did she say anything else?"

"Just that she's calling your dad to let him know she won't be coming home tonight."

Nobody would. As if on cue, my phone buzzed in my hand. It was Martina. "I'm going to take this outside." I stood up and answered, "Hey. How are you holding up?" as I made my way to the hallway and began pacing.

"I should be asking you that," Martina said, her voice strained but still warm. "I know how close you and Zoey are. Are you doing okay?"

I hesitated, then forced the words out. "Not really. But I'm holding it together. We're working on it."

"I'm sorry, Selena. I hate that you're in the middle of this."

"You don't have to be sorry. I want to be here. I need to help find her."

There was a pause. "What have you and Vincent found? Anything yet?"

I pressed my fingers to my temple. "We're still pulling files. Trying to find something useful."

"Good. Just keep going. Call me the second you find a thread."

"I will. I promise."

Martina exhaled on the other end. "If you need a break, don't be afraid to take one."

"I'm not leaving until we find something," I said. "We're not wasting a second. Not with the clock ticking."

"I feel the same way," she said. "If there's anything I can do on my end to help you, tell me."

As if I would add more to Martina's list of things to do. "Thank you. See you soon."

We ended the call, and I stood there for a moment in the quiet hallway, my heart aching. We *had* to find Zoey.

Back inside the room, Vincent met me with a knowing look.

"You didn't tell her."

I shook my head.

"She's going to find out eventually."

"I know. But not until we can find something useful. For now, we give her a reason to hope for the best."

Everything inside me was screaming that we had to find Zoey before the money drop or we'd never see her again. I didn't have to explain that to Vincent. He nodded and turned back to the screen. "Let's get to work."

I dropped into the chair beside him, opened the files on Diego Gentry, and pushed away the gnawing fear in my gut. Zoey was out there. And we were running out of time.

30

SELENA

IT HAD BEEN OVER AN HOUR, and we hadn't found anything useful on Diego Gentry. There was no obvious connection to organized crime or any known syndicate. But then how the heck did he get the car?

"Vincent," I said, turning toward him.

"Yeah? You find something?"

"No, nothing on Gentry," I admitted, leaning back in my chair, "but don't you think it's strange that we haven't found anything on him?"

"It could be harder to make a connection since he hasn't been associated with any kind of violent crime."

"True. But maybe we're looking at this wrong. Maybe we should be looking at low-level associates, see if they connect to someone bigger."

"Makes sense. I'll check in with the rest of the team to see if they dug anything up that we missed." He stood, rubbing a hand over his forehead. "I'll be back."

Vincent bounded out of the conference room, frustration simmering just beneath the surface, not at me but at the case

Before She Said I Do

itself. My attention returned to the six similar kidnappings that occurred over the last ten years. There had to be something connecting them all. I pulled up the files on my screen again and reviewed the notes I had made before we shifted our focus to Diego Gentry. As I reread the cases, my gut stirred. Could it be? It was a hunch. Could it be right? On my computer, I pressed Print. I thought I was seeing a pattern, but I wanted to highlight them on paper, the old-fashioned way, to ensure what I was seeing was real.

I headed out of the conference room toward the printer, which was parked beside the humming coffee machine in the hallway. The scent of burnt coffee clung to the air, and I longed for Betty's fresh brew from home. Vincent was next to the coffee maker, speaking with Stavros. I gave a quick wave.

"Selena," Stavros called out.

From next to the printer, I said, "What's up?"

"The research team is digging into any known associates of Diego Gentry," he said, arms crossed as if trying to hold the stress in his chest. "But we're thinking maybe we need to get some boots on the ground. Start interviewing people." He dropped his voice. "There may not be any associates on the record, but if it's known on the street, we could ask around and learn who this guy's connected to. Do you think you're up for it?"

"Of course," I said without hesitation.

"We can have someone go with you. I want Vincent here leading the research team, but maybe you take a couple of guys. Start with last known address, usual hangouts, and talk to people. Learn anything you can about him and his associates."

"Absolutely. Who's coming with me?"

"Steve and Otto volunteered."

I almost laughed. Of course they did. I'd ignore the fact that they were the two biggest, toughest-looking guys in the office, and I was, well, the opposite. Petite, as people liked to say. But I had skills. I didn't need two giants to save me. Still, we were heading into dicey territory. Having backup wasn't the worst idea.

"Sounds good," I said, collecting the fresh stack of printed reports. "I was just printing out the police reports from the six kidnappings. I might have something... but I want to be sure."

"Connected to Jeremy Santo?" Stavros asked.

"Nothing that obvious," I said, flipping through the pages, "but if I'm right, we'll need to run some background checks."

"If there's something, let me know," Stavros said.

"Will do. Have Steve and Otto meet me in the conference room when they're ready. I'm going to go through these. There's a few I flagged that I want to take a closer look at, make sure what I'm seeing is really a pattern."

"You got it," Stavros said.

I walked back to the conference room. Inside, I laid out the reports, all six case files, then turned to my computer monitor to review the flagged cases. I grabbed a highlighter, popped off the cap, and began marking up the first set of detective notes.

I moved quickly. I'd already read them twice. Now I just wanted to get the key parts down in physical form so I could show Vincent and see what he thought.

For the next twenty minutes, I stayed locked in. Focused. I hadn't realized how much time had passed until I heard a shift in the doorway.

Steve and Otto stood there like statues, each towering around six-five. Otto was bald and stone-faced, and Steve... well, Steve wasn't someone I'd want to meet in a dark alley.

"You ready to go?" Steve asked, eyeing the papers. "Looks like you're working on something."

"I think I might've found a pattern, or at least a clue. Take a look."

They stepped inside. I slid the stack toward them and pointed to the highlighted notes, comments from detectives who had interviewed people near the scenes.

"Am I wrong?" I asked, pulse quickening.

Steve picked up one report, then another. His brow furrowed as he scanned them.

"I think these are the same people, Selena."

"That's what I was thinking," I said. "They're going by different names. One is listed by their last name. Another by their first. This one has both first and last."

Steve nodded slowly. "So, we have two potential suspects in all six kidnappings."

"Exactly."

"Nice work."

"You think it's good?"

He smiled faintly. "It's better than good. Now let's go find these guys."

"Find what guys?" Stavros asked, stepping into the conference room with Vincent close behind.

I stood and gestured to the papers. "I found two potential suspects. Well, two people who were mentioned in all six reports. They're listed slightly differently in each case. Some as part of witness interviews, some as people who were actually interviewed, but none were ever listed as suspects."

"And there's only two?" Stavros asked.

"Weird, right? Different locations, different years, and yet these names keep showing up."

"That's more than a coincidence," Vincent said.

"We need all teams on this," Stavros added, scanning the files. "And of course, still on Gentry. But you three—" he looked at me, then Steve and Otto, "You follow the Gentry angle and call Martina and tell her what you found. I have a feeling she'll be interested in those two names and may want to talk to them herself."

Not wasting another moment, I pulled out my phone and dialed.

31

MARTINA

Pacing the floor of the police station, I kept checking the screen of my phone, over and over, while Hirsch spoke with Lieutenant Blackwell. This was taking too long. We'd been at the station for an hour and a half, and we were no closer to finding out where Zoey was. I didn't like this. We were wasting time.

The lights overhead buzzed faintly, and the walls felt like they were closing in, my pulse ticking up with every passing minute. Hirsch jogged over, his expression tense.

"What's going on?"

Hirsch said, "Gentry's lawyer just arrived."

"This is going from bad to worse. We have to find something."

"You haven't heard anything from the team?"

"No. Not yet."

As if their ears were ringing, my phone lit up with an incoming call. I answered immediately. "Hey, Selena. What's up?"

"We haven't found anything solid on Diego Gentry," she said, her voice filled with urgency. "But the team plans to go and canvas the neighborhood and places he hangs out. See if we can get anyone to talk to us. We're hoping to find out how he's connected to organized crime or if he has ties to more violent players."

"That's smart," I said. "Good luck, and let me know the second they find something."

"There's... more."

"Oh?"

As she explained, my heart sank. Six other kidnappings over the past ten years, each with the same M.O. Each ending in death. *No survivors.* Dread filled my chest like ice water. My breath caught, and I forced myself to look at my watch. 7:30 PM. We had just over fourteen hours—fourteen hours to figure out who had taken Zoey and stop them before it was too late.

"That's something," I said, trying to hold it together.

"That's not all," she continued. Selena went on to explain how she'd found two potential suspects, individuals mentioned in all six cases. The names had been listed slightly differently and in different contexts, but they were there. Over and over. "We haven't been able to find records for Bert Thomas, but we have James Turtle's address and background. I was thinking you'd want to go question him," Selena finished.

A lead? "What have you learned about Turtle?"

"He has a criminal record, but nothing too flashy. No felony convictions. And he hasn't been flagged as gang-affiliated or part of any organized crime syndicate."

"Interesting," I said, thinking aloud. "Maybe he's simply a bad guy for hire and is paid to do whatever job he's given."

"Possibly."

"Only one way to find out." I paused. "Hold on a sec," I said, lowering the phone and turning to Hirsch. "I think they found something."

He met my gaze. "What is it?"

I quickly summarized everything Selena had just told me.

"You wanna head out and question Turtle?" Hirsch asked.

"I do," I said, returning to the phone. "Selena, we're going to divide and conquer. You follow up on the lead with Diego Gentry and find who he might be connected to or something we can use to get him to talk. Hirsch and I will go find Turtle."

"I'll send you everything we have on him so far."

"Great. Who is going to canvass the area Gentry hangs out?"

"Me, Steve, and Otto."

I didn't like that one bit. "Let me talk to Stavros."

There was a shuffle on the line. A beat later, Stavros's booming voice came through. "Hey, Martina."

"Hirsch and I will talk to Turtle. Selena said you're sending her to talk to Gentry's associates?"

"I was planning on sending Steve and Otto with her."

I cut him off. "I can't have both of my daughters taken by these guys."

"Understood. You and I both know she's capable, and Steve and Otto will protect her with their lives. She'll be okay, Martina. Don't worry."

How was I supposed to not worry? "I don't know, Stavros."

"I can have someone else go, but I think she needs to be doing something. She's a lot like you, you know."

He was right. Selena and Zoey were close. It was probably difficult for Selena to be stuck in the office when she could be out there questioning potential leads. And I was grateful Stavros chose some of the most capable on the team to protect her. She was tough, but she wasn't invincible, even though she believed she was. Finally I said, "Okay. She can go. But please make sure you're in contact with her or the guys nearly all the time."

Stavros said, "Will do. And while you're out there, we'll keep digging into all of their backgrounds and see if we can find Bert Thomas. We'll keep in touch."

"My phone's on, and so is Hirsch's."

"Talk soon."

"Can I speak with Selena for a second?"

"Sure."

The phone static sounded, and then I heard her voice. "Hey."

"Did you hear the plan?"

"I did."

"Okay, be careful."

"I will. You too."

"I love you." It was more important than ever to say the words.

"I love you too, Martina."

I hung up and turned to Hirsch, laying out the plan.

He frowned, then stepped in close and pulled me aside, his voice dropping low. We were out of earshot from the others in the station. "I don't know. Are you sure we shouldn't tell someone in law enforcement?"

"You mean Blackwell?" I asked.

"Yeah. I mean, in all six of the other cases, the families didn't go to law enforcement until the body showed up. Maybe we should do things differently. Maybe we tell Blackwell what's going on now."

"No. Not yet." My voice was firm. "Maybe... if we run out of time. But we have fourteen and a half hours to find her. If we fail, we tell him. But not before. I'm not jeopardizing Zoey's life. The other families didn't have the weight of Drakos Monroe."

He looked me in the eye. "True."

"What would you do if it were Audrey? Would you follow the kidnapper's wishes? Or go to the police?" Although technically we already had, but it was before we'd heard the demands.

He hesitated. "Honestly? Maybe. At least let them know what's going on in case we could use them."

"Let's just give it a little more time. If we run out of leads, and we're getting close to the drop time, then we tell Blackwell. We let him know everything we've been up to. Okay?"

My phone pinged. I opened the notification. A message from Selena. All the information we needed on James Turtle: last known address, phone number, known associates, and a driver's license photo. "We've got what we need," I said. "Turtle's address is in San Jose."

I glanced up at Hirsch. His jaw was set. "We do it your way, for now, Martina. I'll let Blackwell know we're taking a break."

Good. *Now, let's find the guys who took my daughter.*

32

MARTINA

THANKFULLY, the address for James Turtle was only ten minutes from the police station. The neighborhood wasn't nice, to put it bluntly. Weeds served as lawns, broken-down cars were piled in driveways, some up on blocks, and people loitered in front yards, drinking from paper bags.

Hirsch nodded toward the windshield. "It's the house right up there. On the left."

"All right. Let's do this."

I parked the car. It was 7:45 PM., and the sun had gone down. It wasn't the safest neighborhood, from what I could tell, and Hirsch still carried himself like a cop. That could be our downfall.

He whipped around from the passenger side. "All right, let's try to remain calm. Don't treat him like a suspect. Just try to talk to him, like we discussed."

Did everyone think I was a loose cannon? "Of course."

"Why don't you go ahead and take the lead?"

"You got it." I nodded and stepped out of the car.

We walked up to the front door. I pounded my fist twice and stepped back. Hirsch stood beside me, his hand near his sidearm, ready, just in case. He'd been carrying since we started searching for Zoey. My weapon was also in place, tucked under my jacket, and one strapped to my ankle.

The door creaked open. An older woman appeared. She had gray hair and was about five feet tall, maybe aged sixty. She looked at us with mild curiosity.

"Good evening, ma'am," I said politely. "My name is Martina, and we're looking for James. Is he home?"

She nodded without a word, turned her head, and yelled, "James!" before retreating back inside.

Maybe his mother? The team hadn't gotten a full background check on James Turtle yet. Just a quick pull. They found he had some weapons charges and a few bar fights, but nothing too serious.

A man stepped into the doorway. About five-foot-five, dark hair, tan skin, wearing a white tank and gray sweatpants. He looked us up and down. "Who are you?"

"My name is Martina," I said. "And this is my friend, August." Better not to use Hirsch's last name. It might give away his law enforcement background. Not that he could really hide it. It was in every fiber of his being. "We just have a few questions for you," I added.

"About what? You trying to sell me something?" His gaze slid to Hirsch, lingering on the way his hand hovered near his hip.

James reached around and casually patted his own lower back, checking for something or making a point.

Hirsch stayed calm, letting his hand drift away.

I took a step forward. "Look, we're not here to cause trouble. We just have a few questions about an associate of yours."

"An associate of mine?" James scoffed. "What do I look like, a banker?"

"Let's call it an acquaintance. Maybe a friend."

He crossed his arms. "Who's your friend?"

"Do you know a Jeremy Santo?"

He looked at Hirsch, then at me. "Nope. Never heard of him."

"What about Bert Thomas?"

James squinted, then smirked. "I don't know those people. Why are you asking about them, anyway?" He took a step forward, locking eyes with Hirsch. "Are you cops or something? 'Cause you look like a cop," he said, eyeing Hirsch.

Hirsch said, "Not anymore, sir."

James squinted at me. "What's your story, lady?"

"I'm a private investigator, and I'm looking for a girl who went missing. I think maybe you know something about that. Or maybe you know somebody who does. Kidnapping for ransom. Lots and lots of money involved."

He scoffed. "I don't get involved in that kind of stuff."

Hirsch stepped forward. "Are you sure about that? We've been going through police reports, and your name comes up quite a few times. It's linked to several kidnappings similar to the one we're looking into right now."

"I think you got the wrong guy," James said with a casual shrug. His tone was relaxed, like this was no big deal, but he was lying. We could both see it. We could also see that he wasn't going to talk to us.

"Okay, so you don't know Jeremy Santos. You don't know Bert Thomas. What about Diego Gentry?"

"I don't know nobody named Diego Gentry."

I stepped forward. "I'm gonna level with you, James."

He raised an eyebrow but didn't interrupt.

"Someone took my daughter. My *25-year-old* daughter. And they've asked for money to bring her back safe. But you know what I think, James?" My voice trembled as I continued. "I think you know that as soon as they get that money, they're going to kill her." I moved closer, my rage bubbling to the surface. "And do you want to know what I'm going to do if that happens? I'm going to hunt you down. I already know where you live. I know about Bert. And Jeremy. And Diego. And I'll find anyone else connected to my daughter's kidnapping and make each one of you wish you were never born. And there won't be anyone who can save you."

"Martina," Hirsch said sharply, grabbing my arm and pulling me back. "Come on."

I shook him off and locked eyes with James. "Mark my words, Mr. Turtle. I will find out who's behind this. And they will pay. Do you understand?"

James chuckled, trying to brush it off. "Hey, man," he said to Hirsch, "you better get your lady under control. She's a little cuckoo-loco, if you know what I mean."

I was shaking, part fury, part fear. "This isn't the last you'll see of me. Mark my words—you will *pay*."

His demeanor shifted, the lazy smirk fading into something darker, more menacing. His voice dropped. "Don't come to my house and threaten me, lady. I'm not someone you wanna mess with."

There it was. His true colors. I laughed, bitterly. "You're mistaken, James. I'm not someone *you* wanna mess with."

Hirsch's hand gripped my arm again. "Thank you for your time, Mr. Turtle. We'll be going now. Come on, Martina," he said under his breath.

He pulled me away from the doorway, but I kept my eyes locked on James. He smirked again, and I surged forward, but Hirsch held me back.

"Come on, Martina," he said firmly. "This isn't going to help."

He walked me back to the car, opened the passenger door, and gently pushed me inside. Then he held out his hand.

"I'll drive."

"He's lying, Hirsch," I said, voice shaking. "He's involved."

"Give me your keys."

I dug them out of my pocket and handed them over. He walked around, slid into the driver's seat, and started the engine. As we pulled away from the curb, the streetlights flickered in the rearview.

"I think he's involved."

"I know," Hirsch said. "I sensed recognition in the names we asked about, except for Diego's. Turtle definitely knows something."

"We should have surveillance on his house."

"Maybe. But going around threatening people, telling them what firm you're with and that you'll hunt them down and kill them, that's not going to get Zoey back." He hesitated. "Put your seatbelt on."

"Fine." I clicked it in and slumped in the seat, bowing my head.

I was full of rage. Full of terror. What if I never got her back? Would I really hunt them down? I wasn't that kind of person. But no one had tested me like this before. But I was sure the people who did this would be brought to justice. Maybe not in blood. But I would make sure they spent the rest of their lives rotting in prison. Even if it was the last thing I ever did.

33

HIRSCH

MARTINA NEEDED TO REST. She needed to slow down and have some tea or something, anything to bring her back to center. She was really starting to worry me. She could've started a firefight back at Turtle's house. She was in no state to be questioning people, not before thinking through the consequences.

I needed to let Stavros know we'd need another team without Martina knowing I went behind her back. There was no way we could let her question another suspect. James Turtle hadn't seemed particularly threatened, but he was armed. And we were civilians. The situation could have ended very badly. I wanted to find Zoey too, but not at the cost of my life or Martina's.

Although if it were Audrey who was missing, would Martina be able to hold me back from questioning people who might know something? Probably not.

But I also believed Martina would make sure I stayed safe. That was just who she was. Martina always had a side to her that was fierce and passionate. But sometimes, that passion tipped into emotion, and when it did, it could take over. She'd been calmer these last few years, but the second they took Zoey, it changed everything. And I was afraid of what she might do and what could happen to her if she started crossing too many lines.

We were already worried enough about Zoey. If something happened to Martina too, if we lost them both, I didn't think I could forgive myself.

And worse, if something happened to me, what would happen to Kim? To Audrey? I glanced over at Martina. Her hands were shaking in her lap, her gaze unfocused.

"Do you want to stop and get some tea?" I asked gently.

She blinked. "Are we heading back to the San Jose police station?"

"Yes."

"They have tea there."

I exhaled, keeping my voice calm. "Look, Martina, this is the worst possible situation. And I get it. I'd be fighting mad if this were Audrey. And I am fighting mad because it's Zoey. But I'm wondering if we should have another team question Bert Thomas when they find him. I don't like the way things went back there."

"I know," she said softly. "I'm sorry, Hirsch. I'm just... I feel so helpless. I'm talking, I'm questioning, and I'm getting nowhere. *Nowhere.*" She turned toward the window, her voice barely above a whisper. "And of all the times I've wanted to save someone... I mean, they've all mattered. Of course they have. These are people. But this is Zoey. What if I can't save her? What if I can't?" Her voice broke. "How will I—how will I go on?"

It was a good question. "We will get her back, but if the worst were to ever happen, you will go on. You're tough," I said firmly. "And you have Charlie. You have Selena. You've got that silly-fluffy little dog, Barney. You've got your mom, your brother... you have me. You have all your family at Drakos Monroe and all the people you help who you haven't even met yet."

Martina stared out the window, silent.

"You know that gut of yours?" I continued. "That instinct you always follow? Well, I've been listening to mine. And yeah, it feels like we're not getting anywhere, but we are."

She turned slowly to look at me, her eyes rimmed red, but listening.

"Let's look at the facts. We've got a guy in custody who was driving a car Zoey may have been transported in. We've got the names of two suspects tied to six other kidnappings with nearly identical M.O.s. And you saw the look on James Turtle's face when we mentioned Jeremy Santo. When we said Bert Thomas. There was recognition. I'm sure of it." I leaned in closer. "I think we're on the right track. We just have to be smart about this. Getting shot won't help anybody."

She took a deep breath. "You're right, Hirsch."

Just then, Martina's phone lit up. She glanced at the screen, then answered, "Hey, Charlie."

With that, I turned the car on and headed back to the San Jose police station. As I drove, my heart went out to Martina. I meant everything I'd said. The clues were starting to line up, and we just had to keep pushing forward. But this was tough. I pulled into a parking stall and turned off the car.

Martina ended the call with Charlie and exhaled a shaky breath.

Before I could give her another pep talk, my phone vibrated in the console. Blackwell.

I answered. "Blackwell, what's up?"

"Where are you guys?"

"We just pulled back into the station. What's going on?"

"We just got the DNA results on the hair we found in the trunk of the black Camry." He paused. "It's a match to Zoey."

Another clue. A sickening one. "All right. We'll be inside in a minute."

Martina turned to me, her voice sharp and electric. "What is it?"

"The hair was Zoey's."

Her eyes darkened, fury flaring behind them. "Let's go have another chat with Diego."

She climbed out of the car without another word.

"Martina—" I called, but she was already halfway across the lot.

I grabbed my things and scrambled after her. The last thing I needed was Martina storming into the police station in that state. I couldn't risk Blackwell throwing us out. We needed to stay close to the suspect. And to law enforcement. But Martina wasn't making it easy.

34

ZOEY

I HAD BEEN TRYING to gauge how much time there was between visits from Mark or Gil or the man in the suit and what they sounded like. I could hear the sounds of them walking above, the creak of footsteps heading toward the door. There were no windows down here. No way to escape other than going up the stairs and out the door. *The door.*

They hadn't been walking around much lately. But if I timed it right, if I listened carefully, I could creep up the stairs when I knew no one was near and crawl out. I had no idea where I was, but surely there was a way out. They came in and out. I was beginning to think it was the only way to survive this. It was clear now what I had to do.

There was no way they were going to let me go after the Ashfords paid them. Did they think I didn't realize that? I'd been acting like I didn't. I'd been calm, too calm, but I was starting to crumble. This was life or death. And I didn't want to die. I had to think of Mom. What she would do, how she would cope. After Dad died, she'd turned to alcohol and nearly destroyed her life. She was in a car accident and was suspended from her job until she'd gotten sober. She had rebuilt everything since then. She said she did it for me. For us.

But if something happened to me, would she go back to drinking? Would she end up in another crash, this time not surviving? And then what would happen to Charlie and Selena and everyone who counted on her? Everyone who loved her? Hirsch would be devastated. They'd all already lost so much. And then there was Henry. Sweet, loving, supportive Henry. I thought he was my soulmate. But if this ended with me gone, maybe I wasn't the one for him after all.

As much as I missed my mom in these moments, I missed Henry just as much—maybe more. His warm embrace. His soft kisses. The way he made me feel like the most special person in the world. It was like when we were together everything else melted away and it was just us.

He'd be crushed. How would he move on? Would Mom help him? Or would she be spiraling out of control again? He at least had his family. I couldn't believe his family's wealth had started all of this. Would the Ashfords feel guilty too?

I couldn't let them go through that, not if I had a chance to stop it. I owed it to them to fight. To get out of here alive. And I would. I got off the couch, my legs stiff, trembling slightly. I crept toward the staircase, stopping every few moments to listen, really listen, for any footsteps above or near the door. I had to be quiet. *Very quiet*. Any extra noise, even my own breathing, could drown out the sounds I needed to hear.

It was already difficult to hear anything down here, but I tried. As I reached the bottom of the steps, I held my breath and listened. All clear.

I took the first step, then the next, and paused, trying to hear past the pounding of my own heartbeat. I was scared, more scared than I'd ever been in my life. Another step, and then I froze. Footsteps.

Oh no. Oh no, they were getting closer.

I spun around, tiptoeing as fast as I dared back down the stairs. My pulse roared in my ears. I hurried to the couch and dropped onto it, lying back, eyes shut, breathing carefully as I heard the turn of the door handle.

Click.

More footsteps. Close. Too close.

But I'd heard them. That was good news. That meant I still had time. They would leave again. I was sure of it. It must be close to dinnertime. Or maybe they were bringing me a snack.

They kept feeding me well, oddly well. Like I was a prisoner on death row, and they wanted to give me my last meal. I guessed there was a bit of kindness in that. Almost humane. *I guess.*

It would have felt better if they hadn't kidnapped me. And they weren't planning to kill me. There was no reason to pretend I didn't hear them, so I sat up and looked at them, pretending to have just awoken.

There was the man in the suit. Mark stood beside him. "Taking a bit of a nap, Zoey?" the man in the suit asked casually.

"There's not a whole lot else to do down here," I said, trying to keep my tone light. My heart still pounded in my chest. I prayed they hadn't heard me on the stairs just moments earlier.

"Sorry about that," he said, giving a thin shrug. "I guess we should've brought you a book or something. It must be quite boring down here."

"It is," I said, attempting a smile. But it didn't feel right on my face. It probably looked just as fake as it felt.

"Well, unfortunately, we're going to need you to make another video for us." His tone shifted. There was no pretense, no friendliness, no smirk. "Some things have come to light, and it means we need to take a more aggressive approach to make sure we get what we want."

The air changed.

My stomach turned.

There was something different about this time. This wasn't just business as usual. I could feel it. Something was about to happen. And I wasn't going to like it. "I don't mind making another video."

"I'm glad to hear it, Zoey. I wish others were as cooperative as you are."

Others.

I flinched inside. The way he said it, the way he casually referenced the "others," made my skin crawl. Mark had said it before too, that I'd been so compliant. Like that made it easier. Like that earned me points. But there was no prize to be won. There was no sense in fighting them, not yet. I knew better. I had to play the long game. But when the time came, when I knew they were really going to kill me, I would fight with everything inside me. There was no way I'd let them just snuff me out.

The man in the suit stepped closer. "We have a script for you. I need you to read it. It's very serious, Zoey. *Unfortunately.* So, please be sure to convey that as you read it. Once you're done, I'll speak, but the camera will stay on you. Do you understand?"

"I think so."

"Good. We need you to be as compliant as you have been. Can you promise me that? No fighting."

A chill went down my spine, ice threading through my veins. "I'll do whatever you want."

"Excellent."

He smiled. It was slick, polished, and hollow. I was beginning to wonder if this man in the suit, this nameless figure, was really just the devil incarnate. Shiny on the outside, but rotted and evil through and through. He handed me a piece of paper.

Mark was setting up the camera on a tripod this time.

That wasn't good. I looked down at the script and a lump formed in my throat. I was right. So right, and I wished I wasn't.

35

MARTINA

As I waited for Hirsch to convince Blackwell to let me back in and talk to Diego, I called Selena to let her know what was going on.

"Hey, Martina, what's up?"

"Did you find anything else on Diego?"

"We've questioned a few people, but nobody's talking to us."

"That's what I feared. Anybody know about the car?"

"No, they're not very forthcoming at all. But we're not giving up."

"If you're running out of people to talk to, head back to the office and help Vincent."

"Okay. Anything else?"

"They tested the DNA on the hair found in the trunk. It's a match to Zoey. I'm about to go in and talk to him again, once I convince Blackwell to let me in."

"Did something happen?"

"He just didn't like that I was getting too close to him. But I'm okay now."

Which wasn't entirely true because I wasn't sure if I was okay.

"How did things go at Turtle's house?"

Shaking my head, I said, "Not helpful at all. Any luck finding who this Bert Thomas is?"

"Not yet."

"I think it's important we find him. I think Turtle knows him, so he may already be alerting him. Anyway, can you tell Stavros I want someone to watch Turtle's house? He could be involved."

"Did he admit to knowing Bert Thomas?"

"No, but you could see the recognition when I said his name. He's probably warning them now. Maybe that's good." Or maybe it was bad. I wasn't sure. Either way, we needed to stay ahead of it.

"I'll let Stavros know we want to watch these guys. Maybe we'll also put surveillance on Diego's house. See who comes and visits."

"Good idea, Selena. Thank you. And… is everyone doing okay?"

"We're all fine. Don't worry about us, Martina."

"Okay. Bye."

Blackwell was still shaking his head when I turned back toward him. I stepped closer and called out, "What's the problem?"

"His lawyer is advising him not to talk to either of you."

"Well, maybe he doesn't need to talk to us. Maybe we talk to him. He's now a suspect, and kidnapping charges are a whole lot more serious than grand theft auto, right?"

"We tried that. Didn't get very far."

"Then just give me one more shot."

Blackwell eyed Hirsch, then looked back at me. "Can I request you keep at least two feet away from the suspect?"

"Fine."

"All right. I'll give you a few minutes, but I'm watching. If it gets too heated, I'm pulling you out."

"That's fair. Just let me talk to him."

He gave a reluctant nod, and we walked back toward the conference room. As we approached, Hirsch leaned in and muttered under his breath, "Are you sure you're okay to do this? I can take lead."

"No. I got this. I promise."

He gave me a tight nod. "Okay."

Blackwell opened the door, and sitting next to Diego was a man in a cheap, rumpled suit. He was probably a public defender. That wasn't helpful for us. If it had been an expensive lawyer, we might have been able to trace some of his other clients and maybe even uncover links to organized crime. That could've been a clue. But this guy? This guy looked fresh out of law school and overworked.

Diego crossed his arms and scowled. "I already said I don't wanna talk to this crazy lady no more. And this guy," he added, with a dismissive jerk of his chin toward Hirsch.

Blackwell sighed. "She just has a few things to say to you. She'll stay two feet away."

I leaned back against the wall to ensure I wasn't too close, just in case anyone got too nervous.

"Whatever," Diego muttered.

Punk. Some people grow out of that ridiculous defiance in their twenties. Not Diego.

"So," he snapped, "what do you got to say?"

I met his glare. "Well, I'm sure you and your lawyer have been informed by now that we found evidence Zoey Monroe was in the trunk of the car, the one with your fingerprints all over it."

I paused and watched him carefully.

He swallowed.

Nervous. *Good.*

He hadn't expected this. When he got that car, he likely

hadn't thought he'd be staring down kidnapping charges. "These are pretty serious charges, don't you think?" I asked, glancing at the lawyer.

The man nodded stiffly.

"Diego," I said, keeping my voice level, "personally, I don't think you took Zoey. We have video of the person who abducted her. It's not you. But what we don't know is whether you were involved after the fact. Maybe the person who took her handed her off to you. And then you did something really bad to her."

I let that hang in the air, my tone as calm as I could manage, even though my blood was boiling underneath. "That'll get you serious time. Maybe even life in prison. If you make it that long. Word on the street is the wrath of her family and friends is harsh," I added. "And we've got a lot of them."

Diego said nothing but glanced at his lawyer.

"Nothing to say to that?" I asked.

He finally spoke. "Lady, I don't know nothin' about your daughter."

I looked at the lawyer. His expression shifted. He was surprised. Maybe this was the first time he realized who I was. The mother of the girl in the trunk. The mother of the missing woman tied directly to his client. I turned to him. "Ever heard of Drakos Monroe Security & Investigations?"

"I have," the lawyer said cautiously.

"I'm Martina Monroe," I said, steady and clear. "Zoey Monroe's mother. Our family and friends are all part of Drakos Monroe. So, if you've heard of us, you know we're going to find out what happened to Zoey. Where she is and everyone who was involved."

I took a small step closer, not threatening, but firm. "Personally, I'm against violence. But I've spent a lot of time working with some serious alpha types. And unfortunately, they're not against violence. I'll do everything I can to protect you, Diego. I really will." I leaned in just slightly, my voice dropping lower. "But honestly, I might be really busy. Maybe I don't get to you in time. Maybe I say, 'Don't hurt these people,' and they ignore me. Maybe they take me too literally. Maybe they go after your mom. Or your girlfriend. Or your brother. I don't know. I hope not. I'll tell them not to. I promise I'll tell them not to."

Hirsch gave me a sharp look, clearly thinking I'd gone too far.

Maybe I had. Yes, it was obviously a threat, but I wasn't the threat. And Diego didn't know that my family and friends wouldn't actually go on some vigilante killing spree. That's not who they were. But he didn't know that. And maybe, just maybe, that uncertainty was enough. "So, what I'm saying is, if you can help me find out who really did this, they'll probably let you go. Forget about the whole stolen car business," I said, keeping my voice calm. "Just tell us where you got the Camry. That's all we need to know."

Diego looked away. He wasn't playing ball. It was time to try another tactic. One he might respond to better. "There is another way. You don't have to be here."

Diego turned back toward me.

"You help me, and I'll help *you*. But this is a one-time offer, Diego, so I need you to listen to me very carefully."

His lawyer stiffened slightly beside him, but I kept my eyes locked on Diego. "The people you're working with, or maybe just doing a favor for, however you got that Camry, those people are *very* bad people. And when I say 'bad,' I think you know what I mean." I paused, watching him closely. His shoulders rose, then fell, as if bracing himself. "They cover their tracks. They don't care about you. You're just a low-level errand boy to them—easily silenced. But you know what I can do?" I leaned in slightly. "I can protect you. You see, I can be your best friend or your worst enemy. Friend is better, don't you think?"

Before She Said I Do

He blinked, uncertainty flickering behind his eyes.

"Your lawyer can't protect you. San Jose PD? Not likely. But me?" I gestured to the window, where I knew the police were watching. "Ask your lawyer who we are. At Drakos Monroe Security & Investigations, we protect dignitaries. Celebrities. High-risk individuals. We don't just find people. We keep them safe." I softened slightly. "We can keep you safe. But you've got to tell me how you got the car."

Diego's voice trembled. "I don't know."

"Look," I said, "my firm already ran your background. I know everything there is to know about you. You've got no violent offenses. Just petty stuff—little things. You're not a murderer. You're not a kidnapper. You're not this guy." I pointed to the chair he was slouched in. "You're just someone trying to make a few bucks on the side. Nothing in your background says you should end up in prison for the rest of your life, or worse, six feet under or dumped in the bay, never to be found again."

He flinched at that.

"I'm the only one who can protect you. So, I'll ask again, how did you get the Camry?"

His eyes flicked to Hirsch, then back to me. "And what about that guy?"

"He works with us now," I said without hesitation. "He's excellent. Ex-law enforcement, but he's cool. We've been partners for—" I glanced at Hirsch. "Almost two decades." I stepped back, hands open. "If anyone can protect you, it's us. Now tell me—where did you get the Camry?"

He hesitated. "You've got to promise you'll protect me."

"I promise," I said. I turned toward the window, knowing full well officers were watching from behind the glass. Then I looked at Hirsch. "Once you're released, we'll move you to a safe house. You'll stay there until this is resolved. They won't get to you."

Diego exhaled shakily. "Okay. As long as you protect me, I'll tell you what I know. It's not a lot, I swear, but I didn't touch her. I never even saw her. I swear I don't know where she's at."

"I promise. How did you get the Camry?"

Diego lifted his chin. "You don't care about the phone?"

"You have the phone?" I asked, my heart racing.

"I *had* the phone," he said.

The phone. The ransom message. "Yes, we care about the phone. Who gave you the phone and the car?"

He nodded. "This dude. A big guy. He said he had a car he needed moved. And a phone that had a message on it that needed to be sent. He said if I dropped off the car and sent the message, I'd get five hundred bucks."

"Who's the dude?"

"I don't know his name. He's like a friend of a friend, you know?"

A sharp knock on the door cut him off. It opened just enough for a peek.

Blackwell's voice came through. "Can I speak with you, Martina? Hirsch?"

I looked at Diego. "I got you," I said gently, then turned and followed Hirsch out.

Blackwell waited outside, posture stiff, his face flushed red with tension. He looked me straight in the eyes. "What message is he talking about?" he demanded. "Have you been in contact with the kidnappers?"

36

MARTINA

I glanced over at Hirsch. He gave me a knowing look, the kind that said it was time to fess up and tell Lieutenant Blackwell the truth. I said, "We've been receiving messages from the kidnappers."

His eyes narrowed. "And you didn't tell me?" His voice was sharp, incredulous. *Understandably.*

I explained, "They gave strict instructions not to involve law enforcement."

He threw up his hands. "It really would've been helpful if you told me. I'm trying to find your daughter, Martina."

"I know." I looked away, shame crawling over my skin. "I didn't want to take any chances. But I have a feeling that kid in there knows who took Zoey."

"You think it's the guy he's talking about? The bigger one, dark hair?"

"Well, it matches the description of the kidnapper in the video."

Blackwell nodded. "True. But Diego didn't even know his name."

"But whoever introduced him probably does."

Blackwell leaned in, his tone intense. "What did the messages from the kidnappers say?"

I took a breath, steadying myself, then told him everything. From the first call to all the research we'd done so far, including the six similar kidnappings over the past ten years and the two suspects we believed were tied to all of them.

Blackwell fell silent for a moment, processing it all. His shoulders slumped slightly. He shook his head. "I really wish you would've told me this sooner."

"What would you do if it was your child?" I asked, my voice catching. "Do you have kids?"

"I do," he said. "But I feel like I just walked into a pop quiz I didn't study for." He straightened. "So, what is your team doing now?"

"My entire firm has been digging into the Ashford family and their past criminal connections along with all the suspects I've told you about. I have people trying to get someone to tell us who Diego is connected to. They've also traced the cell phones that the messages were sent from. One is at the bottom of Almaden Lake and the other pinged in Mountain View, the same location as the Camry. Diego said he had the phone and was the one to send the message. Do you have the phone?"

"If it's the phone he had on him when we picked him up, it's in evidence."

"Have you checked it for prints?"

"Didn't think it would be important."

"It might be," I said. "It could have the kidnapper's prints on it."

"Okay," Blackwell said. "I'll have the lab process it immediately." He paused. "Is there anything else you're leaving out?"

"Nothing. I swear."

"And you haven't found any more damning evidence on the Ashfords?"

"Not yet. It's a lot of data to sift through. My team is going through everything."

Blackwell gave me a scolding look. "You know, if you'd told me sooner, my team could've been helping."

"I understand. I just... I didn't want to do anything that might jeopardize Zoey's life. But now I realize if we don't find her before the deadline tomorrow morning—" My voice cracked. "I think they'll kill her."

Blackwell nodded. "Here's what we're going to do. We're going to keep this quiet. One thing we had discussed was that the kidnapping appeared sophisticated. And it could have ties to organized crime. And if it is that sophisticated, they could have people on the inside, in law enforcement." The weight of his words sank like a stone in my chest. "It's probably not a good idea that you're here."

It hadn't occurred to me. It *should* have occurred to me, but I'd been too focused on questioning Diego. I hadn't gone to law enforcement, not really. I'd filed the missing persons report, sure. But I hadn't told them about the ransom call. We hadn't put anything on the news. There were no activities that would tell the kidnappers we were working with law enforcement.

"You're right."

Blackwell continued. "But I understand you need to be. Once you go back in there, ask him more about the guy who gave him the car. We'll turn off the cameras, so he thinks we're not listening, but we have mics in there. I'll ask the other officers to leave, in the event someone is on the kidnapper's payroll, but I'll stay inside. Try to get anything you can."

"Thank you," I said, my throat tight.

Blackwell nodded toward the door. "Give me some time to set it up. We don't want to tip anyone off."

37

SELENA

BACK IN THE OFFICE, I turned to Vincent. "We're not getting anywhere with James Turtle and Bert Thomas," I said, rubbing my temples. The tension behind my eyes had been building for hours, especially after striking out with getting people to talk to me about Diego and his associates. It felt like a waste of time, when I could have been searching for more clues.

Vincent didn't flinch. He was calm, steady, and methodical as always. "Patience, Selena. We've got a team watching Turtle's house. There have been no confirmed sightings yet."

"It's almost ten o'clock. That's prime time for criminals to make a move."

He nodded. "We keep digging."

I leaned closer to the screen, my eyes scanning the limited background info we'd been able to find. "Turtle's too clean. Nothing recent. And we still can't find anything on a Bert Thomas. It's weird."

"It is. Not what you'd expect for criminals running a kidnapping-for-ransom scheme."

"Unless they're good at it," I said. "Good enough to stay off the radar. Maybe that's how they've gotten away with it all these years. Like Martina suggested, they could be freelancers. And it could be that Bert Thomas is a fake name."

"Maybe."

I looked over at him. "Don't you have contacts at the FBI? Someone within the Organized Crime Task Force that maybe owes you a favor or is just really nice? Maybe they've heard of Turtle or this so-called Bert Thomas?"

"I can reach out," he said. "But it's late. Saturday night. Not everyone's going to be in the office."

"Still," I said, "I've got a feeling about these two."

"All right. I'll call my contact. Off the record."

"Who is it?"

"Old college friend. She's helped us on cases in the past."

I nodded. "I know a few folks too, but most were case connections, not exactly tight relationships." More like we knew each other because they helped save my life.

"I get it," he said, already pulling out his phone. "Let me see what she knows."

I watched him step away, speaking in hushed tones.

My gaze drifted back to the screen. It was the driver's license photo of James Turtle. Dark hair, dark eyes. Five foot five. Not our kidnapper we saw in the video, but that didn't mean he wasn't involved. My stomach twisted at the thought. What if Zoey wasn't connected to a team of investigators? She was just a normal person with normal parents who happened to be engaged to a man with a wealthy family with a criminal past. In some ways, Zoey had an advantage over the other victims. Victim. *Ugh.* We had to find her.

Vincent came back, lowering his phone slowly.

"Jess says she's got something," he said. "She's seen a Turtle in their systems. But no Bert Thomas."

I straightened. "Nothing?"

Vincent smirked. "No Bert Thomas... wait for it... but she has a *Gilbert* Thomas,"

A cold chill passed through me. Gilbert Thomas. "You found him!" Why hadn't I thought to check variations of Bert? I wouldn't dwell on it now. We might have just cracked this wide open. "What does she know about them? What about Jeremy Santo?"

"She's still looking through files. I just wanted to update you with the name, so you can check him out."

"I'll do a search for Gilbert Thomas."

"Cool." He raised the phone back to his ear and stepped away.

While Vincent was on the phone with his FBI contact, I quickly typed Gilbert Thomas into the DMV database. My heart pounded as I hit enter.

Sure enough, the profile popped up: Gilbert Thomas, 6'2", 240 pounds, dark hair, dark eyes. My breath caught in my throat. *Could it be him?*

Vincent ended his call and walked back over, lowering his phone.

"So?"

"She just confirmed it. Gilbert Thomas and James Turtle are known associates."

"That's what Martina suspected," I said quickly. "What else did she tell you?"

"They've both been linked to San Jose and San Francisco organized crime organizations. They're ghosts. Basically hired guns. No formal affiliations, no loyalty. They stay off the radar because they don't operate like gang members. They're freelancers."

Was Martina *ever* wrong? "What about Jeremy Santo?"

Vincent raised a finger, and he stepped away and got back on the phone.

My pulse thundered in my ears. *We're close. So close.* This was really happening. I could feel it in my bones.

I stared at the screen, at Gilbert Thomas's photo, his stats, his cold, unreadable eyes. It had to be him. We could have a team at his house in *minutes*. I needed to tell Martina, but I wanted to wait for Vincent to finish the call.

He stayed in the corner of the room, still speaking with his FBI contact, pacing slightly. The tension in the air was electric, a wire stretched tight and ready to snap.

When he finally hung up and walked over, I didn't even need to ask. "Jeremy Santo," he said. "No criminal record on the surface. But he's flagged in their Organized Crime Task Force files. He's an associate of a San Francisco crime family."

Fighting tears, I said, "We found them, Vincent. We're going to bring Zoey home."

"We have names and connections. That's a start. Now we have to actually find Zoey. Call Martina. I'll tell Stavros."

38

MARTINA

I was finally about to step inside the conference room to requestion Diego when my phone vibrated in my hand. Selena. I answered immediately. "Hey, Selena. What's up?"

"I think we found something, Martina."

My breath caught. "What is it?" I stepped back from the doorway, motioning for Hirsch to hold up.

"Vincent called in his pal from the FBI—Jess or something—and they flagged three names as being connected to organized crime or listed as associates: James Turtle, Gilbert—" she paused, emphasizing, "'Bert' Thomas and Jeremy Santo."

I gripped the phone tighter. "Which organized crime group?"

"Jeremy Santo is tied to a San Francisco organized crime syndicate," she said. "The other two, Turtle and Thomas, have been spotted in connection with both San Jose and San Francisco. Just like you suspected, Martina. Guns for hire."

"Were you able to pull up a file on Thomas?"

"Yes, I did. I'm going to send the details to your phone right now. It could be him, the man who took Zoey."

"Send it now," I said, barely containing the tremble in my voice.

"I will."

I stood there frozen, praying this was it. *Please let this be it.* My phone chimed with a new message. I opened the image, and my heart dropped. It looked like him. The man from the security footage. It was fuzzy with only partial features, but the resemblance was there. Same build. Same posture. The driver's license details regarding height and weight were a near-perfect match. This *could* be him.

Even better, we had a kid in the next room who claimed to have dealt with Zoey's kidnapper. I returned to the call. "This is perfect," I said. "I've been speaking with Diego." I filled her in briefly about our progress. "We were just about to go back in."

"Good," Selena said. "We're sending a team to Thomas's last known address now."

"Thank you, Selena. We're going to find her. We're going to bring Zoey home."

"I think so too. I love you, Martina."

"I love you too," I said softly, then ended the call. I turned to Hirsch and Blackwell. "I think they found something."

Hirsch raised an eyebrow, alert, and I explained to them what Selena had told me.

"Let's go talk to Diego."

"Yes, ma'am."

We stepped into the conference room together. Diego was seated across the table with his lawyer. He looked up as we entered. It was time to get answers.

Blackwell stood at the door of the conference room, addressing Diego and his attorney. "I've spoken with Martina and Hirsch," he said. "We're turning off the cameras, and this is going to be a private conversation between the two of you. Do you both agree to this?"

The lawyer gave a nod. "Yes."

Diego followed with a quiet, "Yeah."

Blackwell nodded, then stepped out of the room, leaving Hirsch and me alone with Diego. I sat down directly across from him, Hirsch taking the seat beside me. I glanced up at the corner of the room, watching the red light on the camera blink. It paused and then turned off.

"We're off," I said quietly to Diego. "Like I told you before, I can protect you, but I need more details about the guy who gave you the car and the phone. I need to know everything. What he looked like. What he said. Everything."

Diego shifted uncomfortably in his seat, then leaned forward, resting his forearms on the table. "Okay. Like I said, I never met him before. A friend of a friend. He was a big guy, probably, I don't know, six-two, six-three? But built. Like, at first, I thought he was fat, but then I realized, no, he's just thick with muscle. Broad. Strong. You know? Big."

He hesitated, searching for words. "Dark hair, dark eyes. Tan skin. He handed me five hundred bucks and said, 'When you get to the location in Mountain View'"—he mimed handing something over—"'send this message, then leave the car.' That was it."

"Is that why you ran?" I asked. "You had a getaway car waiting for you at the shopping center?"

"Yeah," he said. "I planned to ditch it there."

"Why'd you keep the phone?"

He shrugged. "I mean, it's a phone. He didn't say I couldn't keep it."

I studied him a moment. "If I showed you some photos, do you think you could recognize the guy?"

Diego nodded. "I can try."

I pulled out my phone and brought up the photo of James Turtle. Diego took the phone, squinted at the image, studied the face. "No," he said finally. "That's not him. This guy's thinner. And the face, nah. Eyes are too wide. Ears too big."

I swiped to the next image of Gilbert Thomas and handed it back to him. Diego stared at the photo. "I think that's the dude," he said. "Yeah. That's him."

"Did anyone call him Bert?" I asked.

Diego shook his head. "I was told not to ask too many questions, you know what I mean? But he was... he was scary. I knew better than to push."

"Who connected you with this guy?"

"A friend."

I cocked my head in disapproval.

"Okay, fine. It's this guy from my neighborhood. We go way back."

He was stalling, and I didn't like it. "His name."

He slouched. "Keith."

He was starting to irk me. "Last name."

"Santo."

Nearly stunned by the name, it took me a moment to say, "And did Keith say how he knew this guy?"

"Said it was a friend of the family."

"His father's family?"

"Yeah."

After a quick nod at Hirsch, I said, "You've been really helpful. And I'm going to make sure nothing happens to you. Okay?" And I meant it. This kid was only guilty of taking money from a cold-blooded criminal. He didn't deserve to pay for that indiscretion with his life.

"Okay," he said. "Are they gonna let me go?"

"Not yet," I said gently. "But I'll talk to Lieutenant Blackwell and let him know you've been helping us, a lot. Once you're released, we'll put you in protective custody."

He exhaled with relief. "Okay... can you hurry that up?"

"I'll do everything I can," I promised. "Thank you, Diego."

Hirsch and I stepped out of the room. Blackwell was waiting for us just outside. "That went well," Blackwell said.

"I think so."

Blackwell said, "Do you want us to send a patrol to Thomas's house, or..."

"I'll call it in to my people. They're already sending surveillance teams to his house. We need to look into Keith and see if there is a connection to Jeremy, the Ashfords' old criminal partner."

It was too big of a coincidence that Keith and Jeremy had the same last name. It was possible Keith was Jeremy's son or nephew or cousin. The puzzle pieces were finally falling into place, but would it be too late? We may know who was involved, but we didn't have a location on Zoey, and that was what mattered most.

39

MARTINA

Blackwell eyed me and said, "Please keep me in the loop. I'm happy to assist in any way that I can."

"I appreciate that. We have to get going. But what about the kid? Are you planning to release him?"

"We can drop all charges if you're fairly confident he's not involved."

"Well, if we find out that he is involved and knows more than he's told us, we'll have him in our custody."

"True. I'll work on dropping the charges. You'll have someone come pick him up?"

"Someone from the team will pick him up. We'll make sure nobody gets to him and that we have our eyes on him too."

"Okay. Be safe out there."

Hirsch and I moved toward the exit, our footsteps echoing across the polished concrete floor. "Do you want me to drive?" he asked, holding the door open for me.

"Yes, please. I need to make some calls."

And if I was being honest, with myself and with Hirsch, I probably shouldn't be behind the wheel. My hands were still shaking, my chest tight with adrenaline and anger. I had too many thoughts. Too many emotions. Even I could see that. I'd threatened to murder two people today. I didn't mean it. I wouldn't kill anyone. Not that I thought I would. I wouldn't. It's not who I am. I'm not God. I don't get to decide who lives or dies.

Inside the vehicle, I pulled out my phone and dialed Selena as Hirsch eased the car onto the road. "Hey, Selena."

"Hey, Martina. What's new?"

"The kid just ID'd Gilbert Thomas."

"Okay, the team's already on their way to his house."

"We're on our way there too. But he also told us who connected him to Thomas, a kid named Keith Santo. Do we know if Jeremy and his wife had a child named Keith?"

"Yes, they did. And he's in his mid-twenties."

"And do they live in San Jose?"

"Jeremy's ex-wife does."

"Have you talked to her yet?"

"Not yet. I've left messages, but she hasn't called back. I can try again, or we could go out to her house."

"Try calling her. If she answers, question her about Keith and Jeremy. And also, do a background on Keith. Let's try to understand what his life's all about. Is he part of a criminal enterprise like his father? Or pretending to be a plumber like his father?"

"You got it."

"Have you talked to your dad?"

"I just talked to him. He's offered to come into the office. He said he made some snacks."

That almost made me smile. "Okay. I'll give him a quick call."

"Martina, be safe, and let me know if you need anything else."

"I will. Thank you, Selena."

"You got it."

I ended the call. The phone felt cold in my hand, grounding me for a second as my mind continued to spin. "So, is it Santos's kid?" Hirsch asked, keeping his eyes on the road.

"Sounds like it. Selena's going to run a full background. See if he's got any priors."

Hirsch nodded. Streetlights flickered past the windshield in a rhythmic strobe, casting shifting shadows across his jaw. "The pieces seem to be falling into place," he said, his voice low.

"Is it too neat though?"

"I mean, based on the sophistication of the kidnapping, we assumed organized crime. And the most probable criminal in the Ashfords' background was Jeremy Santo. Now we've linked his son to the kidnapping. It wasn't easy to find that connection. I bet they thought we wouldn't."

I exhaled slowly. "They have been careful, I guess."

"Do we have any idea what kind of organized crime Jeremy might be connected to?"

"Not yet. All Selena said was that it was a group out of San Francisco."

"Well, there's more than one crime family in San Francisco."

"Yeah. It'd be nice to know who they're connected to."

A strange feeling bloomed in my gut, and I couldn't shake the idea we were missing something.

Hirsch said, "We're getting closer."

"Closer, like we know who's involved, but we don't know where she is. That's the most important thing."

"My guess? She's local. If they're doing the drop in San Jose, she's probably still here in the Bay Area."

"We've got twelve hours to find her, rescue her, and keep her out of harm's way."

"I know. But look how far we've come, the whole team. Everyone is looking for her. We'll find her. You see that, right?"

I knew he was trying to keep my spirits high and to stay focused. "I hope so."

As Hirsch turned down Gilbert Thomas's street, my phone buzzed in my hand. I answered quickly. "Hey."

"We're in position."

I glanced around the neighborhood. It was quiet. A few vehicles were parked along the curb, one of them a nondescript van, our team's.

"Okay. Hirsch and I are just about to pull up. We're going up to the door."

"We've got your back."

I ended the call and updated Hirsch.

"Okay, we're going to go in calm. Levelheaded. Catch more flies with honey, right?"

"Agreed."

"No more threatening people's lives?"

"I think I've had enough of that for today."

"Good. Now let's do this."

I opened the car door and stepped out into the chilled night air. The street was lined with modest homes, well-kept lawns, and quiet stillness. The neighborhood was nicer than Turtle's, but not exactly luxurious. Still, Gilbert Thomas had to be doing well.

I frowned slightly. "Maybe we should've called Vincent to get more background on him. All we have is what the FBI gave us. A driver's license and criminal history. No work record, no military background... not much else."

"It'll be fine. We have backup in place."

"True."

We walked up the short path to the front door, the porch light still dark. Hirsch stepped forward and knocked. We were met with silence.

He knocked again. This time, we heard faint footsteps from inside.

I glanced at the time. It was 10:02 PM. Whoever was home, if it wasn't Bert, likely wouldn't be expecting visitors. A moment later, the porch light flicked on with a faint click. The door opened just a crack, then wider.

A woman stood in sweatpants and a loose T-shirt, her hair pulled into a high ponytail. Her eyes blinked in the sudden light. Perhaps we'd woken her, or maybe she'd been watching TV. The house behind her was quiet, no sound of voices or background noise.

"Can I help you with something?" she asked.

"Yes, ma'am. I'm sorry for disturbing you so late," I said. "My name is Martina, and this is August. We're looking for Gilbert Thomas. Is he home?"

"No, not right now. What is this about?"

"We have some questions for him about a crime that happened Friday evening. He was identified as a witness, and we were just hoping to follow up."

"Are you cops?"

I shook my head. "No, actually. I'm a private investigator, and so is my partner. We were hired by the family to help close the case."

"Oh. Well, Bert's not here."

"Do you know when he'll be back?"

"Probably not for another few days. He's out of town on business."

"What does he do for business?"

"He's in sales."

"What does he sell?"

"Lab equipment."

My brows lifted slightly. "Do you know where he went?"

"Tampa," she said with a small smile, brushing a strand of hair behind her ear.

Bert Thomas sold lab equipment? Did we have the right guy? I pulled out my phone and showed her a photo of him. "Is this your Bert Thomas?"

"Yes, that's my husband."

"Okay, well, thank you, Mrs. Thomas, for your time. You said you don't expect him back for a few days?"

"He said he'd be back Monday evening."

After he killed my daughter? "If you don't mind me asking, how long have you been married?"

"We just celebrated ten years," she said, the smile returning to her face.

Had Bert Thomas been living a double life? It wouldn't be unusual for someone involved in organized crime, but from what the FBI told us, he wasn't actually a member. I guess that would make it easier to hide a criminal life from loved ones.

"Well, congratulations," I said. "And if you could tell Bert that we stopped by, I'd appreciate it."

"Of course."

"Here, let me give you my business card." I pulled one from the inside pocket of my jacket and handed it over. "So sorry for disturbing you so late."

"Oh, no problem. I was just up watching my shows."

"Have a good night."

On the walk back to the car, the night air was still, and I was more convinced than ever: Bert Thomas was our kidnapper. We knew the identity of our kidnapper, and we knew he was likely connected to Jeremy Santo. But we still had no idea where they were holding her. That was the missing piece. And without it, all of this was just shadows.

Inside the car, Hirsch looked over as he started the engine. "What do you think about that?"

I stared out the window, watching the dark shapes of houses pass in a blur. "Bert Thomas has probably been doing this a long time."

"Yep," Hirsch said. "And he's got the perfect normal-guy cover story for it."

"For now," I said. "But when I'm done with him, everyone's going to know what he's done. Who he really is. A monster living among us."

My hands balled into fists in my lap, the tension in my chest coiling tighter. Now we had to find him. My gut said find Bert Thomas and we'd find Zoey.

In a normal investigation, we'd alert the media. Get his face out there. We'd make him too hot to move, but we couldn't do that. If the kidnappers knew we'd figured it out, if they caught wind that we were closing in, they might hurt Zoey. It was too big a risk.

"Let's go back to the office," I said, voice low but resolute.

"All right. Let's see if Vincent and Selena found anything useful."

I murmured a small prayer under my breath and put in a quick call to Charlie to let him know we were headed back to the office. The race wasn't over. The clock was still ticking, and we were running out of time to find Zoey.

40

HIRSCH

As we strategized on speakerphone with Vincent and Selena during the drive back to the office, we all agreed, financials were key. "We need everything on Bert Thomas," I said. "Aliases, property records, work history, bank accounts, cell numbers, absolutely everything. That's how we're going to find out where Zoey is."

I could feel it. We were close. That tight, pulsing kind of close that wraps around your ribs and makes it hard to breathe. I was glad. But even so, I couldn't help but think about what Martina was going through. If someone had taken Audrey? I'd be out of my mind. I'd probably be just like her, threatening people's lives until they gave me what I needed to find my daughter.

I was confident the team would find everything that could be found. And since Martina and I weren't law enforcement anymore, we were doing things we legally shouldn't be. But I wouldn't rat them out. Not to anyone. Even if I was still a cop, they wouldn't get a peep out of me. Because sometimes working in the shadows was what it took to get the job done. Playing by the rules didn't always give us the desired outcome. Martina had taught me that. It had frustrated the heck out of me over the years, but she was right. We had to save Zoey, by any means necessary.

We hung up with Vincent and Selena, and I was just about to give Martina another pep talk about how close we were when my phone buzzed again. "Do you know the number?" I asked.

Martina glanced at the screen. "I think that's one of ours. Answer it."

I hit "Answer" on the hands-free system. "This is Hirsch. What's up?"

"Hirsch," a voice said quickly. "We just got a call from the surveillance team at your house. They've apprehended someone trying to get inside."

My heart clenched. "What do you mean, someone tried to get inside?"

"Exactly that. They caught him creeping alongside the house. We have him detained. It's not lawful, mind you, but we've got him."

Martina cut in. "How's Audrey? And Kim?"

"He didn't make it inside. And no contact was made with Audrey or Kim."

I said, "We're on our way," and veered toward the direction of home.

Martina asked, "Did the suspect give a name? Say what they were doing there?"

"He hasn't said a word."

"Did he have any weapons?"

"Yes. A Glock and a knife."

I shook my head in disbelief. "We'll be there in ten minutes."

Why would someone try to break into my house? And what if the surveillance team hadn't still been there? We had just been thinking of pulling them off after thinking Zoey's kidnapping wasn't connected to one of our old cases. Martina sat stiffly in the passenger seat, her eyes darting between me and the windshield. "I don't like this at all, Hirsch."

"Something's not adding up, is it?"

"No. Why would someone try to break into your house?"

"Call Vincent," I said.

Martina nodded, already redialing him and updating him on the situation and where we were headed. It couldn't be a coincidence. Not tonight. Not while we were getting this close. Someone was trying to get into my house while we were hunting down Zoey's kidnapper. Why?

We drove in tense silence until I reached my street. I pulled up to the curb fast, barely parked before I was out of the car, racing up the walkway. I unlocked the front door and stepped inside. The house was quiet aside from the sounds of the TV. Kim was sitting in the living room, curled up with a blanket, watching one of those baking competition shows. Her eyes widened in surprise when she saw me. "I wasn't expecting you." She paused the TV, stood up quickly, and rushed over to wrap her arms around my neck. I hugged her tightly, holding her just long enough to feel her warmth.

She stepped back, concern etched across her face. "Did you find Zoey?"

"Not yet."

Her shoulders slumped. "Oh. Then... why are you home?"

Before I could answer, Audrey came padding down the hallway in her pajamas, rubbing her eyes. "Did you find Zoey?"

I brushed her hair back. "No, not yet, sweetheart. But soon." I stepped back, glancing between them. "Everything okay here?"

Kim and Audrey exchanged a strange look before Kim nodded. "Yeah. We were just watching TV. Audrey was on the phone with a friend."

"Good," I said. "Because the surveillance team outside picked up a guy trying to break in."

Kim's eyes widened. "What?"

A knock at the door. I moved quickly and opened it to Martina. She stepped in without a word, her presence calm. *Thankfully.* I turned to Kim and Audrey.

"I was just telling them what happened," I said. "And was about to tell them that we need to move them."

"Yes, we do," Martina said, nodding.

Kim looked back and forth between us. "What do you mean they found a guy? Who was he? What was he trying to do?"

"We're not sure yet," I told her. "But we need to move you. Right now."

"I thought Zoey's kidnapping had nothing to do with you or Martina," Kim said.

"That's our current understanding," Martina said. "It could be an intimidation tactic. Maybe they don't want us to keep investigating. Maybe it's a warning."

Kim's eyes filled with worry. Audrey clung to her side.

With my heart wrenching, I said, "I need each of you to pack a bag. We're moving you. I'm sorry, I don't mean to scare you. But we've got to go."

Kim nodded, pale. "Okay."

As she and Audrey went to their rooms, I turned to Martina. "This is bizarre."

"Agreed."

"Where can I take them?"

"We've got safe houses, but for now, let's bring them back to the office. Charlie's on his way there, too. I'd feel better if we were all together." She paused, then added, "We're missing something."

"Like what?"

She shook her head and said, "I don't know."

She then stared down at her phone as a message flashed across her screen. I watched the color drain from her face.

"Who is it?" I asked.

She looked up at me but didn't say a word. She didn't have to. Her expression told me everything.

41

MARTINA

I STARED at the screen on my phone. The message was a video. I waved Hirsch over and pressed play. There was Zoey. She looked pale, worse than before. Her skin was blotchy and damp, strands of hair stuck to her face. Her eyes were red-rimmed, glassy with terror. She sat on the same old sofa in the windowless room, her shoulders hunched.

"I have a message from the kidnapper," she said, her voice hoarse. "Here goes."

A male voice said, "We told you not to go to law enforcement and you did. Why am I not surprised? Now you've broken the rules, and therefore there are consequences." The video paused, just for a second. Then Zoey's eyes widened in raw panic as a large gloved hand clamped over her face, covering both her mouth and her nose. A sharp blade gleamed in the dim light, pressed against her throat.

The voice, deeper, menacing, cut through the silence. "This is what happens when you don't follow the rules."

Zoey's muffled screams tore through the speaker as the blade dragged down her chest. Blood bloomed beneath the edge of her shirt, soaking through the fabric. She struggled violently against the man's grip, her arms jerking and legs kicking.

Then, in a sudden flash, he released her. She collapsed backward, sobbing, gasping for air. Tears streamed down her cheeks.

The voice returned. "Say it."

Through choked cries, Zoey whispered, "There will be another message. Please follow the instructions."

The video ended. The screen went dark.

My entire body trembled. My stomach lurched. I couldn't breathe.

Hirsch reached over, placing a firm hand on my shoulder. His grip was steady as he guided me over to the couch. He sat me down and said, "She's still alive, Martina. We still have a chance. We will get her back. I'm going to call it in. See if we can get a trace."

I nodded, my voice gone. I sat in silence, frozen. My fingers clenched around the edge of the phone. In the background, I heard Hirsch's voice, measured, calm, and professional, making the call.

Behind him, Kim appeared, her duffel bag slung over one shoulder, Audrey at her side with a small backpack. They stopped when they saw my face.

Kim rushed over. "What's going on?"

I shook my head, trying to speak. "They... they just sent another video."

She stepped back, her eyes searching mine. "Did they hurt her?"

I gave a slow nod.

"Come here, Martina." She sat next to me and wrapped her arms around me.

I pulled back. "She's still alive..." I said, staring blankly ahead. "But it was..." The words wouldn't come. It was too terrifying. Heartbreaking. Something I hoped I'd forget one day, but I knew I wouldn't.

Kim didn't hesitate. "I'll make tea."

Hirsch returned, lowering his phone. He sat beside me, close enough for comfort but not crowding me. "It's a good sign that she's still alive. That they still want to negotiate. They want their money. We just have to avoid law enforcement from now on. Completely."

Kim came back, Audrey holding her hand. Both of them looked pale, shaken. Kim set a steaming cup of tea on the coffee table in front of me. I could smell the faint scent of chamomile.

I mumbled, "Thank you," as I tried to process what I'd just seen. And tried to figure out what to do next. "They must have someone on the inside at SJPD," I said to Hirsch quietly. "Someone leaking information."

"That's what I suspect too. We need to make sure Diego is safe. I'll call Blackwell," he added, standing again. "See where they are with his release."

As he stepped outside to make the call, Kim hovered near me. "Is there anything else I can get you?"

I shook my head. "No. I just... I just need a minute to think."

"Okay," she said gently. "Audrey and I will get out of your hair."

They needed to get to a safe house. I wouldn't let anyone else get hurt on my watch. I brought the teacup to my lips, but my hand shook violently. Hot liquid splashed against the rim, nearly spilling over. I set it down quickly and pressed the heel of my hands into my eyes, grounding myself.

Hirsch was right. They still wanted money. That meant Zoey was still a bargaining chip. That meant we still had time.

A few moments later, Hirsch stepped back into the living room. "He's in holding," he said. "But Blackwell promised he'll personally keep an eye on him until he's released and transferred into our custody."

"Good."

I looked around the room, Hirsch's home. The soft yellow glow from the ceiling light did little to warm the hollow feeling in my chest. And then it hit me like a rocket.

"We have a suspect sitting outside," I said. "The man who tried to break in. We should talk to him. Once Kim and Audrey are moved."

"Agreed," Hirsch said.

"Let's get going."

I stood and was ready to head out when my phone vibrated again.

Another message.

Hirsch and I both turned toward it. I didn't hesitate this time. I pressed play.

The screen lit up.

Zoey sat in the same room. This time, she had a bandage on her chest, white gauze taped awkwardly over the wound, stained pink at the edges.

A man's voice, calm and articulate, spoke off-camera. "Hello, Martina. And I'm assuming former Sergeant Hirsch is by your side. You two, thick as thieves, just as I expected. Truthfully, I assumed law enforcement would be involved a little bit. You had to report her missing, but I didn't think you'd work with them after the ransom demands and instructions were quite clear." There was a pause. "Now my associates and I are feeling a bit exposed."

My breath caught in my throat.

"The cost to get your daughter back has changed."

A chill ran down my spine.

"In addition to the five million dollars, there is something else I want. Rather, what I need. I *need* justice. The two of you took something from me, and now I'm going to take something from you."

I gasped.

The voice continued. "Unless, of course, you'd like to make a deal. Your life for hers."

I froze.

The voice continued. "10 AM tomorrow. Same location. Surrender Martina, and Zoey goes free. No further harm will come to her. You go to law enforcement, or I even smell backup? You die. And, of course, Sergeant Hirsch and his pretty little girl will die too. I hope I'm making myself clear. I look forward to seeing you, Martina."

The screen went black. Zoey's terrified face was gone. I slowly lowered the phone and looked at Hirsch. "This was never about money."

42

ZOEY

Curled up on the dirty couch, I hugged my knees to my chest, trying to steady my breathing. The air smelled musty, like mold and something long forgotten. I wondered if my mom would find me. I had no doubt she was looking.

She was one of the best investigators in the world and so was Uncle August. But no matter how many times I told myself that, I couldn't stop the message from replaying in my head. They would hurt Audrey. They would hurt Mom. They would even hurt Uncle August. I knew this wasn't my fault, but guilt twisted in my gut like a knife. Maybe I should've known better. Maybe I should not have made a surprise entrance to the Bay Area. Maybe I should've asked someone I trusted to pick me up. But wasn't it normal to just take an Uber? That's what nearly everyone else does.

Well, everyone except the people who worry they'll be kidnapped in some bizarre revenge plot meant to punish their mother or extort money from their new in-laws. But I guess my life hadn't ever been totally normal.

Mom tried to make it normal, to give me something like peace. But because of who she was, what she did for a living, normal wasn't something she could promise or deliver. She knew the horrors of this world. And I did too. This wasn't the first time someone had come after her. Or me. Usually, it was just to get to her, to stop her from her relentless pursuit of justice. I should've rented a car. I should've asked Selena to pick me up. Why hadn't I? And now Mom might pay the ultimate price.

I knew, without question, that she'd trade herself for me. She would do it in a heartbeat. But I couldn't let her. I wouldn't let her. I had to find a way out of here. Had she gotten the message yet? Did she have any idea where I was or who these people were?

Mom and her team had worked miracles before. But this time, even if she showed up, would they really let me go? Would she really come alone? I hoped not.

Who were these people? What had my mom done to them? How had she hurt them? *Impossible.* Mom would never hurt anyone. At least, not intentionally. The sound of the doorknob turning snapped me upright. Pain surged through my chest as I moved too quickly, gasping when the gash burned like fire. At least it wasn't deep, just enough to remind me I was at their mercy.

When I'd felt the blade press against my throat earlier, I thought that was it. *The end.* But it wasn't. A pit lodged in my stomach, heavy and unmoving. This wasn't over.

I looked up as the door opened. It was the creepy man in the suit and Mark. I had no idea what time it was anymore. Not that it mattered. The man in the suit gave a tight smile. "How are you holding up, Zoey?" he asked, his tone falsely polite.

"Just fine," I said, my voice sharp with defiance.

He smirked. "Well, I'll have you know the message has been sent to your mother. And no doubt Sergeant Hirsch is with her, considering we haven't been able to make contact with our associate."

My spine stiffened. "What associate? Did you send someone after my mom?"

"Don't worry about that," he said smoothly. "I'm sure your mother will comply. Or... do you think she won't?"

I narrowed my eyes at him. "Do you really want to know what I think?"

He leaned in slightly. "Yes, I would like to know what you're thinking, Zoey."

I stared into his dark brown eyes. They were cold, soulless, like staring into a pool of evil. A gateway to hell. "I think you're messing with the wrong people," I said. "I think no matter how clever you think you are, no matter how carefully you've planned this, you're not going to win. You're not going to hurt my mother. You're not going to kill her. You're going to fail. You're the one who's going to get hurt."

He tilted his head, an amused expression flickering across his face. "Interesting perspective, Zoey. Unfortunately for you, I don't think that's true."

He straightened, pacing the room with a false calm that made my skin crawl. "But at least you have a new mother-in-law, Margot. How's that going? Are you feeling any differently about your impending nuptials now that you know the truth about the Ashfords?"

I scowled. "That they're just as dirty as the criminals my mom has spent her life chasing?"

He raised a brow.

"Well," I said, lifting my chin, "from what it sounds like, it was a long time ago. And as soon as he found out you were dirty, Graham dropped you."

The man's face darkened. His jaw clenched, and a red flush rose to his cheeks. He didn't like that. I guessed he didn't like being reminded that Graham had cut ties. He'd told me all about it, their business dealings and their so-called friendship. And now, what? The man was kidnapping his former friend's future daughter-in-law and demanding five million dollars? *Petty revenge.* But what I didn't understand, what I still couldn't connect, was how it all tied back to my mom and Uncle August. And what they truly planned to do to us.

"Let's just say I remember it a little differently," the man in the suit said with a faint, unsettling smile. "But I just wanted you to know they've gotten the message. You'll be leaving here pretty soon."

Mark stepped forward and handed me a paper bag.

I glanced up at him. "Thanks."

I wasn't hungry, not really. But curiosity got the best of me. Sometimes when I'm stressed, I get the munchies. I opened the bag and peered inside. French fries. *Yeah, I could eat a fry.* Would've preferred red wine, candy, or better yet, something sharp. Something I could fight with.

Mark stepped back. Other than the time he'd carved into my skin, he'd been almost kind. At least he didn't have the same creepy vibe as the guy in the suit.

I looked back at the man, narrowing my eyes. "So, how are you connected to my mom and Uncle August? That's what I don't understand."

He laughed, a sound that made my stomach twist. It was cold. Hollow. Chilling. "No, I suppose you don't know," he said. "And they don't know yet either. But they will. I'll make it very clear why I need justice." He stepped closer. "It's about loyalty, Zoey. And when you're loyal, you do *anything* to protect the people you care about. And that's what I'm doing."

"Are you expecting to get a medal?" I snapped.

His face twisted into a sneer. "Have you decided you don't need to be nice anymore?" He tilted his head slightly. "I never said you wouldn't be hurt further. I just said it was your life for your mother's. So, if you don't want your remaining hours here to be spent in agony and pain, maybe that positive attitude of yours should return."

I bit my tongue. Hard. I wanted to tell him everything I was thinking. About how my mom and the entire team would be hunting them down. That they'd end up in prison for the rest of their lives. But I kept quiet.

"I was going to offer you some comfort," he continued, "but seeing as you've become less friendly, maybe I shouldn't be so friendly either."

"Like what?"

Mark, standing just behind him, shifted and held out another bag.

"Come on," he said. "A reason to be nice."

The man in the suit gave a small nod, and Mark handed me the second bag. It was heavy. Heavier than I expected. *I like that.* I looked inside and saw a few paperback novels. Something to pass the time, I guessed. Better than staring at the wall, trying to piece together an escape plan. But also, those books could be useful. They weren't sharp, no, but together, three thick paperbacks in a weighted bag? It could come in handy.

"Thank you," I said carefully.

"You're welcome, Zoey," the man said. "Mark will be down to check on you, make sure you have everything you need. But as for me, this is where our time ends. Assuming, of course, your mother shows up for the trade. I won't be here for that either."

He turned without another word and walked up the steps, the door creaking shut behind him. I was alone with Mark.

When the sound of the old man's footsteps faded, I looked at Mark. "How'd you get mixed up with that guy?"

Mark's expression didn't change. "Family, Zoey. It's everything."

Then he turned and ascended the steps, leaving me alone again.

Just me. My fries. My books. And a spark of determination lighting in my chest.

Did that mean Mark was related to the man in the suit? Maybe. Maybe not. Didn't matter. What mattered was that I had a weighted object. And the next time Mark came down, I was going to swing. I was going to kick. I was going to gouge eyes and claw throats and run like wind. Because there was no way I was letting my mom trade her life for mine. And I sure as heck wasn't going down without a fight—my mother taught me that.

43

MARTINA

My stomach swirled almost faster than the thoughts racing through my mind. Was I going to be sick? I took a deep breath and told myself, *You have to focus, Martina. Think clearly. If you don't, you can't save her.*

"Are you okay?" Hirsch asked, brow furrowed.

"No, I'm not okay, Hirsch," I snapped, trying to keep my voice low. "These people are threatening us. You. Me. Zoey. Audrey." I kept my tone controlled, even though every nerve inside me buzzed with panic. I didn't want Kim or Audrey to hear. They were already rattled enough after someone had tried to break into their house. And the truth? The intruder hadn't been there to steal a TV or some jewelry. They were likely planning to kidnap Audrey. They were going to put her in the same hellish situation as Zoey. And I was sure Hirsch understood that. I said, "We've got to talk to the guy. The one they've got in custody. We need to understand this situation better. We need to understand the motive so we can figure out who they are and stop them before it's too late."

"I agree. It sounds like revenge, and from what Selena told us about Jeremy Santo, he is connected to organized crime. Maybe the connection to the Ashfords is a coincidence. Think about it. We've helped take down so many different factions over the years. But in a way, they've tipped their hand. We now know it's personal. It will help us find them."

"Who would kidnap and kill for money? Money and revenge?"

He exhaled. "There's a few to choose from, and honestly I'd have to take some time to think about it."

My heart pounding, I said, "We don't have that kind of time."

"I agree," he said. "Let me—" He hesitated, eyes drifting toward the house. His mind was split. He was worried about Kim and Audrey.

"Stay here," I said. "Stay with Kim and Audrey. Get them somewhere safe."

He opened his mouth to protest.

"I'll go talk to the suspect," I added firmly.

"I don't know if you should go alone."

"I won't be alone. The team has him. He's restrained. I'll try to talk to him and get some information." I stepped closer. "You need to keep Kim and Audrey safe. That's your job right now, Hirsch. Mine is to find Zoey."

He paused for a second longer, then nodded slowly. "You're right. As soon as I get them situated, I'll join you."

"Okay," I said, already moving.

Outside, I dashed toward the van parked two houses down. The detainment of the suspect wasn't exactly lawful. These were my guys holding him, and not the San Jose Police Department. Technically, keeping the individual detained could be considered kidnapping.

But let's be honest. If the suspect had been caught trying to break into someone's home, odds were slim he'd run to the police and rat us out. Still, how did we miss this? We'd been so focused on the ransom and on the Ashfords we'd dropped the ball.

But now everything in me was saying this was not about money or the Ashfords. Or it was a two-fer. The people who took Zoey wanted revenge against us and Graham. And why not throw five million dollars into the mix? Maybe the ransom was just so we wouldn't know their true motivations, so we couldn't figure out who they were. They saw Zoey was marrying into the Ashford family and chose her as a target. It was unclear if I was right. It was just a theory, but I *would* find the truth.

I jogged toward the van, my shoes hitting the pavement with determined strides. As I approached, I spotted Wilkes, one of our long-standing Drakos Monroe team members, stationed by the door. He was tall and solid, built like most of our guys: ex-military, trained, and focused. His dark hair was cropped close, his tan skin glowing under the streetlights. He had a boyish smile when he wasn't standing guard, but now, his posture was all business, alert and ready. And I was ready too.

It was time to get answers. "Wilkes, I want to talk to the suspect," I said, stopping beside the van.

"Okay, he's restrained. It should be fine," Wilkes said. "Give me a second."

He opened the passenger door and called out to the people inside, letting them know I was here to question the suspect.

When he returned, I said, "Have they gotten anything from him yet?"

"He won't say a word," Wilkes said with a grim shake of his head. "He fought pretty hard, but there were three of us and only one of him. No name, no ID. He wasn't carrying anything on him, other than the weapons. We have no clue who this guy is."

That wasn't great news. It was always good to know as much

as we could about someone we had illegally detained. "We have his weapons?"

Wilkes nodded. "My take is this guy's a professional, Martina. Not sure what he was planning to do, but it wasn't anything good."

I took a deep breath, trying to steady my nerves. A professional. Armed. At Hirsch's house. Most likely sent to abduct Audrey, his thirteen-year-old daughter, or worse.

I rubbed my forehead with both hands, as if I could push the spinning thoughts out of my brain. My daughter had been kidnapped, and now Audrey had nearly been taken too. This was the worst possible situation. The worst fear Hirsch and I had ever had, realized.

The side panel of the van slid open with a metallic thunk. Inside, the man sat restrained. His ankles were cuffed, and each wrist was shackled to opposite sides of the van. He could still kick, but there was no way he was getting out. Even so, I kept my distance.

His eyes lifted to meet mine, and a smile curled across his face. He was pale, almost ghostly, and his watery blue eyes gave nothing away. He didn't look more than thirty. Maybe younger. Not much older than Zoey.

"Do you know who I am?" I asked evenly.

That smile widened.

My guess was he did, but just in case, I said, "My name is Martina Monroe, and I have a few questions for you."

"I'm assuming these are your friends," he said, his voice smug and calm. "I didn't say anything to them, and I don't have anything to say to you except this: you deserve what's coming to you."

My jaw clenched. He knew the motive for abducting my daughter. For wanting revenge against *me*. "Where is Zoey?"

He stared straight at me, unflinching.

"Who are you working with?"

No response.

Fury rose within me. "Just tell me where she is, and we'll let you go. If not..."

"If not, what?" he asked in a mocking tone.

He was antagonizing me, and he wasn't going to tell me where Zoey was. In that moment, I realized it was likely always the plan to switch Zoey for me. Or to switch us and kill us both and then possibly go after Hirsch and his family. For a moment, I had to consider who had this much hate for us. We'd never done anything but seek justice for the innocent. Had we gotten something wrong?

We would have to go through every case file. Use one of Vincents's programs, his special algorithm. He'd written a code that combed through case histories, looking for patterns and links in electronic files. He'd been teaching Selena how to use it. We'd have to dig deeper until we found someone who felt wronged by Hirsch and me.

We needed to know who these people were. All we knew was they were people sophisticated enough to abduct Zoey and to infiltrate our lives. I looked at the man again. So young. How did he get involved in this? I took a step closer to the van and narrowed my eyes. "I know you won't talk to me, but if I were you, I'd at least give your name to my driver."

His expression twitched.

"So we can give your mother a message," I finished, "when they can't find your body."

And with that, I turned and walked away.

But as I retreated, I wondered if I should have pushed harder. Should I have put a knife to his throat like they'd done to my daughter? Or tortured him until he gave me the answers I needed? The thought roared through me like fire, and before I could stop myself, I spun around and climbed into the van with lightning speed, the ferocity of a mama bear unleashed.

"Wilkes, hold his feet," I snapped.

The man's expression shifted instantly, from smug to something far more uncertain.

While Wilkes pinned him down, the man thrashed against his restraints. I grabbed him by the throat, my fingers closing around his neck with every ounce of fury and grief inside me. "If they harm one more inch of my daughter's body," I growled, "I will personally slit your throat or squeeze the life out of you with my bare hands. And nobody will find your body. That, I can guarantee."

Rage overtook me.

I kept squeezing, my hands trembling, my vision blurring as red hot anger pulsed through me. "Tell me where she is!"

His face was turning purple.

My body shook.

Then—"Martina!"

A voice. *Hirsch.*

"Martina, what are you doing?!"

Suddenly, a strong arm grabbed me, yanking me backward. I released my grip as Hirsch pulled me out of the van.

"What are you doing?" he said again, eyes wide with disbelief.

"He knows where she is," I gasped, my breath coming in shallow bursts. "He won't tell me."

"He can't speak to us if he's dead," Hirsch said firmly. "This isn't you, Martina. You're not like this."

I shook my head, frantic. "He has Zoey. He won't tell me where she is—"

"We are going to find her, but not like that."

I looked down at my trembling hands, and then the tears

came. They poured down my face uncontrollably. "I can't lose her," I cried, my voice cracking. "I can't—"

Hirsch pulled me into his arms, holding me tight as the sobs took over. I cried against him, my body wracked with guilt and desperation.

"I'm so sorry," I choked out. "I'm so sorry..."

"We're gonna get her back, Martina," he whispered, holding me tighter.

I let him hold me. I don't even know for how long. Shame burned inside me as I realized I'd lost control. It left me feeling helpless and weak.

After a few moments, I wiped my face. Wilkes approached with some tissues and handed them to me silently.

Through sniffles, I said, "Thank you"

Wilkes said, "He'll be fine, Martina. No harm, no foul."

I gave him a half-hearted nod.

Hirsch's face was etched with concern. "Do you want to talk about what happened?"

I shook my head, exhaling hard. "I'm sorry. I just... I just kind of lost it in there."

"It's okay," he said. "I know you don't want to hurt anyone, but I understand your actions. *I get it.* I wouldn't want to hurt anyone either, but if he had *my daughter* and he wouldn't tell me where she was? You'd be pulling me off him, too."

I let out a shaky laugh through my tears.

"Let's just take a moment, okay?" he said. "Let's go back to the office. I'm going to bring Kim and Audrey there too. They'll keep our friend here until this all gets sorted out."

I nodded slowly. "Okay," I whispered. "Let's go back to the office. That's what we should do."

"It's gonna be okay, Martina," Hirsch said gently.

I looked up at him, eyes red and tired. "You really think so, Hirsch? After what they did to her?"

He nodded solemnly. "We're going to figure this out."

I exhaled hard and wiped my eyes again. Shame filled me as I thought about what I'd just done. Would I have killed that man if Hirsch hadn't pulled me off? I shut my eyes and said a silent prayer. *God, give me strength.* I'd been tested before, but never like this.

44

SELENA

I SHOOK my head as I ended the call with Martina. She had just told me everything that happened. The thought of losing her, or Zoey, was too much to bear. If I was being honest, I'd rather they take me. But I couldn't do that to Dad. And we couldn't lose Martina. As much as I loved my biological mother, and missed her from time to time, I'd spent more years mothering her than being mothered by her. Martina was the only real maternal figure I'd ever had. She taught me. She protected me. She saved me, more than once. I didn't think I could handle losing her too.

And I knew, without a doubt, she would trade herself for Zoey. Or even for me. Probably for anyone. That's just who she was. We had to find the connection, before it was too late.

I glanced at the clock. It was nearing midnight and only ten hours until the scheduled switch. Ten hours to figure out where Zoey was, rescue her, keep everyone safe, and find out who was behind all of this.

Vincent sat down next to me, balancing a fresh cup of coffee in one hand and his laptop in the other. "What's up?" he asked.

After letting out a breath, I filled him in, repeating everything Martina had just told me. As I spoke, his expression darkened, and he shook his head. "This is so weird."

"No kidding," I said. "It seems like it's been about Martina and Hirsch the whole time or maybe not. We know Jeremy Santo has a history with the Ashfords. He's somehow connected to both Martina's old cases and the Ashfords. We need to figure out how. There has to be a link between Jeremy Santo and one of the cases Martina and Hirsch worked on."

"That's exactly what I was thinking," Vincent said. "I just got off the phone with Jess over at the FBI. She sent over a whole dossier on everyone they believe Jeremy Santo is working with. She said if we find any connection, we need to let them know immediately. He's tied to some really bad people." He opened his laptop. "I ran the algorithm for patterns, but nothing obvious popped up. It needs human eyes, so I figure we can split the files. You take a batch, I'll take a batch."

I nodded, forcing myself to focus. My head felt foggy, but I didn't have time for that. "Okay. Yeah. Let's do it."

I stared at the screen, waiting for Vincent to upload the files to our shared folder on the server.

"Okay," he said, "I'll go through these three, you take those three. Any names that stand out, especially any mention of Jeremy Santo, we flag them. Then we cross-reference every person he's associated with against Martina and Hirsch's case records."

"Got it," I said.

"It's gonna be okay, Selena," he added gently.

"Is it?" The words came out harder than I intended.

Vincent didn't flinch. "There is nobody, and I mean nobody, tougher than Martina."

"Yeah, she's tough, but she's not invincible."

He nodded. "I get it. I've worked with her for a long time. Sometimes... it's easy to forget she's human too. And now they have her daughter. Your sister." He looked at me, serious now. "If anyone can be found, it's going to be Zoey. Everyone's working on it, even Jess. She could get in serious trouble for sending me those files, but she did it anyway. The odds are in our favor." Vincent stood. "You need anything before we get started? Coffee? Water? Tea? Soda? A snack?"

I shook my head. "No. I just want to look at the files."

He nodded.

Martina was tough, but even the toughest people had their breaking point. I knew it firsthand. I'd hit mine more than a few times, but I couldn't let myself think about that now. I needed a level head. I needed to stay sharp. I double-clicked the folder, just about to dive in when a familiar face appeared in the doorway.

I shot up from my seat and rushed forward, wrapping my arms around him. "Hi, Dad."

"Hi, honey," he said, hugging me back. "You guys working hard?"

"Yeah," I said, wiping my face quickly.

"Betty's right behind me with Barney."

As if on cue, Barney, the fluffy little dog, padded into the conference room, tail wagging. For the first time in thirty-two hours, I smiled.

I knelt down and gave him scratches behind the ears. "Hi, Barney! Oh, who's a good dog? You are! Yes, you are."

Betty walked in and I stood up. She gave me a warm bear hug. In my ear, she said, "Ted's coming too. Anything you need we'll get it. We're caffeinated, a little rested, and ready to go."

I hesitated. They hadn't heard the latest update. Martina was on her way to the office, but it wasn't my place to tell them she was likely going to switch places with Zoey. It was better she tell them herself. I looked at Vincent, who caught my eye. He gave a subtle nod.

"We were just going through some files," he said to Betty and Dad. "We think they could be important."

"I can help," Ted said, stepping forward.

As a retired sergeant who had worked closely with Martina and Hirsch for years, he might actually spot names or case details the rest of us could miss.

Dad chimed in, "And Betty and I can head into the lounge with Barney. We'll be in there if you need us."

"Thanks, Dad," I said softly, offering a grateful smile.

Ted took a seat beside us, and Vincent handed him a loaner laptop.

"We're looking through FBI files," I explained, pulling up the shared directory. "Known associates connected to organized crime. Specifically, anyone tied to Jeremy Santo."

"Got it."

"Okay," I said, inhaling deeply. "Now that there's three of us, we can each take two file folders. We'll get through this faster."

"Who do you have searching the cell phone messages?" Ted asked.

"The tech team is on it," Vincent answered. "They're also digging into all the financials connected to Gilbert Thomas."

I nodded, then turned back to my screen. I opened the first file and started reading.

Jeremy Santo wasn't officially linked to any major crime syndicate. No arrests. No convictions. But there were photos. Dozens of them. Surveillance photos of him in San Francisco, surrounded by men long suspected of being part of organized crime. Some of the images went back decades. He'd clearly been bad news for a long time. More recently, he was photographed with the Mancinis, a San Francisco based crime family. They were known for drug trafficking, human trafficking, and grand theft. But none of the photos proved anything illegal.

And I wasn't just looking for photographs. We were

searching for a name, someone tied to Jeremy Santo as well as Gilbert Thomas or James Turtle. I moved on to the second file, trying to keep my eyes focused as the words blurred slightly from fatigue. I kept pushing.

The Mancinis had apparently taken over from another crime family years ago, one that had been brought down nearly a decade earlier. *Interesting.* I scanned the summary again. No mention of Gilbert Thomas or James Turtle, but there were references to other lesser-known associates. Some were prominent figures in the community, people who hadn't been suspected of criminal involvement by anyone but the FBI's organized crime task force. They had all gone to jail after the leaders fell.

I kept reading. One particular detail stood out to me. It was what had spurred the major takedown. It involved a murder. A decades-old cold case. And that, apparently, was what finally put the heads of the crime family away. The idea that you could bury something for decades and it could still rise up and take everything down was chilling. *I guess you really can't outrun your past.* My body stiffened as the realization hit me.

Organized crime.

Human trafficking.

Cold case murder.

I turned to Vincent, heart pounding, and told him everything I had just found. "Is it possible there's a connection? It was in San Francisco but... I mean, it was a cold case that brought them down." Martina and Hirsch had worked cold cases for years and had solved some really tough and really old ones. Vincent's face paled. His eyes widened as he stared at the screen, lips parting slowly. As he began to speak, quietly, urgently, explaining what he knew about that case, a chill ran down my spine.

45

MARTINA

As the group of us stepped back inside Drakos Monroe Security & Investigations, I had a thought. Maybe we needed more than one lounge. Or even sleeping quarters. A secure area, like an in-house safe house. Somewhere people like Kim and Audrey could stay if they were in danger. A safe room sealed off from whatever chaos was unfolding on the outside.

My phone buzzed, pulling me back to the moment. I looked down, saw Selena's name on the screen, and nodded to Hirsch before answering. "Hey, Selena. We just got back to the office. What's up?"

"I'm in the conference room with Vincent and Ted," she said. "We found something."

"Okay. We'll get Kim and Audrey settled in the lounge and then head to the conference room."

"Your mom, Barney, and my dad are already in there," she said. "See you in a minute."

I hung up and turned to Hirsch. "Selena and Vincent found something."

I gave Kim and Audrey a warm smile, trying to keep my face calm and composed. Thankfully, they hadn't seen my earlier breakdown. That moment of weakness had passed, or it was at least buried, for now.

It never surprised me that people saw me as strong. I was the one to call when things went sideways. The one you looked to when you needed a plan. You didn't want to see someone like that lose it. If the strong one breaks, it means things are really bad. And this... this was very bad. There were still so many unknowns.

As we stepped into the lounge, I heard a sharp little yip from Barney, followed by light laughter. That sound, innocent and joyful, made my chest tighten.

Barney came bouncing toward me, his tail wagging like mad. I knelt down, letting his warmth and wiggles ground me for a moment. "Oh, hi, Barney," I said softly, scratching behind his ears. For a heartbeat, I remembered there were still good things in this world.

When I stood up, Charlie came over and pulled me into a hug. I held him for a moment, not ready to let go. I hadn't told him what had happened yet. That I was planning to trade myself for Zoey. I wasn't sure I could tell him.

He stepped back, looking into my eyes. "What else has happened?" he asked gently.

"We got another message," I said, trying to keep my voice steady. "We just need to work fast to find Zoey."

I turned and gave my mom a quick hug too. She said, "We're here if there's anything you need."

"Thanks, Mom. I'd appreciate it if you stayed here until we find Zoey, okay?"

"Overnight?"

"Yes. We think it's important. Audrey and Kim are staying too."

We'd have to figure out where everyone could sleep. Not that most of us would. I knew I wouldn't. Hirsch wouldn't. Vincent wouldn't. Selena wouldn't.

Half the team would stay up all night again. The ones who knew what was really going on, what we were up against—they wouldn't rest. But the others just needed to be safe.

Selena appeared in the hallway and gave me a small nod.

"She says she's got something for us to go over," I told everyone in the lounge. "So, we'll leave you for now, but we'll be in the conference room if you need anything."

I tried to sound upbeat. Cheerful. In control. But if my voice matched how I really felt, it would be low, shaking, and on the verge of breaking. *Not now, I told myself. Not here.* I had to be strong. *I am strong.* I said quick goodbyes and turned toward the conference room, toward whatever came next.

Inside, Vincent and Selena both stood with serious looks on their faces. I shut the door behind Hirsch and me and gave a quick wave to Ted, who was working quietly at the end of the table.

"We think we found the connection," Selena said, getting straight to the point. "We think we know who's behind it."

"Who is it?"

Vincent spoke next. "I've been working with Jess from the FBI, my old contact. She sent over some files. We told you Jeremy Santo had been linked to organized crime. Still no formal charges, but there are plenty of photos of him with known criminals. They've never been able to pin down what his involvement is exactly, but Jess went through everything again and sent us the files to look through. One file stood out."

"Was there a connection to James Turtle or Gilbert Thomas?" I asked.

"No," Vincent said. "But the highest number of sightings of Jeremy Santo were with members of the Mancini crime family out of San Francisco. And here's where it gets interesting. The Mancinis rose to power after the fall of the DeMarco family."

My stomach flip-flopped before I turned to Hirsch, my eyes meeting his. A jolt of recognition passed between us.

Hirsch said, rather calmly, "When we solved my brother's murder, we learned it was Anthony Stanzel who killed Nick. Anthony is the son of Maurice Stanzel, an associate of the DeMarco crime family."

Vincent nodded. "Exactly. So, I went back to Jess and asked her if anything had happened recently that might've triggered this retaliation. Turns out, the head of the DeMarco family, Gianni DeMarco, just died in prison. Word is, it might've been a hit from a rival."

Hirsch's face darkened.

"And now," Vincent continued, "there's some chatter that the Mancinis want revenge as some sort of tribute to the DeMarcos. We think maybe this is their twisted way of getting it because the case that took them all down? It was the one you two solved—essentially making you responsible for his incarceration and eventual death."

Hirsch spoke quietly. "Martina uncovered the connection, and the rest of the team helped build the case. That murder charge against Stanzel unraveled everything—exposed the trafficking, the laundering, the whole network."

I looked back at Hirsch.

His hands were clenched at his sides. "It wasn't enough that they murdered my brother," he said. "Now they're coming after my daughter. After yours. After you."

For someone who had kept his cool this whole time, even when I lost mine and nearly strangled a suspect, it was clear he'd finally hit his limit.

"This is information we can use," I said, my voice gaining

strength. "We know who they are now. The FBI has files on them. That helps, right?"

Vincent nodded. "Yes. Jess and her team are willing to assist in any way they can. I know this gets tricky since they told you not to involve law enforcement for the trade. But Jess and the Organized Crime Task Force have been studying these people for years. We're getting off-the-record intel right now, but she's willing to bring this to the rest of the team." He paused. "Before she goes through official channels, she wanted us to confirm that you're okay with it. She doesn't want to do anything to jeopardize Zoey's life."

I inhaled slowly. My mind flashed back to that case, how it all started with a missing persons file—a woman who'd witnessed a murder decades earlier. A woman connected to the Stanzels. That single tip led to uncovering a massive criminal web and had finally brought Hirsch and his family justice. And now those people wanted revenge because their crime boss died in prison. *As he should have.* It was sickening.

Hirsch exhaled sharply. "If they've got information about their stash houses or safe houses, anywhere they might be keeping hostages, it could help us find Zoey."

I nodded. "We'll take all the help we can get. Just as long as we don't make a single move that risks Zoey."

Vincent looked at me, serious. "We'll be smart. But Jess has people who know the Mancinis inside and out. If they're behind this, she's our best chance at finding Zoey before it's too late."

"But what if they're watching the building?" I asked, pacing. "This building. If they know the feds are coming in, if they know we've alerted them..."

Vincent leaned back slightly. "We've got a pretty smart team here at Drakos Monroe. We'll figure out a way to smuggle them in without detection."

"You're right, we do," I said. "But we have to be sure they're clean. They already had someone inside the San Jose Police Department. How do we know there's not someone dirty inside the feds?"

Vincent didn't flinch. "The Organized Crime Task Force is solid. And so is Jess. I'd trust her with my life."

But would I trust her with my daughter's life?

Jess had come through for us before. She'd been reliable, sharp, and loyal. We'd never encountered dirty feds, but that didn't mean they didn't exist.

Vincent must've read my hesitation. "Jess said there's a strong suspicion the kidnappings, the last six over the past decade, might be tied to this network. If we're right, this could be the thing that takes them down for good."

I let out a slow breath and started pacing again. Could I really trust the feds not to screw this up? Honestly, yes. We'd worked with the FBI on several cases. They'd been professional. Efficient. Strategic. And most of all, they'd been helpful. We'd helped them. They'd helped us. And right now, we needed all the help we could get. I had to remind myself, there's strength in asking for help when you need it.

"Okay," I said finally. "But we need to bring them in covertly. It has to look like they're family members or office staff. It's going to look weird if people show up in the middle of the night in government SUVs."

"I'll call her now," Vincent said, already pulling out his phone.

Hirsch stepped forward. "They'll help us find her."

"I hope so," I said softly, looking at him, and then my thoughts hardened. "The feds will help, but maybe it's time we had a little chat with Jeremy Santo."

Vincent looked up. "We have an address, right?"

I turned to Selena. "We do, don't we?"

She nodded. "We've got one for him, plus his ex-wife and his son, Keith. And no, the ex-wife hasn't called me back."

"Any new information on Gilbert Thomas?" I asked.

"They're still digging. Looking to see if he's got property in his name or any hidden properties he might have put under his name or his wife's," she said.

"Okay." I turned to Hirsch. "You up for talking to Jeremy Santo?"

"Right now?" he asked.

"Right now," I confirmed. "If he's home, I'm sure he'll be thrilled to see us." I said it with all the sarcasm I could muster.

"Let's go," Hirsch said with determination.

Selena chimed in, "Maybe you should bring backup? And we could send another team to talk to the ex-wife. I'll go. I can take some of the guys who are ten times my size."

I nodded. "You talk to the ex-wife. Try to find Keith. See if he'll talk about Gilbert Thomas. Who knows? Maybe Keith will have some useful information that will lead us to Gilbert."

Selena said, "Got it."

"You ready?" I asked Hirsch.

His eyes met mine. "Let's get the backup team," he said. "And then we go."

46

MARTINA

Hirsch crept the vehicle slowly as we parked in front of Jeremy Santo's rather large home in the Blossom Hill area of San Jose. There weren't any lights on, but that didn't mean he wasn't home. I texted the team behind us and got a thumbs-up. They were in position. "Let's go," I told Hirsch as he turned off the engine.

"We need to do this calmly. Rationally."

"I'll try my best."

"Martina..."

With my hand raised, I said, "I promise. Just questioning."

With a nod, we both exited the car and headed toward the front of the house.

As we stepped onto the driveway, the porch lit up. I assumed they were automatic lights with motion sensors. Either way, it startled me, but it shouldn't have. I took a few deep breaths as we walked toward the front of the home.

It was stucco with wooden trim, Spanish style with a tile roof. Jeremy Santo was doing well for himself. *That plumbing company must really be lucrative.* We knew almost for certain he was dirty just like he had been all those years ago when the Ashfords knew him.

Hirsch knocked, but there was no response. The house remained dark.

"I don't think there's anybody home," I said, scanning the quiet neighborhood. "But why wouldn't Jeremy Santo be home? It's almost 1 o'clock in the morning on a Sunday. Is he out of town? Or is he holding my daughter hostage?"

"Maybe we should give him a call."

"Not a bad idea. You got the number?"

I pulled out my phone and copied the information from the email into the field. It rang four times before going to voicemail. Either he didn't want to be disturbed, or he was asleep with his phone on silent. "Well, I don't think he's here. And he's not answering. I'm gonna take a look around."

"Martina…"

"If the cops want to come and arrest me for trespassing, so be it," I said defiantly, trying to peer through the windows. A tall fence surrounded the backyard, making it difficult to get inside. "Give me a boost."

"I'm not boosting you over a fence to break into somebody's yard. We need you *not* in jail, Martina."

"Just for a minute. There's nobody here."

"The neighbors could have cameras."

Out of breath but determined, I ignored Hirsch and tried to hoist myself up onto the fence. Soon, he was beside me. He clasped his hands together for me to put my foot in and hop over the fence. "Fine, but be quick."

"I will be. I just want to get a quick look around. You never know. He might have an ADU or an in-law unit where they're keeping her hostage."

But from the looks of the video, Zoey had been in a basement.

Not likely above ground. But then again they hadn't exactly panned the space to give us a full look at where she was being held. I put my foot in Hirsch's hands, and I hopped over. I landed with a soft thud on the other side. I unlatched the gate and opened it for him.

"We're fine. We have backup," I said.

Hirsch ignored my overconfidence and followed me into the backyard. I turned on the flashlight on my phone.

The yard was nice, professionally landscaped, no doubt. There was a pool and a pool house right next to it. No lights were on, but as I approached, another automatic light flicked on from the small dwelling, illuminating the yard. "If they had attack dogs," I said quietly, "we'd be puppy chow right now."

I looked inside the windows of the small unit. It was dark, but I could make out the faint outlines of a sofa, TV, and a small kitchen. No signs of anyone being held there. I tried the doorknob, and to my surprise, it was unlocked. I let myself in. There was a kitchenette, a bathroom with a tub and shower, and a bedroom with one closet. It was clean with the bed made, and it didn't look like it was being used.

She wasn't there. *Nobody is here.*

I made my way out, shutting the door behind me, and headed toward the back of the main house. The backyard was still lit up. If any neighbors had cameras, we were definitely being recorded. But what was Jeremy Santo going to do? Call the police?

We peered in through the windows. "There's nobody here," Hirsch said.

I let out a breath, defeat heavy in my chest. We'd come all the way out here for nothing.

"All right, let's get out of here and see if the team can figure out where he could be. If he has any hotel reservations or flights, we can find them."

"I'll call it in. Let's head back."

As I reopened the gate, a car pulled into the driveway. I closed it quickly behind me, crouched down, and motioned for Hirsch to do the same.

Just as I glanced down at my phone, a text popped up from the team.

> Someone's approaching.

Super. This wasn't exactly how I wanted to meet Jeremy Santo.

I texted back.

> Description? What are they doing?

A few moments later, I heard footsteps heading toward the front door. Then they paused.

The footsteps were now coming toward the backyard. Another message buzzed in.

> He's headed straight toward you. It's a man. He matches Jeremy Santo's description.

After I showed Hirsch the screen, I pressed a finger to my lips.

We waited, hearts thudding, breath held, as the footsteps crept closer. The grass crunched softly under shoes. We flattened ourselves against the fence, as close as possible, practically fused to the wood.

The fence rattled. Metal scraped. He was testing it. A beat later, his head appeared above the top. I froze. Even blinking felt too loud. But his gaze passed over us without landing, and after a moment, he dropped back down.

Footsteps faded, heading toward the front of the house.

All we needed was a few minutes for him to go inside, then

we could slip out, head to the door, and pretend we hadn't just broken into his backyard.

I texted the team.

> Let me know when he's inside.

A few moments later, the response came in.

> He's inside.

Hirsch reached up and unlatched the gate, crouching low. We slipped out quietly, shutting it behind us.

Once we were out in the open and no longer looking like burglars, I straightened my spine and marched up to the front door. Hirsch gave a sharp knock.

A light flicked on inside, casting a glow behind the frosted glass.

He knocked again.

I shifted from foot to foot, trying to shake the anxiety crawling under my skin. Hirsch knocked once more, and this time, we heard footsteps. A pause. A quiet click. Then the door cracked open, and we were face-to-face with Jeremy Santo.

He looked older than the photos. Wealth had smoothed out some of his edges but not all of them. His eyes were sharp, calculating.

"Good evening, Jeremy," I said, keeping my voice as calm as possible. "My name is Martina Monroe, and this is August Hirsch. We have a few questions for you."

He blinked at us, slow and annoyed. "Ma'am, it's one in the morning. I don't know what your business is here, but if you don't leave, I'm calling the police."

I folded my arms, locking down the fury trying to climb up my throat. "I'll cut to the chase. I think you know exactly who I am. And I think you know August Hirsch. I'm here about my daughter, Zoey."

He stared blankly. "I don't know your daughter. I don't know you."

"You can play it cool in your shiny suit, but I know you know who she is. Zoey Monroe. Her fiancé is Henry Ashford. Ring a bell? Graham and Margot Ashford, your old college friends?" I inched closer. "We believe you may know where my daughter is. And we're not leaving until you tell us where she is."

He raised his voice slightly. "Ma'am, I think you've got me mixed up with someone else. This is your last warning. Leave my property, or I will call the police. Or I'll be forced to defend my home."

His hand came up, and that's when I saw the firearm.

I didn't flinch. "There's two of us and one of you," I said, staring straight into his eyes. "And we've already found you. We know where your ex-wife is. We know where your son is. I'm not scared of your little gun. I don't want any trouble. I just want my daughter back."

I slowly pulled back my jacket, revealing the weapon in my holster. Not the one strapped to my ankle, that was a secret.

Jeremy's jaw twitched. In one hand, the gun. In the other, his phone. He hovered over the dial screen. "I'm going to ask you to leave one more time," he said coldly. "If you know anything about me, you know that when I call the police, they come running. And they'll be on *my* side."

"Martina," Hirsch warned.

"Yes, listen to your friend," Jeremy added with a smug smile.

My body trembled, not with fear but rage. Hot and pulsing. "I will find her," I said through gritted teeth. "And then I'll come back for you."

Hirsch tugged me away. I yanked my arm free, my glare never leaving Jeremy's smug expression.

"I'm fine," I said, walking stiffly down the driveway. The night air felt sharp in my lungs. "He knows where she is."

"Get in the car."

I slid into the passenger seat and slammed the door.

"That may be," Hirsch said as he started the engine, "but he's not going to talk. And we don't need to get in a firefight with whoever he's got on payroll at San Jose PD. Not tonight."

"You're right." I blew out a shaky breath. "Let's check in with Selena. See if they had better luck with the ex-wife or the son."

Frustration burned like acid in my chest, but I was still standing. I hadn't lost control. That had to count for something.

47

MARTINA

Sitting in the car in front of Jeremy Santo's house, I shook my head and ended the call. "Selena talked to the ex-wife," I said to Hirsch. "Apparently Ms. Litman wasn't very friendly this morning, considering the hour, but she told Selena she wasn't surprised her ex was still up to no good and said he'd been dirty for a long time, long before she knew it. Once she did, she tried to keep her son away from him, but Jeremy is his father, and Keith is now a grown-up and can see him whenever he wants."

"Did Selena talk to Keith?"

"No, but he does live with her. She said he went out with his friends and wasn't sure when he'd be back."

"Should we try to track him down?"

"We could try. But you know what's really frustrating, Hirsch? I feel like we've got guys who know exactly where Zoey is. Jeremy Santo—I'd bet money he knows where she is. And that guy who tried to break into your house. He knows. Keith might know too. He might not. It's so frustrating. I feel like we're so close but so far away."

"I understand your frustration."

"We're running out of time, Hirsch."

"We still have almost nine hours. That's a long time. And we haven't checked in with the team yet. Maybe they've found a couple of locations for us to check out and line up a plan."

"They haven't called."

"Doesn't mean they're not finding things. There are plenty of angles. I know they're still looking into Gilbert Thomas and are trying to determine if he owns any properties where he could be holding her. Vincent's reaching out to the FBI, trying to get intel on any known safe houses or places they could be holding her. We're going to find her, Martina."

"Maybe." My voice cracked with fear and exhaustion. "Have we ever solved a case in less than two days, Hirsch? She was abducted at 4 PM on Friday and it's now 1 AM on Sunday. We have nine hours to find her before this all goes very badly and we have to come up with an entirely new strategy. One where I have to go in alone."

"We're not going to let that happen, Martina."

"It will happen if it has to. That's what makes this so maddening."

A heavy silence settled between us.

"Head back to the office?" Hirsch asked.

I hesitated. "Part of me wants to stay in San Jose. I've got a feeling... she's close." There was no proof, but maybe it was my mother's intuition telling me that my baby was near.

He nodded. "We could hit a restaurant that's open 24 hours. Set up a mobile HQ out here."

"Let me call Vincent. See if he's found anything before we make our next move."

"Okay. I'll start heading toward the office, but I can turn around if we need to."

"Understood."

With a little prayer the team had found something useful, I dialed. Vincent answered right away. "Hey."

"Hey. Total dead end at Santo's place," I told Vincent. "Jeremy wouldn't talk. Pulled a gun. Said he'd call his buddies at the police department if we didn't leave."

Vincent swore softly. "Seriously?"

"Yeah. He wasn't exactly thrilled to see us. Keith's MIA, and the ex-wife said she's not surprised he's still dirty but claims she doesn't talk to him anymore." My jaw clenched. "We're spinning our wheels here, Vincent. I'm hoping you've got something, anything. Have the feds gotten there yet? We need a lead, now."

"We just smuggled in a couple of feds," he said. "They're with me now. They're members of the organized crime task force. They're experts on the Mancinis and their associates. Despite being woken up in the middle of the night, they got here in forty minutes. They're solid."

Normally, I'd be ecstatic at such a rapid response, but adrenaline had scraped my nerves raw, and I didn't have time to celebrate. "What do they suggest we do? Do they have any known addresses we can check out? I've got a gut feeling she's still in San Jose. That's why we haven't left yet."

"I'm putting you on speaker."

I did the same, so Hirsch could hear. A soft click, then a new voice broke through. "Martina, it's Special Agent Honeycutt. Vine's with me too—we're both with the San Francisco Organized Crime Task Force."

Hirsch and I exchanged glances. We'd worked with both agents when we were investigating Hirsch's brother's murder. "It's good to hear your voice. Thank you for helping."

Honeycutt said, "Yours too. Wish it were under better circumstances."

Me too. "We believe members of the Mancini family have taken my daughter, Zoey."

"We're aware. Vincent filled us in. We've had our eyes on the

Mancinis ever since the DeMarcos fell. These guys are colder, meaner. But they love money, and that could be their weakness."

"We're technically off-book here," Agent Vine added. "But Vincent saw our names on the file, asked us for a favor. Jess did too."

"I appreciate it. Anything you can do to help us get Zoey back, we'll be grateful. We're running out of time."

Agent Honeycutt said, "We're combing through known assets and hideouts, cross-referencing Mancini connections, and—"

Suddenly the line crackled. A rush of static cut through, followed by faint movement and voices in the background.

"What's going on?" I asked, my pulse spiking.

"I just got something from the team." Vincent's voice returned, sharp and urgent. "A property in Campbell. Technically registered under Gilbert Thomas's wife's maiden name."

"Campbell?" I echoed, already opening the maps app on my phone. "We're close. Send the address."

Vincent said, "I just texted it to you... Honeycutt, could that be where they're holding her?"

There was a pause.

Honeycutt said, "Thomas is slippery as all get out. But if he's involved, it's plausible they'd stash someone there."

Hirsch said, "We'll head there now."

Vine said, "You've got backup, right?"

"Two vehicles. Solid people."

Honeycutt said, "Good. We'll head out now and meet you there too." He paused. "Vincent, while we're out, can you work with Jess to continue cross-checking properties? Vine will be riding shotgun. He can be in communication while we're en route."

Vincent said, "You got it."

Honeycutt continued, "Martina, we'll be on our way. We've got your back."

"Thank you."

"Be safe."

The call dropped. My phone buzzed with the address. I opened the map, and my stomach twisted when I saw how close it was. It was a ten-minute drive, maybe less.

"Let's go," I said.

Hirsch turned the car around without a word.

I stared out the windshield into the dark. Streetlights blurred past like ghosts. My heart pounded, not with hope but with dread. We were so close. But what if we were already too late? I said a silent prayer, one I'd said a dozen times already, but this time, it came out like a plea from the bottom of my soul. *Please let her be there. Please don't let it be too late.*

48

MARTINA

THE NEIGHBORHOOD WAS QUIET, maybe even too quiet. Even in the dead of night, you'd expect to hear a dog bark, a car pass, a rustle of wind. Anything. But as we pulled onto the street in Campbell, we were met with silence. Maybe it was my nerves. Maybe the thoughts of what we might find were smothering every sound. The houses were older, mostly well-kept. Not as nice as Jeremy Santo's neighborhood, but I guess as far as secret houses tucked under your wife's maiden name go, it was decent. Except for the one at the end of the court. "That's it," I said. "Number twelve."

I stared at the dark, two-story structure, its silhouette hulking beneath the dark sky. Overgrown hedges crawled up the front like they were trying to hide it, and the driveway was cracked and crumbling. My gut twisted.

Hirsch slowed the car to a stop a few doors down. Our second vehicle with our backup team was already parked behind us, lights off. Without a word, I opened the door. The chill in the night air hit my skin like a warning, and I shivered.

Resting my hand on the grip of my firearm, I stepped out. My shoes pounded faintly against the pavement as I made my way to the sidewalk. The house looked empty. There were no lights on, no shadows moving behind curtains. *Nothing.*

What if this wasn't where they were keeping her? I had to remind myself that the FBI was checking out other locations, so this wasn't the end of the story. This was just one page. At least, I hoped so.

Hirsch walked silently beside me. As we approached, a strange kind of knowing settled over me, heavy and absolute. "She's here," I whispered.

"You see something?"

"No. I can't explain it... but I can feel it."

I stopped and texted our backup.

> Meet us at the target.

As I crouched near the edge of a hedge, waiting for their confirmation, a flash of my daughter filled my mind, my Zoey. Beautiful inside and out. Smart. Funny. Obsessed with all things glitter. About to be married. And now, being held in a basement. Every single person I knew was looking for her. Helping me. Fighting for her. Others weren't so lucky.

Maybe I was hoarding all my luck for this very moment. The moment I'd see her again—stare into her bright blue eyes, alive and safe.

A buzz in my hand.

> Affirmative.

I moved forward, Hirsch shadowing me. Soon, I heard the soft, controlled footsteps of the backup team behind us.

We were at the house.

"No visible movement inside," Hirsch said. "Blinds are

drawn. Looks like blackout curtains. Even if something's going on in there, we can't see it."

The garage door was closed. No light seeped from underneath. I edged toward the side, checking for a window. There was one, but it was covered, like everything else.

"This could be a trap," Hirsch said. "Jeremy Santo knows we're onto him. Maybe he warned them. Maybe they moved her."

But I didn't feel like they had.

I felt like she was still here.

Waiting.

I turned to Gemini and Rocket and motioned for them to flank right. Hirsch and I would take the left.

"Don't you want us to take a look around first?" Rocket asked. "Considering you're one of the targets?"

He was right, but I wasn't about to stand down. "No. Go ahead."

Gemini and Rocket peeled around to the back of the house. The fence was low, barely waist high. Easily scalable. I glanced up toward the eaves of the home. No visible surveillance cameras, but that didn't mean there weren't any. Whoever lived here, if anyone did, might be watching from inside.

I scanned the rest of the neighborhood. Most houses were dark, a few porch lights glowing faintly in the distance. No movement behind the curtains, no signs of life. But that didn't mean we weren't being watched. If these people were as sophisticated as we thought, they could be careful enough to remain invisible.

We continued along the narrow left side of the house. It was overgrown with ivy curling up the siding, weeds creeping over the walkway. The smell of damp earth and mildew hung in the air. I brushed back a branch and crept forward, careful not to snap any twigs or rustle the bushes.

Then, a motion sensor light flicked on.

Hirsch and I froze in place.

A pool of white light spilled across the dead lawn, illuminating a sliding glass door. And beyond that, light. A faint glow from inside the house. It wasn't abandoned. I signaled for Hirsch to retreat.

We regrouped at the side yard just as Gemini and Rocket returned. My heart pounded, not just from adrenaline, but from something deeper. A mother's instinct. A primal knowing that my daughter was close. Still alive.

"There are a few entry points on the right," Rocket said. "We spotted a light on in the back. Someone's inside."

Zoey. And whoever had taken her. "We saw a slider on the left," Hirsch added. "We triggered a light."

"They might know we're here," Gemini said.

He glanced toward the house, eyes scanning the shadows. "We don't know how many people are inside. I think we should go with a team approach. One person stays outside to guard the perimeter. The other three go in, quiet and fast. Subdue anyone we find, secure the area. Then we bring you in."

"Or," Rocket added, "you and Hirsch stay back. You're both targets. Let us go in first."

Could I just stand by while my daughter might be feet away? Everything inside me screamed no, but I had to be smart. "Let's call Stavros," I said, nodding toward Hirsch. "Let the team know we're going in."

My hands trembled slightly as I grabbed my phone from my pocket. I wanted to run to my daughter, but I also needed to bring her out alive and not blow the entire operation out of desperation.

Still... as soon as the team was notified?

I was going in.

49

MARTINA

AFTER BEING HEAVILY CAUTIONED to stay back while the others searched for my daughter, I politely, or not so politely, declined. Weapon in hand, I said, "Let's go."

Gemini nodded. So did Hirsch.

"Rocket, stand guard. Let me know if anybody comes in."

"Yes, ma'am," he said without hesitation.

I crept back to the side of the house. The motion light still beamed harshly across the wall and the overgrown path. The sliding glass door stood in front of me. It was mostly dark beyond the glass, but the low light inside made it so I could just make out a small room with fast food wrappers scattered across a table. A laptop sat open, glowing in the dark. There were no people in sight, but that didn't mean no one was there.

I reached out and gave the slider a gentle tug. "It's locked," I whispered, glancing at Hirsch.

Gemini stepped forward, already unrolling a slim pouch of lockpicks. He crouched low, steady and practiced, while the rest of us stood guard. Somewhere in the distance, a car engine revved, then faded. The metallic click of tools against the lock filled the silence.

Each second crawled. Finally, the soft click of success. Gemini slid the door open just enough for us to slip through. The smell hit me first.

Stale sweat. Mildew. Something faintly metallic. Blood? The air inside was thick and humid despite the cool night.

I stepped inside.

The living room was dim, lit only by the glow of the laptop screen and a small lamp on the table. A couch with torn upholstery sagged in the middle. Empty takeout containers and a few bottles of water were piled on the table. The space had the feel of transience, like someone had been there, not living but hiding or holding someone against their will. Maybe it was where they'd kept other victims or did other dirty deeds.

I re-scanned the space. No signs of struggle, but the energy here was wrong.

To the left, a narrow hallway stretched deeper into the house.

I pointed to the staircase just beyond the kitchen. "Check upstairs," I mouthed to Gemini.

He moved silently, climbing step by step, weapon drawn. I waited, tense, every creak in the walls sounding amplified in my ears. Then he reappeared at the top, eyes scanning down at us. A quick hand signal: All clear.

I exhaled, just once.

Then I turned down the hallway.

The walls were a pale yellow, stained near the floorboards. A single overhead light illuminated a soft glow. I passed one door and twisted the knob. Inside the closet were stacks of boxes. They weren't labeled. I shut the door and kept going.

My heartbeat thudded in my ears as I continued. The silence in the house was oppressive, like it was listening. Then another door. I opened it slowly. A mattress lay on the floor. It was stained and had no sheets. It smelled of mildew and human sweat. I swallowed against the tightness rising in my throat. *Zoey had better not have been held here.*

I glanced back.

Hirsch was across the hall, checking what looked like another small utility closet.

I turned around, and I saw *it*. A second, narrower hallway, partially hidden behind a jutting wall. I raised my hand and pointed.

Hirsch nodded.

Together, we moved forward, trying not to make a sound. At the end of the hall, I reached for the doorknob, and that's when I heard it.

A soft sound. It was barely audible. Was it a scrape? A footstep?

I stilled. Finger to my lips, I signaled for silence once again.

My pulse jumped, adrenaline spiking through my limbs. I motioned for Hirsch to get Gemini.

This was it. We were walking in blind, and we needed to be smart and fast. Gemini appeared behind me, weapon raised, eyes alert. With the three of us ready, I tightened my grip around the doorknob, held my breath, and turned.

50

ZOEY

Mark was talking again, this time about how he grew up in the area. I'd guessed right. He was in his early thirties, not *too* much older than me. At least his rambling gave me something to focus on while I quietly plotted my escape. I was fairly certain it was just Mark in the house now. The man in the suit, the one who liked to hear himself talk, had left earlier. And Gil, the man who had drugged me and brought me there? I didn't know where he was or if he was still nearby.

Mark told me he liked to fish. His parents had a place near a lake where he used to spend summers. "Still do," he added with a shrug. "It's quiet. Peaceful. I'd catch trout off the dock before breakfast," he continued. "The place hasn't changed much."

Suddenly, he stopped talking. He tilted his head toward the hallway, eyes sharp and focused. "Did you hear that?"

My heart raced. "What?"

He put his fingers to his lips, telling me to be quiet as he reached behind him. He pulled a gun from the back of his pants. He wasn't expecting anyone to be there, so that meant no one else was there.

This is my chance.

The door creaked above, and Mark turned toward it, distracted. I grabbed the bag of books beside me and, with all the strength I had left, swung it straight at his head.

The blow landed with a solid crack. He stumbled, cursing, but didn't go down.

He spun toward me, gun still in hand.

And then—

BOOM.

A gunshot rang out. *Deafening.* Like firecrackers exploding inches from my ear. I dropped the bag and froze.

Then I saw her.

At the bottom of the stairs.

Weapon raised. Eyes wide.

"Mom?"

My knees nearly buckled. But I used all of my strength to run toward her as Uncle August and another man burst toward Mark. There was a loud thump, and I glanced to see they'd pinned Mark down. Blood was pooling around him.

Mom lowered her weapon and caught me in her arms just as I collapsed against her. Her grip was tight, and her body was shaking as much as mine. "I knew you'd find me," I cried.

51

MARTINA

My heart pounded as I held my daughter. *She's here and she's safe.* And I never wanted to let go of her ever again. I stroked her hair, still tangled and damp with sweat. She stepped back just enough to look at me. "Honey, are you okay?"

She nodded quickly. "I knew you'd find me. I knew it. I told him they were going up against the wrong people."

That was my daughter. Always defending me. Always believing.

Tears began to leak from the corners of my eyes, but I forced myself to pull it together. I had to be strong for her and for the team.

Off to the side, I caught movement. A man lay bleeding on the ground. He was handcuffed and pinned beneath Hirsch and Gemini. Hirsch held a second gun, likely taken off the suspect.

"Is there anybody else here?" I asked. "Who else has been with you?"

"There was Gil and the man in the suit. Those are the only people I've seen. Gil's the one who took me. He drove the Uber, but I don't think he's really an Uber driver."

"He's not, honey. You're safe now."

I pulled out my phone, ready to alert Rocket and the others, but the screen showed no signal. I exhaled a frustrated breath. "I'm going to take her outside," I said to the team.

"Okay. Be safe," Hirsch said, still crouched over the bleeding man.

I knelt to check Zoey again, brushing a strand of hair behind her ear. Before we could move, Hirsch hurried over and Zoey pulled him into a hug.

"Thank you for finding me, Uncle August," she said.

"Of course, sweetheart," he whispered. "I'd go to the end of the earth to find you."

My daughter smiled through her tears.

"Come on," I said gently. "Let's go."

With her hand in mine, I started up the stairs. As we climbed, my phone vibrated to life. A message from Rocket lit up the screen.

> Someone just pulled into the driveway.

I stopped and looked at Zoey.

"Change of plans," I said. "I need you to stay here with Uncle August and Gemini."

She blinked, confused, but followed me back downstairs. To the three of them, I explained the message I'd just received.

Gemini stood, alert. "You stay with her and watch this guy."

Zoey spoke up. "His name is Mark."

Hirsch said. "You two stay with Mark. Gemini and I are going up to see who just arrived."

"Call for backup. There's no reception down here until you get to the top of the stairs."

"Okay. Be alert. We'll be back after it's all clear," Hirsch said, as he and Gemini stepped toward the door and up the stairs making a swift and quiet exit.

I glanced at Zoey, then down at Mark who was still cuffed, still bleeding. He wasn't moving. He might be bleeding out, but he wasn't my concern at the moment. All my energy was reserved for protecting my daughter. I turned to Zoey. "You stay down here. I'm going to wait at the top of the stairs so I can get a signal and see who's outside."

She nodded slowly, but her eyes darted to Mark's limp body. "Mom..."

"It's going to be okay. Just stay here, and don't look at him. Promise me?"

With a grimace, she said, "I promise."

I rushed up the stairs, every step echoing with the weight of everything I'd almost lost. And that's when I heard the gunshots. Three sharp cracks. I froze at the top of the stairs, adrenaline crashing through my body. "Stay there," I shouted back. "I'll be back!"

Zoey's voice trembled behind me. "Mom, don't leave me—"

But I couldn't stop. Not now. I had to make sure no other monsters got anywhere near my daughter.

52

MARTINA

MOVING AS QUIETLY and quickly as I could, I raised my weapon and headed toward the sound of gunshots near the front of the house. My breath caught in my chest as I inched forward, crouched low, until I reached the front window and peeked from behind the curtains to the outside of the house. Rocket stood to the side, weapon drawn and pointed toward the ground. He looked tense but alive. Where were Hirsch and Gemini?

I unlocked the front door and burst outside, adrenaline slamming through me. Rocket was now crouched over a man in a suit, two fingers pressed to his neck. I slowed when I saw Rocket's grim expression. He looked up at me and shook his head.

Jeremy Santo was dead.

Just off to the side, I saw someone on the ground and another kneeling next to them.

There was blood on the path.

Gemini turned his head and looked up at me as his hand applied pressure to Hirsch's side. I cried out and ran over, dropping to my knees. Hirsch's face was pale, his breaths shallow, but his eyes fluttered open at the sound of my voice.

"Martina," he gasped. "Call Kim..."

Footsteps pounded behind us. I looked up to see two men in FBI jackets running toward us. Honeycutt and Vine, the special agents who had come out to help us. Relief flooded through me.

"We need an ambulance now!" I called. "He needs a hospital!"

Honeycutt pulled out his phone. "Dispatch, this is Special Agent Honeycutt. We've got a wounded officer. Looks like a GSW to the abdomen. Suspect down. We need EMS immediately!"

"Call Kim," Hirsch said through gritted teeth, though I could see the pain twisting his features. "Martina," Hirsch said, gripping my wrist.

Honeycutt said, "What's the situation?"

"Zoey and a body are downstairs. She's fine. He's not. He aimed at me. She hit him with something, he went down. She distracted him, gave me the shot." I blinked back tears. "She saved me. I don't know if he's dead," I said. "We swept the house. It's clear. Jeremy must've come to move her after we went to his house."

"But they were too late," Honeycutt said softly, "and you weren't."

I looked up at Honeycutt. "I need to get Zoey out of here. And Hirsch needs to get to the hospital. *Now*."

Vine yelled out, "Car approaching!"

I turned and looked as a dark sedan took in the scene. Our eyes locked. It was Gilbert Thomas. I said, "It's Gilbert Thomas! Get him!"

"I'll call it in," Vine said, as he ran after the vehicle, presumably to check which direction it was headed.

We needed to get out of there. There was no telling who would show up next. I crouched beside Hirsch. I took his hand as I dialed Kim. I whispered, "You're gonna be okay."

He gave a faint nod. I dialed. The moment Kim answered, I said, "Hi, Kim, this is Martina."

"What's wrong?" she asked, instantly alarmed.

"Hirsch is right here," I said, holding the phone to his ear.

Hirsch's voice was hoarse. "Kim... I love you. Is Audrey there?"

I turned away, blinking back tears. *No. There will be no goodbyes. This can't be goodbye.*

Zoey was going to be fine.

Hirsch was going to be fine too.

"Hi, honey," he said. "I love you too. I'm gonna see you soon, okay?" After a moment, he said, "Bye, honey." He nodded slightly and I took the phone from his trembling hand.

I told Audrey to put her mother on the phone. "We're heading to the hospital," I told her. "He's going to be okay. As soon as we know more, I'll call you back. We found Zoey. Everything's going to be fine."

I wasn't sure if I said it for Kim or myself. But I had to believe it because everything had to be fine. Hirsch had to make it. We hadn't come this far, risked this much, just to lose him now. I ended the call and looked at Honeycutt. "Let's get Zoey out of here."

We rushed back into the house and stormed down the stairs.

Zoey was standing at the bottom, arms wrapped around herself. Her eyes wide. Pale.

"It's okay, honey," I said, rushing to her. "It's okay. We're getting you out of here."

"I think he's still alive," she said, glancing toward Mark, who lay on the floor, motionless.

"We'll get him help," I said. "Come here."

I pulled her into my arms, holding her tight as Honeycutt stepped forward.

"I'll take care of this," he said, nodding toward Mark.

Zoey nodded slowly. "FBI?"

"Everyone was looking for you, and we found you," I said. "You're safe now."

Honeycutt looked at me, and I mouthed, "Thank you."

I led my daughter, my brave, beautiful daughter, out of the basement where she'd been held since late Friday afternoon.

As soon as we stepped outside, we heard the distant wail of ambulance sirens growing louder. Zoey gasped. Her eyes darted toward the sound, then down where Hirsch lay on the ground. She ran to him and knelt down next to Gemini and clutched Hirsch's hand. "Uncle August... you're going to be okay! Hang in there."

He was pale and losing too much blood. His lips parted. "Good to see you..."

"Come on, honey," I said gently. "The ambulance is coming. They'll take him to the hospital."

I wrapped my arms around her, trying to guide her away, but I couldn't stop looking at Hirsch either.

He reached up, just barely. His voice labored, he said, "Go, *now*."

I nodded, gave his hand one last squeeze. "I'll see you at the hospital."

Zoey and I rushed to the car. My hands trembled as I started the engine and said a quick prayer for Hirsch. I thought all I wanted was to take my daughter far away from this place, to erase this nightmare from her life, but I needed more than that. I needed Hirsch to be okay.

53

MARTINA

AT THE HOSPITAL, Zoey had her wound examined and properly cleaned and disinfected. The doctors wanted to run more tests, but she swore she was fine. That was the only time she raised her voice. She didn't think she'd been drugged, not beyond the moment they grabbed her when she'd tried to flee the Uber. I thanked the Lord every second I could. Zoey was safe. But Hirsch...

They'd rushed him into surgery the moment the ambulance arrived. The doctors said they wouldn't know how bad it was until they opened him up. They'd need to see exactly where the bullet had struck.

Part of me wondered, again, if this dangerous job was worth it. Maybe it was time to walk away. Not that any of this felt like work. This wasn't a case. This was personal. There was no way I could've stayed back while Zoey was missing. And there was no way Hirsch would've let me go in alone. We always took risks when we worked together. But Hirsch had never been shot, not when I was there. That would continue to eat at me.

Like Zoey, I was terrified for Hirsch. She kept asking about different scenarios. All I could do was keep saying the only words that made sense, that "everything is going to be fine." Because it had to be.

Kim was on her way with two armed security guards. I'd told Charlie to stay back at the office with Mom and Ted and the Ashfords. Zoey was able to say a quick hello to everyone. She said she wanted to hear their voices and no doubt they wanted to hear hers.

Zoey was desperate to see Henry, but I didn't want to put anyone else at risk. We knew this was organized crime, and that meant they had people everywhere. Just because we got Zoey back didn't mean they were finished with us. They could still come after me. After Hirsch. After his family. After the Ashfords. But Kim and Audrey needed to be here. They needed to be near him, in case... of the worst.

I didn't know what I'd do if we lost him. He was more than a former partner. More than a friend. Hirsch was family. A brother. My best friend. I couldn't lose him. *I won't.*

Heavy boots echoed down the hospital corridor. Kim and Audrey appeared, flanked by two of our most trusted security experts, both tall, broad, trained to take a bullet for anyone they protected. Zoey and I stood and met them with tight embraces. None of us wanted to let go.

"Where is he?" Kim asked, breathless. "What did the doctors say?"

"He's in surgery," I said softly. "They said they'll come talk to us when they're done."

Kim turned to Zoey and wrapped her in a hug. "I'm so glad you're safe. We've been praying for you."

"Thank you," Zoey said through fresh tears.

Audrey stood frozen, pale. Her hero, her father, was fighting for his life. I had no words for her. No comfort that would make this easier. Guilt settled deep in my chest. Why him? Why not me? I'd been shot before. I could take another. But he'd taken a bullet for my daughter. "He's going to be okay," I said again. I didn't know if I believed it, but I had to say it. For her. For all of us. Zoey slipped her hand into mine and gave it a squeeze.

"Maybe we should all sit down," Kim said with a strength I envied.

I nodded, and we moved to a row of chairs. Our guards took their positions, silent and alert. While we waited, no one spoke. There weren't words for all of the emotions. The terrible possible outcomes. Then, finally, a voice cut through the quiet. "Family and friends of August Hirsch?"

All four of us were on our feet in an instant.

"This is his wife, Kim, and his daughter, Audrey," I said quickly as we rushed forward. "We're all family."

The surgeon nodded. "He's out of surgery."

The room stood still and silent surrounded us. You could have heard a hair pin drop.

A moment later, the doctor spoke. "The bullet nicked his liver. Thankfully, it missed the major arteries. We were able to cauterize and repair the damage, and the bleeding's been controlled."

Kim let out a gasp, a half sob, and a half breath of relief.

"He got very lucky," the doctor continued. "It could've been much worse. He's stable now. We'll be moving him to recovery shortly. The next 24 hours are important, but as of now, we're optimistic he'll make a full recovery."

"How long will recovery take?" I asked.

"He'll be in the hospital for a few days, then a few weeks of rest. Maybe four to six weeks before he's back on his feet fully. No lifting. No stress. But he should be fine."

Kim, with her arms wrapped around Audrey, said, "Thank you so much."

The surgeon gave a small smile and nodded. "You can see him once he's moved into recovery."

Then he turned and disappeared back through the doors. The weight in my chest loosened for the first time since this nightmare started. I let out a long, shaking breath and nearly collapsed into the nearest chair. "Let's sit down," Zoey suggested.

Kim, Audrey, and I sat quietly in the waiting room, our bodyguards still stationed nearby. I don't think there was a dry eye between us.

Kim wiped her cheeks. "He's going to be okay. That's good." Her voice trembled slightly. "But... how did this happen?"

I gave her a very shortened version of the events that led to the shooting. I left out most of the details, how close we came to losing Hirsch, how it all nearly unraveled, but even the edited version left them horrified. Still, they deserved to know the truth.

Hirsch was a hero.

There was no getting around it. He'd saved my daughter and me. Audrey leaned forward, her hands clasped tightly in her lap. "I'm so glad Dad's okay. And you too, Zoey. We were so worried."

Zoey offered a tired smile. "I was too. I still can't believe I'm not in that basement anymore." Then she grinned and added, "I mean, I can believe it. Come on, my mom is Martina Monroe."

That earned a round of soft laughter. A moment of levity we all needed. Audrey turned toward her. "You're still getting married on Saturday, right?"

Zoey glanced at me, then at Kim and Audrey. I saw the hesitation flicker across her face, and it surprised me.

"What is it, honey?" I asked gently.

She hesitated, then said, "I mean... I think so. Yeah. It's just, while I was there, they said some things about Henry's family."

What had they told her? Kim leaned forward, calm and firm. "Henry is not his father's past. Henry loves you. And from what we can tell, his family is respectable now. You know that, right?"

Zoey and I hadn't had time to talk in detail since we found

her. That would come later. There would be a full investigation. Honeycutt and Vine would lead on the federal side, but local law enforcement would need to question her, too. It wouldn't be easy and all of it was happening less than a week before the wedding. "It's okay if you want to postpone the wedding," I said, brushing her hair behind her ear. "No pressure, sweetheart."

Zoey looked at Kim, then Audrey, both of whom nodded in agreement.

Kim reached out and took her hand. "It is okay, trust me. Henry loves you. But if you need time, if you need space to process and do what's right for you, he'll understand. There's no rush."

Zoey smiled faintly. "But I already have my dress. And he's... he's my perfect guy. Right?"

I slipped my arm around her shoulders. "Of course he is."

She looked up at me. "When do I get to see him?"

"After we see Uncle August," I said. "Then we'll go back to the office and you can see him."

"Okay," she said, her smile warming her entire face.

And just like that, as if it were a blessing, the topic shifted. Kim, Audrey, and Zoey began talking about the wedding and the idea of a rescheduled bachelorette extravaganza. There were discussions about the flowers, the dress, music, and the cake. It was exactly the distraction we needed. For a little while, it let us pretend everything was back to normal.

Then the surgeon reappeared. "You can see him now," he said, smiling. "He did great. He came through it all with flying colors."

All four of us, along with our bodyguards, made our way into the recovery room. Technically, only two visitors were allowed, but the nurses, understanding the kind of night we'd had, turned a blind eye. We let Kim and Audrey go first. They rushed to Hirsch's bedside, each grabbing one of his hands. His eyes fluttered open, and a weak smile tugged at the corners of his mouth.

Kim leaned down and kissed his cheek. Audrey followed, blinking through tears.

Zoey and I stood side by side, watching quietly. "I told you you'd be fine," I said gently.

Hirsch smiled, his voice groggy. "Of course. It'll take more than a silly bullet to take me out."

"They said you're going to make a full recovery."

"Yep. And then I think I'm going back to my boring, retired life. No more investigations for a while... unless you need me."

Kim gave him a look. "They'll go on without you." And then her gaze landed on me. "He's not going to be needed for a long time, right, Martina?"

Message received, loud and clear. "I think it's time we all took a break. Don't you?"

Hirsch nodded.

Zoey stepped to Hirsch and squeezed his hand. "I'm so glad you're okay."

He smiled. "You too, kid."

She stepped back, "I'm going to call Henry, okay?"

I handed her my phone. "Go ahead."

Her smile lit up the room as she stepped aside and began speaking to her fiancé.

Watching her now, after everything she'd been through, I couldn't help but feel overwhelmed with gratitude, relief, and love.

This family, this beautifully tangled, fiercely loyal family we'd become was more than anyone could ever ask for. And, at least for tonight, we were all safe.

54

MARTINA

Zoey and Henry's big day went off without a hitch. Zoey shined in her sparkling ball gown, and Henry stood beside her, a happy, deeply in love groom. The only noticeable additions to the otherwise flawless wedding were the armed guards and the full security sweep we did before the ceremony and again before the reception.

The FBI had taken over the investigation, not just into Zoey's kidnapping but what they believed was a much bigger case including the murder of Jose Juarez, the rideshare driver whose account was used to kidnap Zoey. Agent Honeycutt believed it was a strong possibility that the house they kept Zoey in may have been used for multiple kidnappings, and God only knows what else.

Mark, her captor, had survived, but barely. The FBI explained Mark was a blood relative of the Mancini crime family. Jeremy Santo, whom we learned from Zoey was "the man in the suit," had made the videos with her. Santo hadn't been as lucky as Mark and died at the scene, but I didn't shed a tear for him.

The FBI eventually caught up with Gilbert Thomas, after

Zoey positively ID'd him as her kidnapper. After he was arrested, he flipped on the boss, Antoni Mancini, who ultimately had given the order to kidnap Zoey, in order to seek revenge for DeMarco. Rumor had it Mancini wasn't going to ask for ransom, but at the urging of Jeremy Santo who had read about Zoey's engagement to Henry Ashford in the newspaper, said the Ashfords owed him. It was theorized that the desire for a ransom had actually saved Zoey's life. The original plan was to capture me and kill Zoey in front of me; Hirsch and his family were next on the list. The thought made me shudder.

The Feds were still building their case against the Mancinis and their associates but expected a whole slew of arrests since we'd uncovered the hideout they suspected was used for years. They were already closing in on the family for ties to human trafficking and other crimes the FBI had been tracking. It was out of our hands, and for that I was grateful.

Because today, none of that matters. Today, we celebrate.

A small but very welcome addition to the wedding reception was the little fluffball curled up in my lap, Barney. Zoey insisted he had to be there, even when the venue initially said no dogs allowed. When we explained the week we'd had, the venue made an exception. He'd been through as much as any of us, and now he slept soundly in my arms. Charlie sat beside me, his hand resting gently on my back.

It couldn't have been a more wonderful day. Well, except, of course, if Hirsch hadn't been shot. But, as he said, it would take more than a "silly bullet" to take him out. And he was there, alive and well. Audrey and Zoey approached our table. Audrey bent down and gently petted Barney's head.

"He's so cute. Daddy, can we get a dog? Please? Please, please, please?" she begged.

Hirsch smiled. "We'll talk about it later."

Kim raised an eyebrow at him, and he gave a tiny, reluctant nod. I guessed they were getting a dog.

Audrey squealed, clapping her hands as she threw her arms around her dad from behind. "Oh, sorry, Daddy."

"It's okay, honey." He chuckled, hugging her back. Then she hugged her mom.

"Well, that's exciting," Zoey said, grinning. "How is everything? You guys having fun?"

We nodded.

She turned to me. "Mom, I haven't seen you on the dance floor yet."

"Soon. I promise."

"Well, Grandma and Ted are already out there. They're really showing you up. And I *know* you can dance."

Hirsch raised an eyebrow.

"It's true," she added.

I said, "That's right. Charlie and I danced at our wedding."

"Not just then. I still remember our living room dance parties!"

Charlie smiled. "I'd love to dance with my wife, if she'll have me."

Audrey quickly said, "I'll look after Barney!"

Barney lifted his head as if he knew we were talking about him. I chuckled, as did most of the table.

I said, "Of course…" But before I could accept my handsome husband's offer, Zoey pulled up a chair from the neighboring table and sat beside me. "You look stunning, Mom."

"You too," I said, brushing a hand down her arm. "I think it runs in the family."

She smiled, then her expression grew thoughtful. She glanced over at Hirsch and then back at me.

"You know," she said slowly, "what you guys do, what you did

—it makes me wonder. Am I really doing the right thing, becoming a veterinarian?"

That was a surprise. "What's wrong with being a veterinarian?" I asked gently.

She shrugged. "Nothing. I love animals." She smiled down at Barney. "But while I was... while I was in the basement, one of the men asked what I wanted to do with my life. I told him I wanted to help others. And it made me think. I mean, animals are great—but should I be helping people, too?"

"Are you thinking about becoming a doctor?" I asked.

"No... I don't know. Maybe. Maybe something more. Or something different. Maybe something like what you do."

I raised my brows. "And you're thinking about this right now?"

She laughed softly. "Maybe."

My concern over her going forward with the wedding so soon after her kidnapping was quickly returning. After such a traumatic event, she should have taken time to process everything. She was an adult, and she was so excited, I didn't want to take it away from her. But now, questioning her career choice on her wedding day? I said, "Take some time on your honeymoon to rest and have fun. You've got a few weeks before vet school starts again. You don't have to make any decisions right now."

"But is it enough?" she asked. "Is being a veterinarian enough?"

I looked down at Barney, who was snuggled against my lap, then back at her. "Veterinarians are incredibly important. Just ask Barney."

She smiled.

I continued, "Animals help people heal. They bring joy and comfort when everything else feels dark. You know how many smiles Barney brought during this whole ordeal? He was at the office with all of us. I think the only moments of light we had came when Barney was around. *That matters.* Not to mention, all of the service animals and the amazing work they do." I gazed into her baby blues. "Taking care of animals who take care of us? That's doing a lot with your life. And I don't think some criminal who kidnapped you should make you question that. Think about the source, Zoey."

"I guess you're right."

Just then, Henry walked up, slipping a hand into hers. "What am I missing out on?"

"Just talking about being a veterinarian and how important it is," I said.

Henry nodded. "I agree." He kissed her cheek. "Two animal lovers who love each other. What more could we ask for? Is everyone having fun?" he asked the table.

Everyone nodded, big smiles all around.

What a difference six days could make. From fear and chaos to music, laughter, and light. Life could turn upside down in a second, but we were all still here, happy and healthy.

And if the FBI was right, the ones who wanted revenge, the ones who targeted me, Hirsch, and our families, would all be behind bars soon. And maybe, just maybe, they'd forget about us. Or at least leave us alone.

Suddenly, music filled the air. Zoey gasped. "Mom! You know that's my favorite song. You have to come dance with me. It's my wedding day. I think I get to boss you around a little, right?"

With a grin, I said, "You absolutely do."

I stood up, handed Barney over to Audrey, who immediately cradled him like a baby, which he loved, and took my daughter's hand. Charlie followed close behind. I still owed him a dance, too.

We stepped out onto the dance floor. And we danced, not

just to celebrate the day, not just to toast the bride and groom, but for everything. For family. For survival. For hope. Because no matter how dark things had gotten, we had made it back to the light. Just like we always did, and we always would.

ALSO BY H.K. CHRISTIE

The Martina Monroe Series —a nail-biting crime thriller series starring PI Martina Monroe and her unofficial partner Detective August Hirsch of the Cold Case Squad. If you like high-stakes games, jaw-dropping twists, and suspense that will keep you on the edge of your seat, then you'll love the Martina Monroe crime thriller series.

The Val Costa Series —a gripping crime thriller with heart-pounding suspense. If you love Martina, you'll love Val.

The Neighbor Two Doors Down —a dark and witty psychological thriller. If you like unpredictable twists, page-turning suspense, and unreliable narrators, then you'll love *The Neighbor Two Doors Down*.

The Selena Bailey Series (1 - 5) —a suspenseful series featuring a young Selena Bailey and her turbulent path to becoming a top-notch private investigator as led by her mentor, Martina Monroe.

A Permanent Mark A heartless killer. Weeks without answers. Can she move on when a murderer walks free? If you like riveting suspense and gripping mysteries, then you'll love *A Permanent Mark* - starring a grown up Selena Bailey.

Please Don't Go She thought she left the past behind. Until a long-buried secret pulled her back—and turned her into a killer. A fast paced and addictive revenge thriller.

For H.K. Christie's full catalog go to: **www.authorhkchristie.com**

At **www.authorhkchristie.com** you can also sign up for the H.K. Christie reader club where you'll be the first to hear about upcoming novels, new releases, giveaways, promotions, and a **free e-copy of the prequel to the Martina Monroe Thriller Series, *Crashing Down*!**

ABOUT THE AUTHOR

H. K. Christie watched horror films far too early in life. Inspired by the likes of Stephen King, Jodi Picoult, true crime podcasts, and a vivid imagination she now writes suspenseful thrillers.

She found her passion for writing when she embarked on a one-woman habit breaking experiment. Although she didn't break her habit she did discover a love of writing and has been at it ever since.

When not working on her latest novel, H.K. Christie can be found eating & drinking with friends, walking around the lakes, or playing with her favorite furry pal.

She is a native and current resident of the San Francisco Bay Area.

To learn more about H.K. Christie and her books, or simply to say, "hello", go to **www.authorhkchristie.com**.

At **www.authorhkchristie.com** you can also sign up for the H.K. Christie reader club where you'll be the first to hear about upcoming novels, new releases, giveaways, promotions, and a free e-copy of the prequel to the Martina Monroe Thriller Series, *Crashing Down*!

ACKNOWLEDGMENTS

Many thanks to my Advanced Reader Team. These wonderful readers are invaluable in taking the first look at my stories and helping find typos and spreading awareness of my stories through their reviews and kind words.

To my editor, Paula Lester, a huge thanks for your careful edit and helpful comments and proofreader Ryan Mahan for catching those last typos. To my cover designer, Odile, thank you for your guidance and talent.

To my best writing buddy (aka the boss), Charlie, thank you for the looks of encouragement and reminders to take breaks. If it weren't for you, I'd be in my office all day working as opposed to catering to all of your needs and wants such as snuggles, scratches, treats, and long, meandering walks. To the mister, thank you, as always, for being by my side and encouraging me.

Last but not least, I'd like to extend a huge thank you to all of my readers. It's because of you I'm able to live the dream of being a full-time author.

Made in the USA
Las Vegas, NV
20 November 2025